AMBUSH!

Archie jumped backward as the VC leaped at him. The fingers of Archie's left hand closed over the grip of his K-Bar knife. The right hand reached for his Browning. The 9mm pistol came free first and roared a fraction of an inch from the chest of the Cong. Flung backward by the muzzle blast, Archie crashed into a small palmetto. Pain exploded in his wrist a moment later and he dropped the Browning.

A grinning VC raised his Type 56 for another buttstroke when Archie's K-Bar came out. With a short forward lunge, Archie drove the keen-edged blade into his enemy's abdomen at an upward angle. His shoulder behind the thrust, he buried it to the hilt. Instantly, the grin left the face of the VC as steel pierced his diaphragm and the razor edge sliced through his aorta.

Archie gave a hard twist and let the cadaver drop off his knife. *What happens*, he wondered, *if every Charlie charges into our ambushes from now on?*

SEALS

TOP SECRET #1

Operation: Artful Dodger

CHIEF JAMES "PATCHES" WATSON
and MARK ROBERTS

AVON BOOKS ◆ NEW YORK

AVON BOOKS
A division of
The Hearst Corporation
1350 Avenue of the Americas
New York, New York 10019

Copyright © 1998 by Bill Fawcett & Associates
Published by arrangement with Bill Fawcett & Associates
Visit our website at **http://www.AvonBooks.com**
Library of Congress Catalog Card Number: 97-94309
ISBN: 0-380-78712-1

First Avon Books Printing: March 1998

AVON TRADEMARK REG. U.S. PAT. OFF. AND IN OTHER COUNTRIES, MARCA
REGISTRADA, HECHO EN U.S.A.

Printed in the U.S.A.

WCD   10 9 8 7 6 5 4 3 2 1

SEALS

TOP SECRET #1

Operation: Artful Dodger

CHAPTER 1 ———————————————

ANOTHER NIGHT of nasty tricks was winding down for the SEALs of Alpha Squad, First Platoon, Team 2. As usual, it ended in a hastily laid ambush to break off contact with the VC enemy. The platoon expected a brief firefight before the PBRs that would transport them back to Tre Noc could come in close to shore and scoop up their human cargo. Only this time, it didn't go like it should have.

Quartermaster First Class Kent Welby suddenly found himself up to his ears in little brown men. Kent had been trained to run forward into an ambush, rather than hitting the dirt. He didn't think the VC knew that. He grudgingly gave them credit for learning fast. Unlike their usual tactic of melting into the jungle undergrowth, these Cong came right at him after the SAW (Squad Automatic Weapon) opened up and Archie Golden popped his pair of claymores. At once, the fighting grew fierce.

With a sideward sweep of his XM23 Stoner, Doc Welby wiped three Cong off their feet and out of the world. A blur of movement, caught in the corner of his right eye, made him turn in that direction. A five-round burst of 5.56×45mm slugs cut across the bellies of two more black pajama-clad enemies. *Damn! Where were they all coming from?* as he brushed back a lock of sweat-dampened, sandy-blond hair with long, thin fingers. He swung center again in time to put a slug between the eyes of a determined VC. Quickly he slapped a 150 round belt onto the feed tray and racked the bolt back and forth to chamber another round, then spun to face a new threat.

Machinist's Mate Third Class Richard Golden blinked in disbelief. No sooner had he popped his first claymore than all that remained of Charlie's patrol rushed forward with a shout. When he fired the second one, only three others went down. That left more than enough for the squad to deal with. Archie hefted his CAR-15 and cut a three-round burst into the onrushing Cong. Two staggered and one of them went down. A moment later, Archie Golden found himself in hand-to-hand combat with a pair of Cong.

One of them smashed aside Archie's CAR-15 with the butt of his empty Chinese Type 56 assault rifle. Archie quickly regained his grip on the CAR and guided toward the mouth of the second VC. He squeezed the trigger and Charlie flew away in the muzzle blast. At once Archie ducked and pivoted on his left heel. He saw the astonished expression of his enemy a moment before he sent him off to Viet Cong heaven with a short, hot burst.

At once, two more came at him, bellowing curses in Vietnamese. *Noisy bastards* flashed through Archie's mind. Usually they fought as quietly as mice.

With the last rounds in his CAR-15, he stitched one Cong from right hip to left shoulder. Charlie's shout ended abruptly. By then, the other Cong, his weapon dry, had closed with Archie.

Archie jumped backward as the VC leaped at him. For the moment, his carbine was useless. The fingers of Archie's left hand closed over the grip of his K-Bar knife. The right hand reached for his Browning. The 9mm pistol came free first and roared a fraction of an inch from the chest of the Cong. Flung backward by muzzle blast and a reflex knee-jerk, Archie crashed into a small palmetto. Pain exploded in his wrist a moment later and he dropped the Browning.

A grinning VC raised his Type 56 for another butt-stroke when Archie's K-Bar came out. With a short, forward lunge, Archie drove the keen-edged blade into his enemy's abdomen. His shoulder behind the thrust, he buried it to the hilt. Instantly, the grin left the face of the VC as steel pierced upward through his diaphragm and the razor edge sliced his aorta.

Archie gave a hard twist and let the cadaver drop off his knife. *What happens*, he wondered, *if every Charlie charges into our ambushes from now on?*

Chief Quartermaster's Mate Tom Waters had enough problems of his own. The VC they had ambushed showed a degree of tactical knowledge on a par with NVA regulars. Troops can survive an ambush, although not all of them, Tonto Waters mused. The trick was in running forward and shooting really fast. This batch might have made it, QMC Waters considered, as he dumped one with his 12-gauge Ithaca.

Hell of a mess No. 4 buckshot makes at close range,

he observed dispassionately. He had been back from his vindication at the court-martial for less than two weeks when this operation got put on the squad's plate. As platoon chief, technically he did not have to go out on individual squad actions, but no matter how scary it got, he had to admit he had become a combat junkie. This one, designated as a two-night search and destroy mission to interdict supplies and fresh troops coming into the Delta region, had turned into a toe-to-toe slugfest.

Tonto admitted that the first night had gone like clockwork. Although Tonto never considered himself a pessimist, this second night along the winding trail back to the Bassiac River could sure as hell make him one, he readily acknowledged. Swift, black shapes flitted through the leafy undergrowth in front of Tonto and he fired again.

''I'm hit,'' shrieked a surprisingly young voice in Vietnamese. Strange, these Cong had seemed hardened veterans, not mere boys.

He pointed his shotgun at the source of the thrashing vegetation and fired again. A brief howl ended in a gurgle and silence in the bush. ''That one won't need a corpsman,'' Tonto muttered to himself.

From his right, he heard the excited voice of Chad Ditto, their RTO. ''Over here. Jeez, they're comin' at us like ants from a pissed-on hill.''

''Save that radio, say again,'' Tonto shouted to him.

''Fu'in' A,'' Repeat Ditto riposted as his Matt-49 stuttered to life.

Platoon Chief Tom Waters broke off his engagement with three more Cong with a quick, two-round discharge of his Ithaca. Brushing sweat from his walnut eyes, he began to work his way through the thick underbrush toward young Chad. *Tonight, we made contact with our intended targets readily enough*, Tonto thought. Only so much action, in so short a time and small an area, had attracted the attention of these dudes who seemed determined to do in Alpha (First Squad). Always willing, Tonto prepared himself to do his part to see Charlie failed.

Twin diesel engines throbbed as the Patrol Boat, River (PBR) *Juan Diego* cruised the muddy brown waters of the Bassiac River. The bass vibes gave good feelings to all aboard. The coxswain and boat commander, BMC Alfonso Gutierrez, peered into the darkness ahead. His flak jacket felt like it weighed a ton. Sweat had turned the green skivvy shirt underneath to a sodden mass. The crotch of his dungarees had dampened from the heat and humidity. Why in hell couldn't it cool off at night?

That question had been asked a million times by tens of thousands of young Americans in the steaming stewpot of Vietnam. Al Gutierrez asked it every night they had river patrol. Tonight they had a pickup mission, which made it even worse. Bad enough that any inexperienced VC out along the river took potshots at them from time to time. Those who knew better avoided the superior firepower of the PBRs. When the boats went in to take out SEALs from an operation, a whole lot of highly pissed off VC usually came right behind. A light touch on one arm from his engineer brought Al Gutierrez back to the present.

"Skipper, Charlie's all along the bank over there."

Engineman Second Class Hal Vincent had raised his
night-vision goggles to try to read the expression of
Chief Boatswain's Mate Gutierrez in the soft red glow
of the instrument lights.

"They're smart little *cabrónes*. They're not firing
on us." He stuck a foot through the open hatch and
tapped lightly on the shoulder of the gunner riding the
M-60 machine gun. "Lou, keep an eye on those *chin-
gaderos* on the bank. If they so much as twitch, blow
'em into the weeds."

1C/GM Lou Roftus did not even turn his head, only
nodded grimly and swung the barrel of the M-60 machine gun toward the portside bank of the river.

"Looks like those SEALs are in for some heavy
shit, Skipper," Vincent said.

"I think they've already got it. Grab a look at those
flashes about half a klick from the river on the port
side."

Unable to hear the distant gunfire over the engine
noise, Hal Vincent could only guess at the intensity
of the firefight he witnessed. At last he drew a shud-
dering breath.

"Jeez, someone's sure catchin' hell over there."

A moment later, the radio began to crackle.

There was another reason for Tonto's urgency to
reach Repeat Ditto. The Radio-Telephone Operator
would be cheek to tail with Lieutenant Carl Marino,
the team leader of Team 2, who had come along with
the Squad for the sheer sake of getting into the action.
Further, Chad Ditto had seen enough combat not to
panic without good reason. Tonto wanted to know
what that reason might be.

Chad crouched behind a rotted palm log that lay at an acute angle, parallel to the trail where they had set up their L-shaped ambush. Cobalt eyes wide, he peered into the darkness beyond. He sweated profusely under his cotton cammo shirt and behind his ears. The grease paint on his face prevented all but a thin sheen from forming on his cheeks. He sensed, rather than heard, movement to his front and the next instant a dozen VC burst out of the thick vegetation and rushed directly at him.

Biting back the fear that every reasonable man felt in combat, Repeat Ditto cut neat three-round bursts from the French 9mm submachine gun. It took all his concentration to maintain accurate bullet placement. Puffs of dust and cloth flew from the chests and bellies of the Cong. All the while, Lt. Carl Marino talked earnestly over the radio strapped to the back of Chad Ditto.

"Moonshine, this is Champion One. What is your ETA? Over."

The receiver crackled against Pope Marino's ear. "Champion One, Moonshine. We're about ten minutes out. Over."

"Get your buns in here and light up this fuckin' place. Over."

"Champion One, do you have unfriendlies? Over."

"Moonshine, we've got 'em eatin' our goddamn' C-rats. Over." Carl Marino looked up to see a VC diving at Chad Ditto. "Your left, Repeat!" Marino shouted, then went ahead and shot the Cong with the 5.56mm barrel of the CAR-15 above his XM148 tube. Immediately the VC fell away from the muzzle of the combo weapon, Lt. Marino triggered the 40mm grenade tube slung under the slender barrel of the modified CAR-15.

Three VC died and two more took heavy doses of shrapnel when the small grenade exploded directly over them. A moment later, Tonto Waters appeared, pumping round after round through his 12-gauge Ithaca. The din of fire from the entire squad drowned out the screams of the wounded and dying. Lancing orange flames made Hell pay a visit to the narrow tongue of land between the Bassiac and its larger, sister river, the Mekong, which it joined farther on.

Reduced to OO buckshot now, Tonto Waters splashed part of a load into the shoulder of one VC and put three pellets into the eyes of the one behind. The .33 caliber balls jellied the brains of the unfortunate Cong. At the end of the long side of the ambush, Tonto heard the sharp crack which served notice that Archie had moved his position and gotten another claymore into action.

Beside Tonto, he heard the crackle of the radio. Pope Marino keyed the switch. "Okay, go."

"Champion One, can you pop flares to mark your position? Over."

"Roger that, Moonshine. Over."

"Do it now an' you'll have some friendly incoming, Champion One."

"None too soon, Moonshine. Over."

"Where are the unfriendlies?"

"Hell, they're just about on top of us."

"I'll advise when they're in the air. Break off and fall back a hundred meters. Over."

"Roger that, Moonshine. Over."

"Moonshine, out."

Doc Welby unwound a 150-round belt from his shoulder and slapped the lead cartridge in the feed tray into the Stoner, checked the guides, and charged the weapon. He had a slight breather, thanks to the claymore Archie Golden had fired off. The whizzing steel balls of the M-18 antipersonnel mine, propelled from the curved surface by a charge of C-4 plastic explosive, had trashed six Cong in one frightful instant. Doc used his respite to reach into a cargo pocket of his tiger-stripe cammo pants and press a thumb against the gold crucifix that he had taped to his dogtags. The rule was, nothing made a sound. Not a clink, not a jingle.

Accordingly, the SEALs always removed the beaded chain from their dogtags and taped them together to put in a pocket. Kent Welby added the heavy gold crucifix his wife Elizabeth had given him on their wedding day. *Estranged wife,* Doc corrected himself, with less bitterness than relief. After all, there was Francie.

Francie Song of the lovely, black almond eyes, heart-shaped face, long, ebony hair and graceful curves. Francie, who loved him with even more intensity than Kent could return. At least until this mess with Betty had been cleared off the deck. Introspection nearly cost Kent Welby his life as a VC rudely interrupted his stream of images.

A short burst of 7.62x39mm rounds tore the hat from the head of Doc Welby and cut away some bristly strands of his sandy, crew-cut hair. The Stoner in his hands bucked and snorted, seemingly of its own accord, as the startled SEAL responded in kind. The slugs trashed broad palm leaves and liana vines and smacked into flesh, ending the career of another Viet Cong guerrilla.

"Jesus, Mary, and Joseph!" Kent blurted aloud. That was close. Something had better happen soon.

It did. The sky lit with pop-up flares at both ends and the center of the ambush.

Sailors aboard the PBR *Juan Diego* quickly tore off the covers and struck the bases of the green pop-flares with the palms of their hands. With soft explosive pops and airy whooshes, the illumination pyrotechnics sped from their tubes on the aft deck. Along the port rail, the elevated barrels of two Honeywell 40mm, hand-cranked, repeating grenade launchers chuffed out their cargo of death. Al Gutierrez keyed the mike in his hand and spoke tersely.

"Champion One, break off. They're on the way. Over."

"Roger, Moonshine. Breaking contact now."

By then, six more 40mm antipersonnel rounds had left the tubes of the Honeywells. An instant later, the jungle washed a vivid white in the glare of the sizzling, smoking flares. On the *Juan Diego*, the crew cheered. Dark, malevolent blossoms rose in the green canopy of the three-tiered rain forest as the 60mm mortar opened up. The Fourth of July pops of the 40mm grenades quickly followed. Two more mortar rounds dropped out of the sky onto the suddenly disorganized VC. Then the PBR coasted toward shore.

*   *   *

Doc Welby let out a gusty breath he had been holding, breaking the hushed silence that followed the mortar attack. They had done it. They had held the damned VC until help arrived. And what help! -

Doc rated a PBR in full blitz mode as being right up there with Puff the Magic Dragon and an ARC-Light. Even before the bombs fell, a guy could not hear the B-52s way up there where they made their release of a broad, long, carpet bombing.

But Charlie had other ideas. The squad had no sooner stepped out of the thick underbrush and started down the narrow, mud-slicked trail than a Chicom Type 56 on semiauto cracked and Zoro Agilar let out a soft cry. From ahead of him, Doc Welby heard Archie Golden's CAR-15 stutter a three-round burst. Other weapons quickly joined in.

Doc Welby reached Porfirio Agilar at the same time as Fil Nicholson, the platoon corpsman. Fil kneeled to inspect the wound.

"Hey, Zoro," said Fil softly, "you got yourself a sweetheart wound here. No doubt all the way back to the Philippines for you."

"*¿De veras?*" He repeated, "Is it true?"

Cloth tore and Fil Nicholson gently probed the area of the wound. "Naw, I guess it ain't. Cut the outer edge of your deltoid. It's just a nasty scratch. Three days and all you'll have is a scab."

Porfirio Agilar affected to look disappointed. "No pretty Filipino girls for Zoro?"

Fil commiserated with his patient. "Sorry, pal. Maybe next time."

Pope Marino appeared at their side. "We got 'em. Two of them. Just kids. They must have been scared witless when the PBR hit them.'' To Agilar, ''Too bad, Zoro. We came through this one clean, except for that. Fil, patch him up and let's get on the move. That boat won't wait all night.''

After that small incident, the squad made an easy stroll to the riverbank and boarded the PBR. The engines thrummed with renewed power as the patrol boat fought the current upstream toward Tre Noc. Tonto Waters and Kent Welby began to unwind as their AO faded into obscurity behind them. Yet, they both knew this was not the end of it. They would relive every desperate second as it all happened again . . . and again.

CHAPTER 2 ————————————

AT HIS CIA Station office in My Tho, Jason Slater did not believe the Eyes Only document that lay on his desk. He knew it was genuine. It came from Langley, and the authentication code was correct. Yet, the contents seemed too preposterous to accept. He pushed back the padded leather swivel chair and pulled a pack of Camels from the snap-fastened pocket of his Western-cut shirt. He lit the white cylinder and stared up at the paneled wall, and the highly treasured, framed, autographed photograph of John Wayne.

"To my good friend—Jason Slater, a trusted man to ride the river with any day," it read, and it was signed in a large, rolling scrawl. Slater had met Wayne five years earlier, while on a recruiting stint to the campuses of California universities. Wayne's son, Patrick, was in the cinema school at USC and had flirted with giving the Agency a try. The Duke stopped by the classroom loaned to the CIA for its interviews, and attempted to talk Slater out of accepting an application from the younger Wayne. Sla-

ter, his dark gray eyes and square chin giving him a steely appearance, interrupted him in mid-appeal.

"I have already rejected Patrick, Mr. Wayne," Jason told him. "Oh, not because I think he might be a fag, or a twit, or a lint-brained campus Marxist. It is because of his vulnerability. He is *your* son. If that ever became known to the other side, he would become a target. The Wet Affairs people of the *Komitet* might make a try on your life, and they would surely be all over him like stink on crap. I don't think you want to see your son die at an early age."

John Wayne drew himself up into his film persona and spoke with the familiar drawl. "Waall, goddamnit, why didn' you say so in the first place, Pilgrim? Instead of draggin' it out like this." Slater saw the flood of gratitude in the graying screen star's eyes. "If there's ever anything I can do for you, just say it."

Encouraged, Slater ran fingers through his longish, blond hair and blurted out, "There is one thing. I would appreciate it if you could sign a photograph to me. My name really is Jason Slater."

At the door, the Duke turned back. "Consider it done."

Early the next morning, the signed picture arrived by messenger, installed in the silver frame that still held it. Jason Slater sighed heavily. Not even the Duke could help him now. The US Air Force could not have lost something like that and no one know about it until now. It had to be a bad joke.

Yet, he knew that the Director—a former admiral— had little sense of humor. Which made it real, and he was stuck with it. The big question still bugged him.

How did it get into that part of the world? Slater slammed a palm on his desktop and spoke aloud to the Duke and himself.

"And why the hell put it in *there*?" He would have to verify everything before deciding what to do about it, he concluded with another hefty sigh.

Cyclos—the pedal-powered cabs of Vietnam—darted through the swarm of pedestrians in downtown Saigon. Everyone carried net bags, many had yokes across their shoulders, bearing square, bright metal ammunition cans converted into water buckets. Hawkers extolled the quality of their wares in loud, singsong voices. The variety of what they sold was staggering.

Everything from fruit and vegetables to car parts and medicinal herbs could be found. Hole-in-the-wall restaurants sold bowls of noodles, rice, Chinese style barbecued pork, broiled eel, and mixed fruit from their doorway stalls. Kiosks at street corners sold *Bamibah* and quart bottles of LeRoux beer. The "33" was brewed with formaldehyde, and tasted of it. And the next morning it gave one a powerful reminder of that. However, among the taverns most habituated by US military personnel, better potables could be obtained.

At the Sea Horse—obviously a navy bar—on Truman Key, Anchor Head Sturgis and the SEALs of Bravo Squad, first Platoon, Team 2 were availing themselves of such quality libations in copious quantities. Granted three days in-country R&R, they lapped up bottles of Tiger from Singapore, San Miguel from Manila, and Sapporo from the Toyko suburb of the same name.

Being good sailors, and especially SEALs, the volume of their imbibing could be more accurately described as monumental. What proved most astonishing to the small, slender, young native women who served them was the Americans' capacity. Not a one showed signs of intoxication—at least not while they remained seated. Only when one or more roused from their comfortable, high-backed rattan chairs to visit the head did the room spin around them.

Such was the state of alcohol-floated good humor when four youthful lads in Air Force blues rolled in through the beaded curtain that covered the doorway. Dead silence hit the room at their arrival. Eyes large and wide, small and narrow, swiveled their direction. For a moment the flyboys hesitated. Then, taking the lead of the senior man, a burly sergeant, they advanced on the bamboo-fronted bar.

Chin Yee, the owner, a Vietnamese of Chinese extraction, rushed toward them from the open doorway of his office. His braided queue bobbed with agitation. ''You go some prace erse. You be happiest some othza bar, hay-yah!''

Fists on hips, the beefy sergeant surveyed the large, dimly lit room. ''We kinda like it here.''

''No—no, prenty tloubre come you stay here. This sai'or bar, hay-yah!''

A nasty sneer spread on thick lips. The sergeant reached out and pushed Chin Yee from his path. One of the airmen beat it to the door and set out to find reinforcements. ''It is, huh? How'd squids ever git a place of their own? Ain't enough muscle among a hunnard of 'em to clean out a place this size.''

Eyes wide with alarm, Chin made a final appeal. "You go now. I carr mir'telly porice."

Belligerent now, Sergeant Howard Lamb pushed Chin Yee aside. "You will not call the military police. We got a right to drink any damn place we want."

Anchor Head Sturgis came to his feet. "We'll take care of this Mr. Chin."

Sgt. Lamb gave Anchor Head a long, slow go-over. As he did, he took in the size eighteen neck, the bulging lats and traps, the big fists and thick wrists. Anchor Head's huge, bullet-shaped cranium shone even through his ample thatch of bristly sand-colored hair. Large, even by SEAL standards, Anchor Head towered over Sgt. Lamb.

The man who had apparently risen to challenge him wore civilian clothes, so Sgt. Lamb did not have the advantage of seeing the UDT badge, which would have aided him in making the correct decision. So it prevailed that he inserted foot in mouth with the next words to pass his lips.

"Ain't no fu'in' swab jock gonna tell me what to do."

Anchor Head Sturgis gave him a hard right to the mouth. Sgt. Lamb rocked back, then came on in raging determination. What he lacked in style, he made up in ferocity.

"Get him, Howie!" a USAF corporal cheered Lamb on.

Sturgis sidestepped him and slammed a ham fist into the space between exposed shoulder blades. Lamb went down, sputtered, and pushed himself off the meticulously clean floor, a raw curse on his lips.

He looked up in time to catch a looping left to his forehead.

Anchor Head's knuckles stung and shot lines of pain up his arm. He should have kicked the flyboy. Lamb's eyes rolled up in his head and he flipped over backward. Groaning, he came to his feet slower than before. By then, his fellow fliers had gotten into the act. The two of them grabbed Anchor Head by the arms, which brought instant retaliation from Mickey Mouse Norton and Little Pete Peterson. Smacking them first, they grabbed the airmen and flung them toward opposite ends of the room. Lamb threw over a table and made a dive at Anchor Head.

Laughing, Anchor Head chopped him behind the neck. Howard Lamb ate the floor again. A commotion at the front door attracted the attention of the SEALs. Fully a dozen airmen struggled to force their way inside all at once. Well, that still left the flyboys outnumbered, Anchor Head surmised. But it would be bound to attract the attention of a roving patrol of Military Police. That would never do.

Batting away a frothing-mouthed Air Force corporal, Anchor Head called out to Tom Killian. "Long Tom, go get the white mice!"

Killian split out the back door. Half a dozen US airmen swarmed inside and rushed the sailors at the bar. So far they had stayed out of it. Now they gleefully entered the fray. Fists flying, the opposing sides waded together. A mad cackle of laughter came from Big Ben Gates, a SEAL who had placed second in the fleet boxing championships. This was his element.

His fast flurry of lefts and rights turned an Air Force corporal's head into a speed bag. The guy went out before his brain got the message to his legs, so Gates took a couple of totally unnecessary extra shots, then watched as the corporal crashed in a heap.

"Heee-yaaah—heee-yaaah—heee-yaaaah—hooooo!" Piercing, the Rebel yell filled the room. The chilling war cry came from the lips of SEAL "Colonel" Ernie Culpepper, the squad clown. He stood on a table with either hand at the back of a flyboy's head. As his bellow echoed across the ceiling, he flexed his shoulders and slammed their foreheads together.

Their bodies dropped to the floor as whistles began to shrill. Seconds later, a squad of South Vietnamese military police stormed into the brawling throng inside the Sea Horse. The Americans had given them the name *white mice* due to their small stature, white "flying saucer" hats, and the gloves they wore. That didn't make them any less formidable. Quickly sizing up the situation, they waded in with batons flailing.

Not restrained by the customs, regulations, and traditions of American law enforcement, they ruthlessly separated the participants and hurled them to opposite sides of the barroom. Anchor Head noted with satisfaction that the sailors received less punishing treatment. When the fury had been quelled, Chin Yee pointed out Anchor Head to the lieutenant in charge of the Vietnamese police. He walked directly to where Anchor Head stood and looked upward.

"Very bad trouble, *Daiwi*." The peak of his garrison cap came to the center of Anchor Head's chest.

Anchor Head took note of being addressed as "Captain," and smiled. "Yes, very bad." He pointed to the subdued air force crowd. "Those men should be made to pay for the damage done to Chin Yee's place.'' He pulled a droll expresssion. ''And, naturally our people feel it is only right to compensate you and your men for taking you away from your usual duties and wasting time stopping the fight.'' To the other SEALs, he appealed. ''C'mon, guys, pony up. All the piasters you've got. We can buy more. We've got to give these whi—er—these loyal policemen something for their trouble, right?''

When the flyboys had been shaken down to cover damage in the Sea Horse, the Vietnamese lieutenant returned to where Anchor Head stood. The big SEAL handed over two large handfuls of piasters and solemnly nodded toward the door in subtle suggestion.

The lieutenant caught it at once. ''We will go now, *Daiwi*. Ah—everything is in good order. I do not see any reason to file a report with your military authorities, do you?''

Anchor Head tried his best to look totally innocent. ''Nooo, you're certainly right about that, Lieutenant. And—ah—thank you.'' When the White Mice departed, Anchor Head heaved a huge sigh of relief. ''What say we go someplace else, buds?''

General Hoi Pac of the Army of the Democratic Republic of Vietnam was perplexed. He knew he was being cut out of the loop. Something big was happening and he'd not been informed. His flat, moonface shined with a skein of perspiration brought on in anticipation of the passion he would soon enjoy. With an impatient gesture he slammed his teacup on the tabletop. A thick, blunt finger stabbed the third button on a Soviet-made intercom. When an answer crackled from the speaker, he spoke from his pique.

"Dak, get in here at once."

Colonel Nguyen Dak, the intelligence officer for Hoi's command, responded crisply. "Yes, sir, immediately."

After a brief rap on the door, a slightly built, ferret-faced individual in a neatly tailored uniform entered. He marched smartly to the desk, studiously ignoring the child crouched at the side of Gen. Hoi's chair. The general looked up at him.

"Sit down, Dak."

"Yes, sir. What is it you wished?"

Gen. Hoi examined the face of his intelligence officer with flat, black eyes. "Our army is not so different from others that it lacks a rumor mill. Of late, I have been listening to these anonymous sources quite a lot. They say that something important, something crucial is going on. That it involves Vinh Province. And I don't know a damned thing about it officially or otherwise." Hoi's fist struck the desktop with such force that the teacup on the table beside him jumped.

"What, if anything, can you tell me about this?"

Col. Dak turned a mild expression on his superior. "I know nothing more than you do, General. You have heard that it involves the Soviets?"

"No—no, I had not. Tell me about that."

"A month ago, a Soviet vessel offloaded a highly secure crate at Haiphong and it was transported to Hanoi by closed rail car. I have not heard anything about its destination, but it is said that whatever the crate contains will eventually come here."

Fury at being kept in ignorance darkened the face

of General Hoi Pac. "Look into this at once. I want to know everything you can find out."

Col. Nguyen came to his feet, preparatory to leaving. "Yes, sir, of course. I will put my best men on it." He shrugged. "Naturally, you realize, if the high command wants this kept secret, there's nothing you or I can do about it. That's the beauty of our system. When someone is told that something they saw or heard of didn't happen . . . it never happened."

Hoi's eyes narrowed. "And the Soviets, if they really are mixed up in this, are masters at rewriting history. When someone falls into disfavor in their country, he simply ceases to exist. I heard once that when an arms manufacturer was charged with using inferior materials and sent to a reorientation camp, his name was removed from all accounts, private and public. They even went so far as to file his name from the weapons he had already made." Gen. Hoi fought off another scowl, brightened his mood. "But you will do your best. I am confident of that."

After Col. Nguyen had left the office, Gen. Hoi resumed his seat and let a small, neatly manicured hand drop to the shoulder of the sweet young thing that crouched at his side. His touch made the girl cringe, and tears sprang to her eyes. He stroked her raven hair as he addressed her.

"You know, you are the youngest blossom to have ever graced my love bouquet. Your gift to me will be exquisite, I can sense that already. Come now, bring me happiness."

Trembling, the twelve-year-old reached up, as was expected of her, and put a tiny hand on the inner surface of his thigh.

*   *   *

Francie Song put the cover over her IBM typewriter in the Riverine Force S-3 office and left her desk. Outside the Plexiglas cubicle she went directly to the time clock in the small entranceway. She pulled her card from the rack beside it and a small square of folded white paper came with it. Quickly she pocketed it, with a nervous glance from side to side. She inserted her time slip and pressed the plate so that the machine stamped the time in the OUT column: 1745.

She had stayed late to finish an operations order for the 3142 Boat. Now all she wanted was to get home, have a glass of white wine and a long, steaming bath with her son, Thran, then fix dinner. The note could only be bad news, she knew, so she avoided reading it until she was clear of the naval base at Tre Noc. Alone on the street, she unfolded the paper and looked numbly at the neat block letters.

MEET ME IN THE PAGODA GARDENS, 1830 HOURS.

It was signed with two initials, EY.

That confirmed the identity of her expected, and dreaded, correspondent. The note had come from Sergeant First Class Elmore Yates, USMC, her Control. Her face contorted into an expression of disgust, Francie hurried off to her apartment. She would not make the meeting at the Pagoda. Her Kent would be back tomorrow.

Starshii Lortyant Alexi Maximiovich Kovietski returned the vodka bottle to the freezer unit of the refrigerator built into the sideboard of his wet bar.

Stolichnaya, not the best Mother Russian produced, but it would serve. And *sava Vory!* it was 100 proof. He lifted the chilled tulip glass to his lips and sipped deeply of the nearly frozen liquor. Elegant brass table lamps gave off a soft glow, reflected by the highly polished mahogany and teak panels of the room's walls. Captain Dmitri Ivanovich Vlady drank also and smacked his thick lips.

"So, it is all in readiness," he spoke to his superior, Kovietski.

Kovietski ran long, tapered fingers through his white-blond hair and drank more vodka. "Yes. I leave tomorrow for Station Ca Mao. You will see that anything of importance is forwarded to me there, Dmitri Ivanovich?"

"Certainly, Colo—er—" Dmitri glanced around self-consciously, then broke out a big grin. "Congratulations on your promotion to *Podpolkovnik*, Comrade Rudinov."

Of all the persons in the network, only his fellow Soviets knew the true name and rank of supposedly Senior Lieutenant Kovietski. He was, in fact, newly promoted Lieutenant Colonel Rudinov of the *Komitet Gosudarsvannoy Bezopastnosti*, the KGB.

"Thank you, Dimi. I'm certain you will. What I cannot figure out is why my superiors want me in South Vietnam at this particular time. We have already received an alert message that indicates a major operation is about to get underway. I would think this the worst time for me to be away from Shangrilah Station."

" 'Ours not to reason why . . . ' " Dmitri quoted.

"That was the Brits, not us. *Our* glorious army

kicked the hell out of the Light Brigade, remember.''

"Oh, yes. Of course, Alexi—er—Colonel. But, what is it they say? 'The *Komitet* proposes and the *Komitet* disposes.' You will learn the reason why when they will it. And I . . . well, if it's *that* big, if it's a need to know affair, I'll never know.''

"Poor boy." Rudinov polished off the last of his vodka and reached for the handle to the freezer. "We might as well enjoy this while we can. The vodka and beluga are all in aid of celebrating my promotion after all. Do have some more of the caviar. It loses something of its character when it gets close to room temperature.''

"Always the connoisseur, eh, Comrade Colonel?''

Rudinov nodded in acknowledgment. "Yes, but right now I'd gladly kill for a bowl of borscht and a plate of *blinis* swimming in crushed strawberries and sour cream.''

Capt. Dmitri Vlady produced an expression of mock-horror. "Think of the calories, Maxim. Such rich food would do terrible things to your weight.''

Tall, trim, broad-shouldered and narrow waisted, *Podpolkovnik* Rudinov had the blond hair, fair complexion, and clear blue eyes one would have expected to find on an old recruiting poster for the Nazi SS. Laughing, Lieutenant Colonel Rudinov slapped his hard, flat belly with a large hand. "I don't have to worry about that.''

Vlady agreed. "Not for a decade or so, I'd wager.'' He scooped caviar onto a toast point, sprinkled it with chopped onion and hard-boiled egg, and bit off half of it. "Mmmm, this is really good.''

A smile spread across Rudinov's lips. "An Amer-

ican capitalist freebooter would have to pay fifty of
their dollars for just the amount you heaped on that
toast, Dimi. While I receive all I want for our officers'
lounge, free of charge, from our benevolent Soviet
government. Think of that, Dimi.''

"It's stunning. Tell me, when we conquer them,
will beluga be as inexpensive there as it is here for
us?''

Rudinov laughed out loud. "I don't know. We'll
have to find out.''

CHAPTER 3 ───────────────

BACK AT Tre Noc, the tired SEALs of Alpha Squad took it easy following their close call with Charlie. Word had gotten around, as it always did, about the fight in the Sea Horse. Tonto Waters, a can of Miller High Life in one big, hairy paw, swaggered over to where Anchor Head Sturgis sat in the platoon bar.

"I hear the blue-suited fairies cleaned your clock in Saigon, Anchor Head."

"They did like hell. Sit down, Tonto, if you're gonna smirk like a ninny."

"I hear, too, that you had to call in the white mice."

"Now that I did do. Didn' have it in mind to spend my liberty inside a cell."

Tonto nodded, a stray lock of his dark hair swaying on his forehead. "Smart, that is."

"Why is it our own military police can't see reason the way those little gooks can?"

With a sigh, Tonto made a one-handed gesture of uncertainty. "Too full up on regulations, maybe? We've got our ways and the Vietnamese have theirs."

Anchor Head put on a pained expression. "Most of those MPs in Saigon are clodhoppers. Ain't right to git our heads thumped by other than shore patrol."

Tonto chuckled. "You've a point there, and a right fine one at that." Tonto studied the yellow-green bruise on the face of Anchor Head. "You sure you didn't come out on the dirty end of the stick on this one?"

Groaning, Anchor Head emptied his beer. "Get outta here. You spoil my day."

Kent Welby occupied a chair under the shade of a neatly trimmed, round-leafed "dollar" tree. He lifted his beer and then nodded at two riverine sailors who approached and passed his table.

"How's it hangin', Doc?" one of them asked.

Kent answered through a grin. "Like a flagpole at high noon."

"You got a date?" the other sailor asked.

"Now, that would be telling, Spence."

A moment later Francie Song came to the table and beamed him a wide, warm smile. Still neat and trim, she did not yet show, but her mind was fixed on the baby she carried, Kent Welby's baby. "We could have eaten on base," she said.

Doc Welby noted her apparent distraction, and ascribed it to her job. "I get all of that stuff I ever want. Speaking of which, I'm starved. Shall we order?"

"Yes, *mon cher*. I have to get back by thirteen hundred. Lots of work to do."

Doc patted the bench beside the one he occupied. "I thought something had your attention other than me."

Francie looked shocked, her mind still on the missed meeting with Elmore Yates. "That's not true. I think of you . . . all of the time. It's only that they've doubled up my workload. I was in the office until nearly eighteen hundred last night."

Doc grinned and patted her arm. "That's my girl. Nose to the grindstone."

A perplexed frown dented Francie's brow. "What does that mean? Nose to the grindstone. Wouldn't that hurt?"

"It's a figure of speech, sweetheart."

"You Americans have so many of those. I think I will have a bowl of prawns and noodles, and some steamed garlic and bok choy."

Doc wrinkled his nose. "You don't figure on going out tonight?"

Francie loosened up then with a giggle. "You've kissed me when I've eaten garlic before."

"Yes, but I've eaten garlic then, too."

"Have some of my bok choy."

"Anything you say. Are we going to Phon Bai tonight?"

Should I tell him now? He seems so happy. Perhaps in the restaurant later on. "I hoped so."

"Good, then we will. I've asked them to do something special with lamb. I hope you'll like it."

"Anything you suggest is delicious. I know I'll love it. Have you seen that——" She had almost asked if he had seen SFC Elmore Yates. "——that new patrol boat that came in while you were on patrol?"

"Yes. We tied up alongside it. More armor plate and two mortars on the fantail. It'll bring scalding pee on Charlie." Doc noted her sudden pinched expression. "Sorry. I didn't mean to be crude."

Francie took his hand in hers. "It's all right, Kent Welby. That isn't what bothered me."

"Then what is it?"

"I—I cannot say."

Doc eyed her hard. " 'Cannot' or will not?"

"Can we . . . please talk of something else?"

"Sure, like dinner . . . and after?"

Her smile warmed an already hot day. "Especially the after. Go order for us now, *mon amour*."

Lieutenant Carl Marino hopped a ride to Binh Thuy in a truck. He was eager to visit his assistant officer in charge (AOIC), Cyrus Rhodes. Recently, Dusty Rhodes had been captured and tormented by a North Vietnamese general named Vinh Toy Giap. Since he had been liberated from the POW camp in the shoot and scoot operation, Dusty had been slowly recuperating in the hospital. Hopefully Dusty would be rational enough now to hear the good news about Giap.

Lieutenant (junior grade) Cyrus Rhodes sat upright in his bed, leaned back against the pillows, when Pope Marino entered the room. "Hey, you're lookin' good for a goldbrick," Lieutenant Marino said as he entered.

"Where'd you get the idea I was screwin' off? If I had my way I'd been out of here a long time ago. D'you ever use one of those urinal things? It's like pokin' it down the metal tube of a vacuum cleaner." Dusty gave a little shudder. "And I'd like five minutes alone in a room with the man who invented the bedpan. It's clearly cruel and unusual punishment."

"Hang in there, buddy. I've got good news for you."

Dusty cocked an eyebrow. "Yeah? What's that?"

"General Giap is now in the tender hands of the company cowboys. Jason Slater bagged him up and sent him off to Langley. There's some rooms on the subterranean levels there that would whiten your hair in a hot tick."

Dusty brightened noticeably. "Now, that is good news. So, tell me, what did happen on that raid?"

Pope Marino settled in a chair beside the bed. Everything smelled crisp and new and bore a heavy aroma of disinfectant. He rubbed his hands together and launched into his account of the raid on the POW camp.

"We went in hot, in a full-sized Parakeet operation. The gunships trashed the guard towers and blew up their fuel and ammo dumps. You trained with us, up until that last week, anyway, so you know how we handled it. We went in before the last round had left the barrels, each man to his assigned objective. We got 'em all out, Dusty. Even the badly injured ones."

"Like me?"

Marino looked pained. "Yeah. Like you. You weren't reasoning then. Couldn't have much registered on the exfiltration. We windmilled out of there slicker than snot on a glass doorknob. Took the camp commandant and General Giap. We lost only one KIA and seven slightly wounded. No way it could have been cleaner."

"That's great, Pope. And what about the camp itself?"

"It's history, Dusty."

Involuntarily, Dusty shivered. "Good. I couldn't face the idea it was still out there."

"No sweat, guy."

"Excuse me, Lieutenant." A navy nurse in crisply starched uniform stood in the doorway. "Your time is up. Mr. Rhodes still needs his rest."

Dusty frowned at her. "Not that I notice. I've just had the best news a guy can get."

Firm, confident in her authority, the nurse entered the room and fluffed up Dusty's pillow. "Then, let's not overdo it, shall we?"

" 'We?' You got a frog in your pocket?"

Her stern expression vanished in a flash of smile. "You're such a tease, Mr. Rhodes. Now, lay back, it's time for your medication."

"I don't need any more painkillers. But, I'd sell my soul for a bottle of single malt."

A frown put a gully at the top of her nose. "You just might, if you tried that. Now say good-bye to your visitor and close those eyes."

"Boo and hiss."

"I'll see you again, soon, Dusty. And that's a promise. Say, the day after tomorrow?"

"Good. I'll be here."

Bouncing precariously from water-filled pothole to mud-slimed rut, the transmission of the duce-and-a-half whined in protest. For a brief moment, Marino caught a glimpse of three small boys at the side of the road, wheeling a bicycle. At the approach of the truck, they dropped the bike and bolted into the undergrowth. A couple of seconds later, Pope caught sight of them again, running through the abandoned, swampy fields.

"What are they doing here?" Marino asked the driver.

Before an answer could be given, the bicycle exploded.

The truck lurched violently from the shock wave. Shards of glass from the side window filled the cab. Pope Marino felt a hot stinging on his right cheek. Instinctively, he reached up and touched the pinpricks of pain. His fingers came away smeared with blood.

"What the hell!" he blurted. Then, to the driver, "Does that happen often?"

"Yep. Gettin' to be more common. Be thankful their timing was off. They've creamed a couple of trucks, wasted half a dozen guys." Thinking of that, he added eagerly, "Them li'll fuckers ain't far off. What say we go after 'em?"

"There's little chance of catching them now. And, there might be an ambush laid over there."

A glum expression covered the driver's face. "Yeah. A couple of Sixteens an' a pistol ain't much if we run into something like that."

Carl Marino agreed entirely. Come to think of it, he had heard about the kiddie killers. There was something in the last intelligence summary. *If they're getting this close to home, might be something to look into.*

Votive candles flickered in their red and green glass containers on the little shelf in front of a gaudy Oriental representation of the Virgin. It made Doc Welby decidedly uncomfortable at first, considering what he and Francie Song did on the big, downy bed. He eventually overcame his reluctance, drowned as he was in the voluptuousness of Francie. They had come back to her apartment over the Chinese herbal doctor's shop after a meal at Phon Bai.

Jacques Xeong, the chef, had outdone himself. The crown rack of lamb had a crisply brown exterior and a perfect, lemony-mint flavor, offset by just the slightest hint of garlic. It had been a total pleasure for Francie, who had never eaten the popular European delight. She had clapped her hands when Kent had carved off a loin riblet and placed it, pink side up, on her plate. The vegetables were crisp and stir-fried, arranged around a mound of mashed potatoes. A gravy boat held the warmed lemon-mint sauce. Yet, all of it had been only a preliminary for what came after.

They walked to the apartment, hand-in-hand, and climbed the stairs in silence. Inside the door, Kent kissed her, their mutual passion soaring as he prolonged the embrace. When he released her, Francie tiptoed to the small refrigerator and produced a bottle of French Sauvignon Blanc and two chilled glasses.

Doc Welby pulled the cork from the green glass neck and they went directly to the bedroom. There they sipped wine while they disrobed lazily. They embraced and Doc felt Francie's nipples erect and demanding against his bare chest. With one hand, she reached down to touch him. Moaning softly, they sank to the bed.

Francie bit playfully at Doc's lower lip and they caressed each other with growing hunger. With one leg cocked over him, Francie began to rub the small of Doc's back. He shuddered in pleasure and kissed one of her breasts. Francie sighed in contentment.

"Oh, my Kent Welby, you are so wonderful to me."

At last they were inflamed to the point of desperation. Just as Doc was about to enter her, a disturbance at the side of the bed drew the attention of both lovers. There stood Francie's small son, Thran, who knuckled one eye with a tiny fist and spoke through a yawn.

"I heard a noise, Momma," he said in Vietnamese.

Kent flushed crimson and hotly from toes to the roots of his fine, blond hair. *How long was Thran there?*

Although likewise aghast at the unexpected interruption, Francie handled it with calm dispatch. "That's all right, darling. It was nothing." Rising, still entirely naked, she reached for his hand. "I'll take you back to bed."

"I'm thirsty. I want a drink."

"All right. We'll get that first, then it's back to sleep for you."

Nodding, the seven-year-old started for the kitchen alcove of the apartment. Abruptly he paused and glanced back over his shoulder. "G'nigh', Kent Welby."

Doc Welby wanted to melt right through the soft futon mattress. His face blazed with chagrin. Mother and son padded barefoot through the apartment, and Francie put the boy down on his pallet. Smiling wistfully, she returned to the arms of Kent Welby.

All of a sudden Doc's distress grew by major bounds. Not even the usually thrilling touch of Francie's silken skin against his could work its magic. Doc groaned in frustration.

"This isn't going to work," said Doc wretchedly.

"What—what is wrong?" an alarmed Francie probed.

"I don't know ... well, it's just ... well, it's Thran, coming in here naked as a jaybird and finding us like—like we were."

Francie sought to make light of it. "It's not the first time he has seen me making love. When his father was still alive, Thran slept in the same room with us. We tried to keep quiet ... but then, that is not always possible. Thran would wake up and see us. It's—it's only natural."

A note of a pout sounded in Doc's voice. "Not the way I was brought up. We don't take all this nakedness as casually as you do. Everything is supposed to be done behind closed doors. In secret. And children are never, ever to know what adults do together."

Misreading him, Francie teased, "How odd. My sister, my two brothers, and I slept in the same room with our parents. I knew in detail what a man and a woman do from the time I could talk. In our culture there is no shame about the human body, or about sex."

"But—but, you're *Catholic*, the same as I," Doc objected weakly.

"I know what the Church teaches, Kent Welby. But, Asian wisdom is so much older. Why make taboo something as beautiful as the human body? As beautiful as your body?"

"Or of celebrating life by making love?"

That cheered Francie. "Exactly. It is such a splendid thing to do."

Somewhat mollified, Doc made an answer. "I agree with you . . . in principle. Although in practice, I prefer our culture's way of doing things."

Francie put a purr into her voice as Doc began to respond to her ministrations. "Oh, my darling, darling Kent Welby, let us not make comparisons. Tonight we should listen to the dictates of our hearts."

A sudden rush of renewed passion surged through Kent. Taking Francie in his arms he entered her with a powerful thrust. "Yes—yes, I really think we can."

Riding in one of these things always made him queasy. Not that *Podpolkovnik* Pyotr Rudinov suffered motion sickness in any other form. These small sampans wobbled so erratically that he could never stabilize his inner ear. As a result, his stomach kept telling him it wanted to ride up and sit on his tonsils. Although the most direct and secure way to reach the Viet Cong command post at Ca Mau, Rudinov would have much preferred to travel overland.

Trusted Viet Cong guerrillas stood in bow and stern, with long poles to propel the craft through the shallow water. They wore the characteristic black pajamalike garb and conical, woven palm-frond hats, the thongs tight under their chins. They were barefoot, their sandals rested on a thwart close by each man. Matting of cabbage palm covered their Type 56 rifles. Two more, ranking cadre, sat on the low benches like Rudinov. They wore Western-style suits and white Panama hats, as befitted their importance. One clutched an American-made Sampsonite attaché case.

Rudinov broke the silence to observe in Vietnamese, "It is too bad we cannot fly to Ca Mau."

"We can," the elder cadre responded. "Once we drive the capitalist pigs and their American lackeys out of the Delta, Comrade Senior Lieutenant."

Pyotr Rudinov still wore the gray-black-and-green cammo uniform of a Senior Lieutenant in *Spetznaz*, the Soviet special forces, and was known to the Viet Cong as only an advisor. He produced a broken smile as he fought back another bilious attack. Would this trip never end?

"It is a day to which we all look forward," Rudinov said.

The younger cadre spoke up. "Let us hope that your visit presages that it will soon be a reality."

"Would you believe me if I told you I had not the least idea why I am coming to Ca Mau?" Rudinov said. "No, I suppose not. Your curiosity is unbecoming, but I will satisfy it, at least in part.

"There is a major operation coming up that might alter the entire complexion of your struggle for liberation of the South. I, least of all, do not know the details as yet. It might have something to do with my coming here, and again it might not. When it is decided by our superiors that it is time to tell us, we will know."

"Wisely said, Comrade Lieutenant Kovietski," the elder cadre approved. "Now, how about a sip of this *Ca Bok*? It does wonders to settle a troubled stomach, I am told."

What arrogance! Rudinov's mind rebelled. He knew all the time. The only reason that made sense for him to be sent to this forsaken part of the marshy

Delta would be to put an end to those meddlesome SEALs. *What a pleasure it would be, Rudinov thought, to personally rip out the throat of that smug* ooeludok, *Lieutenant Carl Marino.*

CHAPTER 4 ─────────────────

TONTO WATERS and a dozen men from First Platoon sat around on grenade cases, which had been converted to serve as stools in the platoon bar. Nothing more than a room in one of the concrete block barracks buildings, the improvised saloon sported a jestful sign outside that read:

PETTY OFFICERS' MESS
(OPEN)
HOURS: 0001-2400

Of course the establishment was never open around the clock. It was only the dream of every sailor who had gained a crow on his sleeve to have a saloon where he could slop suds day and night. The bar and tables were made from packing crate boards, still rough-hewn, although showing signs of smoothness from much use. A single, bare forty-watt lightbulb hung down from the center of the room and cast feeble light into the dark corners. A refrigerator "requisitioned" by Pope Marino sat to one side of the

40

pseudomahogany. Taped to the door was a chartlike list inscribed with the names of everyone in the platoon. No money changed hands over the bar; the beer and sodas came on the honor system, and a SEAL was expected to mark a picket-fence slash by his name for each one he bought. They paid up once a month when payday came and a supply run was organized to Binh Thuy. Tonight, a radio sitting atop the cooler blared rock. A steady buzz of conversation nearly drowned out the music.

When the Rolling Stones ended their number a heavy silence came over the assembled SEALs. Then, a voice on the radio floated softly, cloyingly, enticingly. "Good evening all of you American boys. I have sad news for the men of Detachment Two, Company B, Fifth Special Forces. The men you sent out to the Ho Chi Minh Trail won't be coming back. Heroic soldiers of the Army of the Democratic Republic of North Vietnam engaged them and killed all but five of them, whom they took prisoner. It saddens me that you are still led into these disastrous defeats by your officers who are the running dog lackeys of the capitalistic military-industrial complex. I appeal to you once more to lay down your arms. Reject the false credo of the evil men who have deceived you. Accept the offer of safe passage to the North. Confess your war crimes and you will be welcomed with open arms by your comrades of the Democratic Republic of Vietnam, to join with them in solidarity to world peace."

"Hanoi Jane," one SEAL spat.

"Yeah, that *puta*," said Zoro Agilar.

"Fuck her," growled Chad Ditto.

Archie Golden stood and downed the last of his Miller. "Hey, I wouldn't screw her with someone else's *schmuck*," he declared.

After several minutes of heated discussion, Randy Andy Holt took center stage and expressed the general consensus. "If I could have my way, we'd pull off a black bag operation. Before she goes back to Hollywood, we could hit her convoy somewhere outside Hanoi. Then waste that traitor bitch and extract by sea."

Two dozen SEAL voices rose in eager accord.

Five large bunkers had been connected by tunnels. Set deep in the marshy jungle outside Ca Mau, the major VC command post served to direct actions of guerrilla teams in the Delta and train new members for the battles ahead. Lieutenant Colonel Rudinov was greeted warmly by the area commander, Colonel Voh Daong.

"Welcome to our humble compound, Comrade Senior Lieutenant Kovietski. We are honored by your visit."

"Perhaps you could honor me with some idea of why I have been sent here?"

Eyebrows diverted only a fraction of a millimeter upward at this rudeness, Colonel Voh smiled and gestured toward his office. "Perhaps the message that awaits you in my office will provide an answer. Shall we?"

Inside, Colonel Voh handed over a sealed packet. It was marked with the red star and black hammer and sickle of the Soviet Army. Rudinov thanked Voh for keeping it secure for him and broke the seal.

Inside the outer wrapping the five page document had emblazoned at its top the Cyrillic characters for TOP SECRET. Below it was the emblem of the KGB.

The first line of typescript informed Rudinov that the document came from the Asian Affairs Directorate at KGB headquarters. Quickly he read through the first paragraph.

Podpolkovnik *Rudinov, you are to take personal supervision of a highly sensitive program of this Directorate named* Dystvne Vecher Ogan. *Three days after receipt, but not later than 21 March, you are to travel with all due speed to North Vietnam and assume control of the project. Since Operation Night Fire will take place in Vinh Province, you will make a courtesy call at the headquarters of General Hoi Pac of the Army of the Democratic Republic of Vietnam.*

The purpose of this visit is to make an initial briefing of General Hoi regarding Night Fire. Under no circumstances are you to reveal to him that the final choice of employment of Night Fire is vested in yourself.

Lieutenant Colonel Rudinov did not like any of that at all. Privately, he considered Hoi to be incompetent, and worse, a fanatic. To make the prospects of the new assignment worse, Rudinov read on to discover that the subject of Night Fire was currently concealed at the Thran Lon Dong Prison. *Why there?* he asked himself. Then his cynical side asserted itself. *Perhaps it is because the Americans never bomb the POW camp*, he thought cynically.

Although the communique did not reveal the nature of Night Fire, Rudinov strongly suspected it had something to do with the rumors currently going around KGB circles. Something about a highly sensitive item recovered recently by a Soviet submarine from the ocean off the coast of Spain. He reread the orders and noted that future communications would come through the Soviet Embassy in Hanoi.

Then he ran the message form through a hand-cranked shredder and put the results in a burn bag. A slight frown still on his high brow, Rudinov rejoined his host, who had more news for him.

"We also received a message for relay to you in Cambodia. Since you were coming here, I took the liberty of holding it for you. It is in a code I am not familiar with," Colonel Voh added in a prompting tone.

Lieutenant Colonel Rudinov took a quick glance at the sheet from a one-time pad. No wonder the colonel did not recognize it. It was in the system used by his Cambodian wet affairs detachment. "No doubt," he agreed. "It is a Soviet Army code." He put the message form in his pocket to read later.

Later, it pleased him greatly to watch the words spill out onto paper. "Comrade we are pleased to advise you that your operatives are ready to proceed at Binh Thuy," it read.

A peach fuzz–cheeked Yeoman First Class looked up from the desk in the S-2 Office of NAVSPECWARV in Binh Thuy. He saw a naval lieutenant in a freshly starched and pressed tiger-stripe camouflage uniform, with a cluster of taped-down white squares of gauze on his face. "Yes, Lieutenant. Did you have an appointment with Commander Lailey?"

Marino flashed a smile. "No. But, why don't you see if he can squeeze me in for a minute? The name's Lieutenant Carl Marino."

Pope Marino kept the smile plastered on his face as he heard the bearlike growl from inside the private office of the S-2, LCDR Barry Lailey. "What the hell does he want?"

A squeaky voice answered from the yeoman. "I don't know, sir. He didn't say."

"Then go find out."

Pale and shaken, the sailor/secretary returned to the anteroom. "Commander Lailey would like to know the purpose of your visit, sir."

"Tell him it's about the kiddie killers who put these bandages on my face."

"I—ah—beg your pardon, sir."

"I doubt if you know it, Yeoman, but there are little Vietnamese kids running around out there with exploding bicycles. I'm here shopping for an assignment to do something about it."

"*Bicycles*, sir?"

"Do you have a hearing problem, Yeoman?"

"No, sir. I'll tell him, sir."

When he returned a moment later, he made a sweeping gesture toward Lailey's door. "The Commander will see you now, sir."

Pope Marino went to the door, put his boonie hat under his left arm, rapped sharply on the upper panel and entered. "Good morning, Commander Lailey. I'm here seeking to be put in harm's way again."

"What's this about bicycles blowing up in your face?"

Still keeping the forced smile in place, Marino spoke in a pleasant tone. "You can see for yourself. One of those took four stitches." Then he quickly described the incident. He concluded with, "Three young boys ambushed a truck I was riding in yesterday. I'm told it is getting worse."

An old enemy of Pope Marino, Lailey looked up at the lieutenant, while sunlight glinted off the large bald spot at the back of Lailey's head. He was well aware of the rising incidence of the terroristic bombings. And certainly the CO wanted something done about it. Lailey laced short, thick fingers over his growing paunch and reconsidered. Of course, if Marino's First Platoon got the assignment, it would put him in an exposed position once more. Odds said Marino could not go long without taking a bad hit.

Therefore, Lailey exhibited only mildly bad grace when he left his desk to withdraw a slim file from one battleship-gray cabinet. "Here's what we have so far. Give it a going over and let me know what you think."

After he read the scope of the activities of the kiddie terrorists, Pope was even more determined. He returned the file to Lailey's desk. "I really want to take this one, Commander. I want a free hand to look into the cause and source of the attacks."

Lailey considered it a moment. Grudgingly, he nodded. "All right, I'll authorize it. Subject, of course, to orders from the G-3."

For the sake of shoving in the needle a little further, Lieutenant Marino beamed back his gratitude.

"Thank you, sir. You have no idea how much I appreciate this."

"Wait and see, Marino," Lailey grumbled. "This may be more than you can handle."

"You are certain you are five months pregnant?" Dr. Xohn Kao Key asked the slender young woman seated on his examination table.

Francie Song looked at her physician. "Yes, Doctor, I am sure of it. I have another child, he is seven, and I remember how I felt in the early days."

His next words electrified her. "I think it would be wise for you to not have this child."

Eyes wide, showing a lot of white in her outrage, Francie shouted her answer. "No! I will not, I cannot, abort this child. You see, I am Catholic. *We* honor the sanctity of life."

Shaking his head sadly, the doctor advised further. "Abortion is as old as Asia itself, my dear young woman. There are herbs, infusions that can accomplish it without physical harm to the fetus."

Hands over her ears, Francie hastily jumped from the table. She rearranged her clothing as she spoke. "I don't want to hear anything about that. I will have this baby. I *must* have him."

Eyebrow cocked, the doctor tried another tack. "How are you so sure it will be a boy? What if it is a girl? Girl babies are of little value in Asia."

Determination hardened the features of Francie Song. "It is a girl I will love her and care for her every bit as much as I love and care for Thran. Besides, the baby's position is the same as when I was carrying Thran. It will be a boy,'' she concluded with smug certainty.

Quickly she paid the doctor and hurried from his office. Why had she come? She knew how important people considered it to have proper care for an expectant mother. Yet thousands of women who lived out in the jungle and high in the mountains had dozens of babies and never saw a doctor, let alone talked with one. *Yes*, her common sense told her, *and most of those babies die before their second year*. She would have to tell her Kent Welby. It could not be put off any longer.

Rotor blades whipping the air into a noisy turmoil, the 0730 mail chopper from Binh Thuy settled onto the helipad inside the SEAL compound at Tre Noc. Out came the sacks of letters and packages from friends and family for the Riverine Force sailors and SEALs alike. Also on board were five green-as-grass replacements for men killed or seriously wounded. Three of them went to First Platoon.

"All right, you newlies, gather around," brayed Tonto Waters. "I'm the platoon chief, Chief Quartermaster Thomas Waters. In a minute, you'll stow your gear in one of those concrete block buildings over there. The rules are simple around here. You keep on the alert at all times. You keep your personal weapon and sufficient ammunition with you at all times. And you are ready to fight off the enemy . . . at all times. Are there any questions?"

"No, Chief," came a chorus.

"Then welcome to Tre Noc. There is a curfew at twenty-three hundred every night. Charlie likes to drop in a few mortar rounds shortly after that and we don't like any of you guys to be out and about where you can pick up some stray chunks of hot metal. The only exception to that is when you are on liberty R and R in Binh Thuy or Saigon.

"In other words, every night is a Cinderella liberty unless you're on an op or far away from the base. Do I make myself clear?"

"YES, Chief!"

"You will draw specialized weapons immediately prior to training or a mission. There will be a briefing on what's shakin' around here after morning chow. Now, here's your bunk assignments." Tonto read off names, building and bunk numbers. "Right, then. Now you're squared away . . . dismissed."

Jesus, Tonto thought as the young SEALs dispersed, *they grow them younger each replacement allotment. Before long, they'll be in knee pants and not yet shavin'*. Tonto Waters did not take into account that, although only twenty-four, he had aged ten years for the one he had spent in Vietnam. Maybe, just maybe, this crop would get a chance to shake down on the Train-Fire and Vil ranges before they went out on an op. No matter how good the training, it all went out the window when they faced the reality of the Viet Cong. It made inexperienced men a danger to everyone.

Kent Welby met Francie Song at the My Flower Laundry. It actually was a laundry, although much of its revenue came from an unlicensed bar, which served beer all the time and some wines when available. It had quickly become the off-base hangout for the SEALs. The couple had a drink with friends, then went off to dinner in the Phon Bai restaurant.

After a delicious meal, something Vietnamese and highly aromatic, they strolled the main street of the mushrooming village to Francie's apartment. Francie put a protesting Thran down for the night and she and Doc sipped wine while the boy dropped off to sleep. When she checked on Thran and found him in deep slumber, she came eagerly into Doc's arms.

Their kisses grew more ardent and Francie resolved that tonight would be the time to tell him. His hand inside her dress rested comfortably on one small breast. She had early on learned to like this American way of prolonging the act until both parties burned with unbearable desire. Then the delightful game of extending it farther began.

How sweet their passionate joinings, she thought as Doc slid his other hand up her thigh. *Everything would be good, perfect, in fact. If only . . . if she could somehow escape the clutches of Sergeant Elmore Yates*. The cold, unwanted thought broke her ascent to ecstasy and she shivered involuntarily.

"What's the matter?"

"Nothing, my precious Kent Welby."

"Hummm. Maybe if I move . . . here?"

Francie's eyes went wide and she squeaked her response. "Oh! Yes, yes, that is lovely."

"Or if I move . . . here?"

Breathless now, desiring him more than she had ever wanted any man, Francie gasped. "Oh, yessss, yessss. Please, hurry, carry me to the bed."

Her slight weight proved insignificant to the superbly conditioned SEAL, although he noted that she might have put on some pounds of late. Eager for their joining, he lifted her and padded barefoot to the bedroom. They disrobed with the eagerness of amorous youths. Embraces and kisses followed, then Doc eased her onto the bed.

Everything continued to go well up until Kent Welby tried to penetrate her. Francie found herself left with shriveled nothingness in her hand. Beside her, Kent groaned in misery.

"Damn it, why does that have to happen? We talked about it, I thought I understood. But—but the thought of Thran popping through the doorway and catching us at—at—"

Francie put a hand on his bare chest. "Easy, darling. We have a lot of time. Here, let me try something very Oriental and very exciting."

She tried and failed to arouse her lover. "Oh, damnit, damnit," Kent groaned. "I keep seeing his face, so wide-eyed and curious about what we were doing the other night."

Francie tried something else. It, too, did not bring results. She found herself growing as frantic as he had become. This simply would not do.

"He didn't know what he was seeing. And if he did, he wouldn't care. He loves you, Kent Welby, nearly as much as I do. Please, let us try again."

Half an hour of intense effort brought no satisfaction. Tears of self-contempt welled up in Kent's eyes. Embarrassed, humiliated, and frustrated, he dressed and started to leave in a black, gloomy mood. Francie sprinted to him from the bed and wheedled with him, toying with his hair and stroking his neck. At last she brought him back to the bed, where she did her best to comfort him.

"It's only temporary. Perhaps you have caught some jungle malady that saps your vigor? We don't know, but we can find out. Please, let us try again."

They did, up until nearly curfew with no satisfactory results. Kent Welby left the apartment with his head hanging. Worst of all, Thran never stirred. And tomorrow they were to take the newlies out on a simulated operation.

CHAPTER 5 ——————————

"BACK WHEN they were organizing Team Two, we didn't know who was gonna be the skipper," Tonto Waters told the audience of newlies during the noon chow break. "We sure didn't expect it to be Pope Marino. Now, Pope goes way back with the UDT. And he'd been AOIC when Barry Lailey had it. But that's another story."

"It sure is," growled Archie Golden. "Hey, I remember one time back at Little Creek. I had me a good set of charges laid among some hedgehogs. Gonna blow 'em sky-high. And I damn near did. When the time came to turn the crank, the chunks went up like rockets. Put one of them a meter off the starboard bow of an admiral's launch. Needless to say, he was sorely pissed. Wanted to know the name, rank, an' sexual habits of the idiot who had tried to scuttle him. Well, Pope stood right up for me.

"He said it must have been someone from another team, or maybe one of our UDT instructors showin' what damage could be done." Archie's freckled face glowed with the respect he had for Marino. "The ad-

53

miral—I forgot which one it was—didn't buy it whole, but it put him off the scent enough. Ol' Tonto here verified what Pope said, and I wound up buyin' the beer for the two of them for a month.'' He gave the rapt newlies a broad wink. ''And that, boys and girls, is one hell of a lot of brew.''

One of the replacements, Jordan, whose cuphandle ears stuck out from his nearly hairless head in such a manner that it had already bought him the nickname Jughead, piped up. ''Hey, did you guys know that they're forming a UDT/SEAL association back at Little Creek?''

''Naw. Tell us about it,'' urged Tonto.

Jordan shrugged. ''We didn't hear too much detail before we shipped out for here. Anyway, they plan to hold annual reunions at Little Creek. All of the East Coast teams, like what they do at Coronado.''

Archie considered that a moment. ''I'll betcha one thing. When they get it going and hold their first meeting, the whole amphib base will be awash to the scuppers in beer.'' His laughter barked through the trees around the Train-Fire Range.

Tonto clapped a hand on Archie's shoulder. ''I won't take that bet, Arch. Because you an' me will be there and that means they'll have to bring in an extra truckload to keep up with us.''

Lieutenant Marino approached and halted in front of the new SEALs. ''Okay, let's go through this exercise again. And remember one thing. It's our guiding principle out here. Less is better. And try to keep your heads down and be quiet.''

*　　*　　*

At least the first part of his journey on water was not as disturbing as the previous one. Lieutenant Colonel Rudinov had taken passage on a motorized patrol boat—a small, armor-plated junk actually. It did not roll side-to-side in the precarious manner of a dugout sampan. They would proceed, running only at night, up the Mekong River to its headwaters in the mountains.

From there it would be a two-day foot march before he could rendezvous with a convoy of trucks. Why couldn't he have been flown directly to Hanoi? The momentary thought of that galled him. Built-in paranoia permeated every level of the *Komitet*. He accepted it, but he did not have to like it. Sighing at the incongruity of "evasive approaches," he sipped from his glass of tea, which had grown cold.

"Comrade Senior Lieutenant." The captain of the vessel invaded his thoughts from the open hatchway. Not even he was aware of Rudinov's true identity. "We are approaching our daytime place of concealment."

Rudinov frowned. "Very well. Make certain that the American river patrols cannot find us."

"Of course, Comrade, we always do."

"Yes, or you wouldn't be here, right?"

"What is that, Comrade?"

Rudinov snorted in contempt. "Never mind. Just see that I am delivered to my destination undetected, in one piece, and on time."

Late the following night, Sergeant First Class Elmore Yates stood in the shadows across the muddy street from the apartment of Francie Song. He shivered and turned up his collar against the chill rain that drove down from a black sky. He could well imagine what went on inside. Images of Francie's naked body seared his brain.

He had seen her lovely, amber flesh only twice, when he had boldly climbed onto the roof of the building next to her dwelling and peered in through an unshuttered window. The first time she had been toweling herself dry before she squirmed tantalizingly into a filmy night gown. The second, and his loins ached and throbbed at memory of it, she had been cavorting in a steamy tub with her son. *If I could have been in the boy's place, I would have shown her a thing or two*, Yates told himself now. When she climbed from the wooden basin, all shiny and slick in the lamplight, she stretched like a cream-filled cat. He almost lost it. Then the boy had joined her and ruined his happy vision.

Now, he could imagine the squirming, churning bodies, coupled and surging toward blissful release. *Goddamn him!* he thought angrily of Kent Welby. The couple's relationship infuriated him for more than one reason. Not only did it flood him with jealousy to imagine her divine body in the arms of Kent Welby, the knowledge that their alliance could jeopardize both himself and Francie haunted him. Somehow, Yates decided angrily, he would have to do something about ending it.

"I'm sorry, honey, really I am. I don't understand it. This is two nights in a row. And all I can think of when we're right in the mood is Thran walking in on us. It's just . . . the way I am."

"Tell me about it," Francie urged as she lay in frustration beside Kent on her bed. "Tell me why you are like you are."

They had been over this before. Kent made a pained expression, still vexed by the experience. "Once when I was little, I peeked through the bathroom keyhole at my sister taking a bath. My Mom caught me and gave me a whale of a licking. She said it was a mortal sin for little boys to look at little girls when they were undressed. My butt stung all day and I lived in fear of ever encountering Sally naked, even by accident."

Francie Song sighed in exasperation. "Why is it sinful to look at something so beautiful as the human body? I know, I've asked you that before, but your answer did not make sense to me."

Kent groaned in his embarrassment. "In America, we Catholics, and I think most kids, are taught it is not only a sin to look, but it's a sin to *want* to look."

"*Mon bien Dieu*, how do your people ever have babies?"

Abruptly, that struck Kent as funny. He laughed softly. "It just . . . happens."

"But, don't you learn things from other boys, ones who are not brought up the way you were?"

"Oh, yes. By the time I was eight, I knew all about *doing* it. Only I didn't have the least idea how one managed to do it. And the priests scared you to death about even *thinking* about anything connected with sex, though the word was never mentioned."

"Silly," Francie dismissed. Then, "How does this feel?"

"Good. Very good."

"Do you think we can try again?"

"Yes, I think we can. Yes—yes, I *know* we can."
Then after a few long, intense, silent minutes, "Aaah,
Francie—Francie, this is soooo wonderful."

Lieutenant Carl Marino stepped out of his phone
booth–sized office a minute before the first muster
formation. Squinting, he stepped into the bright light
of the Tre Noc compound. He took his position and
formally received the report of the team chief, then
gestured with the papers in his left hand.

"Now hear this. Guys, you know about how I got
my face cut up. Well, I had a little talk with our good
friend Commander Lailey about it, and orders have
come down for us to dig into this kiddie terrorist activity. They are leaving bicycle bombs all over the
place. I didn't know there were that many spare bikes
in this country."

"They're stealin' 'em, LT," Chad Ditto offered.

"That sounds reasonable, Repeat. They're using
them to kill people, so a little theft shouldn't matter
much. Bravo Squad is to go out on a sweep and grab
some area VC to interrogate. You will draw equipment and depart the base at sixteen-forty-five hours.
Stay out until you can bring back enough Cong to get
more than one or two slants of what is going on. Briefing will be at fourteen-thirty. That's all. Dismiss the
muster, Chief."

QMC Tom Waters snapped to attention. "Aye aye,
sir."

Later, over a cup of dissolve-the-spoon coffee,
Tonto Waters and Archie Golden compared notes.
Archie cut a slantways gaze at the officers' table. "I

wonder why we aren't going out on this op?"

Tonto had a quick, though unsatisfactory, answer. "We have two of the newlies, remember?"

"So? They've got to get their feet wet sometime, right? Why not now?"

"Be thankful for small favors." Tonto drank deeply from the bitter brew. "The idea is to take Charlie alive and not get anyone hurt."

"Hell, you an' me could do it by ourselves. Maybe take Doc along. Or am I just being touchy?"

Snickering, Tonto finished his coffee. "At least you're not touchy-feely." He stood up. "Let's get over to the machine shed. I've got McGonigal workin' on hushpuppies for our long guns. Maybe he has enough for those guys of Anchor Head's to take along."

Garrity McGonigal had the rolling gait of a fleet sailor and the round, smile-wreathed face of a man from County Cork. Born and bred in Boston, he had the dockside, chowderhead accent implanted in his soul.

"Fot in a codbowad cottin, if it ain't the Jehzey Kid. How's it hangin' Tonto?"

"Low and lonesome, Garry. Say, do you have those suppressors finished yet?"

"Naw. We machined all the tubes. But I cou'n't get enough washehs of the right size. I have a dozen, though. Will that help?"

Tonto beamed his satisfaction. "Yeah, for what I've got in mind."

"What might that be?"

Tonto put tongue in cheek. "Just like them hush-puppies. It's all very hush-hush."

McGonigal nodded sagely. "Some of your guys goin' after another big shot?"

Deliberately letting the machinist go astray, Tonto played along. "Bite your tongue, McGonigal."

"Hope it's the fucker who's been teachin' those gooks to shoot straight. We've been up to the gunwhales in armor plate to repair."

"Maybe it is. I'll never tell."

Tonto and Archie gathered up the custom-made suppressors and took them to the armory vault. It would help considerably if the Cong could be taken silently.

Petey Danvers paced in a long oval in front of the gate to the UDT School on the strand of Coronado Island. The neat white buildings beyond the fence that separated the demonstrators from the naval base lumped together in a blur to his drug-fuzzy eyes. Petey chanted lustily with the others.

"Hell no, we won't go! Hell no, we won't go!"

Petey carried a placard that blazoned forth with bold, red letters:

BABY KILLER SAILORS
CONFESS YOUR WAR CRIMES!

Petey reveled in satisfaction at how successful the demonstration had been so far. A dropout from UDT/R School, and dishonorably discharged from the navy for smoking pot, the World Peace Foundation had become his home, and Petey repaid them with his enthusiasm at every march and picketing. He had even traveled as far as San Francisco for the cause. No one in the WPF knew that he had been a volunteer for military service. And Petey would never admit that his inability to accept the authority of anyone over him, or to take responsibility for his actions, had gotten him ousted from the service he had entered with such high hope. It had embittered him and he turned to the antiwar movement for consolation. At least they had good sources for primo weed and really boss LSD. Some of the chicks were cool, too.

Petey looked up from his pot-fogged reverie to see a growing number of trim, fit, muscular young men along the inner face of the chain-link fence. He didn't like that much. If they got pissed off enough, and the older guys would sure as hell do that, they might come out here and bust a few heads. At least if the stuff hit the fan they would not have to go back to the ferry through the gauntlet of NAS North Island. They could split south to Imperial Beach and San Ysidro. Might even skip over to TJ for a while. Marla, the chick he was sleeping with this week, would groove on that. Lots of grass, and even some blow over there. Petey began to shake his fist at the UDT students.

"Murderers! Baby killers! Killers ... killers ... killers!" The others took up his new chant.

Only a single SEAL recruit lost patience and answered them. "Aawh ... go ... fuck ... yourselves!"

Lieutenant Commander Barry Lailey was having second thoughts about getting the mission to break up the child terrorist ring assigned to Carl Marino's SEALs. If they went out there and did a good job, it would only reflect credibly on Marino. It was one thing to have the man take the chance of getting blown away. It was quite another for him to come out of it smelling like a rose.

No matter how much time had gone by, Marino's actions, and his later testimony before the board of inquiry, still rankled Lailey. Hell, Marino had been a kid officer, not even dry behind the ears, when that op went bad down in Central America. John Kennedy had only signed the authorization to organize the SEAL Teams eight months before that crucial test of their ability had been devised. Extract a deep-cover agent who had been infiltrated into a large band of Marxist guerrillas operating in the mountains that divided Nicaragua from El Salvador. Piece of cake. Then it turned sour.

Three guys bought it, including the CIA spook. For all of Marino's twisting the facts, Barry Lailey remained convinced that it had been Marino who had caused the death of those men. What else could it be? Marino was the most junior, least experienced officer. Logic pointed to him as the cause. It *had* to be.

Then why is it that you were the one transferred out of the SEAL program, given a desk job, and passed over for promotion every time? Lailey's mind mocked him.

Barry Lailey slammed his fist on his desk and blurted out his perplexity. "Goddamnit, he has to screw up this time! Has to!"

CHAPTER 6 —————————————

ANCHOR HEAD Sturgis put Walter Redfern on point. The young Navajo from Arizona had the best eyesight and quickest reactions Sturgis had ever encountered. Soft-spoken and impeccably polite, the twenty-year-old SEAL had been a boon to Bravo Squad's operations since UDT/R training.

His visual acuity had contributed greatly to the embarrassment of a group of junior officers. While training on the islets around Puerto Rico, Walt Redfern's keen sight picked out a group of ensigns and j.g.s from the local naval base who had thought this particular island cove to be ideal for an afternoon of skinny-dipping with some of the local lovelies.

Redfern not only saw them, he photographed them cavorting in the surf with their young ladies, all of them mother-naked. Redfern had the film developed and saw that copies of the photos got around to the naval personnel involved. He could imagine the howls of anguish, albeit silent ones, that must have gone up among the fleet sailors and navy aviators involved.

Always the gentleman, Redfern did not offer the

negatives for sale. He simply assembled all concerned, let them examine the evidence, then burned the negatives before their eyes. Unwittingly, he also bought a great deal of affection and respect for his brother SEALs. Today, he faced a far grimmer assignment.

Drifting as silently as possible through the lianas and cabbage palms, the short, stocky QM/1C kept his eyes in constant motion. Although definitely night, enough weak starlight filtered through for Redfern to make out the figures of unfriendlies, if any were to be found.

Walt Redfern liked the two-foot-long metal cylinder that hung on the muzzle of his CAR-15. Built on the Worbel principle, the suppressor and its end-wipe cut off nearly all sound of the cartridge firing, and also reduced the muzzle bloom to a mere flicker that lasted a fraction of a second. After Tonto Waters had distributed them, the SEALs of Bravo had tested their effectiveness right inside the compound. Not even the sentries in the guard towers heard anything.

It would give him the advantage, Redfern knew, over any Viet Cong who might be around. Local assets had advised the SEALs of a small encampment the VC had established on the ridge they now swept from end to end. So far nothing, which Redfern knew did not mean a thing. The Cong could rise right out of the ground and ambush any slack patrol with disastrous results. His uncle, *Hosteen* Naugay, had told him of how clever the North Koreans and Chinese had been at doing such things during the Korean War. Walt Redfern had taken the lessons to heart.

An out of place aroma caught the attention of his nose. He halted and sniffed.

"Yeah," he whispered to himself. "*Nuoc Mam.*" There was no hand signal for *enemy in smell*, and only Anchor Head, who wore night-vision goggles could have seen it if there had been.

Being careful not to disturb the undergrowth, Walt Redfern eased backward fifty meters and waited for the rest of the squad to catch up to him. When they did, he eased up and whispered into each available ear.

"We've got company up ahead. Spread out and hold what you've got."

Anchor Head asked the key question. "How many?"

"I don't know. I just smelled them."

"You're shittin' me."

"No. Fish sauce. It came to me clear as could be."

"Okay. Here's what we do. You go ahead and get a fix on them. We'll come along, and spread out in a half-circle. Bring us in real close and I'll pop a round to get their attention. Then we roll 'em up and take 'em home."

"What if they resist?"

Anchor Head shrugged, a darker movement in the blackness. "Do what you have to. But the skipper said to bring back more 'n two to question."

Walt Redfern went ahead to locate the VC. It did not take him long. They had a neat little camp, under a large, spreading mahogany tree. The thick branches and a high ring of rocks effectively hid the small fire over which they cooked their food. The odor of *Nuoc Mam* and broiling fish came stronger to Redfern's nostrils. He edged in to where he could get a good look.

Six men sat around the tiny fire. Four of them faced outward, whether to guard against discovery by an American patrol or to warn of the approach of their own kind, Redfern did not know. The others tended their food. All of them were violating regulations about fires at night. Crouched close by, Redfern saw two small boys, on the younger edge of their teens. *Perfect. Now if the squad can only scoop them up.* Walt Redfern eased himself away and went in search of his buddies.

It took twenty minutes for the squad to move into place. A moment later, Walt Redfern heard a soft *phuttt* and the tin pot of rice went flying from the fire.

"Do not move, we have you surrounded," the PRC—Kit Carson Scout—assigned to the squad said in Vietnamese for Anchor Head Sturgis.

One of the men's hand closed on the forestock of his Type 56 assault rifle. Anchor Head put a stop to it with a neat, blood-rimmed hole in the forehead of the VC. His comrades still had no idea where the bullets came from. Worse, they heard no shot. One of the little boys turned away from the scene and began to cry. The older kid tried to comfort him. Slowly, the five Cong raised their hands.

With that, the SEALs came out into the clearing around the huge tree. Expertly they lashed the hands of the enemy behind them. Then they cut and threaded poles of monkey palm between arms and bodies.

"Tell 'em to keep quiet if they don't want to be

gagged,'' Anchor Head told the Vietnamese interpreter.

One by one, the boys were secured. The one who had started to sob and whine had also wet his trousers, which shamed him out of his state of terror. ''Put them in front of the other prisoners, Walt, then join me at the head of the column,'' Anchor Head instructed Redfern. ''Long Tom, put out the fire and take position on my six, in front of the prisoners.'' The rest of the SEALs fell in behind the captives and all started back to their pickup point.

Long Tom Killian, the RTO, sounded greatly relieved when he observed in a whisper to Anchor Head, ''Like Pope said, 'Piece of cake.' ''

Anchor Head studied the face of Long Tom as best he could in the darkness. He wanted to know if the cocky bantam rooster was joking.

Early the next morning, back again at Tre Noc, the interrogation of the five VC lasted an extraordinarily short time. They refused to answer any questions. One by one they sat alone in the jury-rigged interrogation room and remained silent. Every legal technique known to the SEALs failed to produce results. At last the Cong were brought together in the room. A PRC interpreter translated the comments of the Americans.

Tonto Waters had joined the questioning. When none of the group wavered, he spoke in a casual, off-hand manner to Anchor Head Sturgis. ''Why don't we call in a chopper and take 'em up? You know, climb about a thousand meters and question them Marvin-the-ARVN style. Ask a question. If none of them answers, kick one out the door.''

Anchor Head grinned, enjoying the role he played. "That's a good idea. Let's take 'em out now."

From there the prisoners, including the two small boys, were taken to the edge of the helipad. Their nervousness became immediately obvious. When the man they had seen with a radio out in the bush trotted up, the Cong grew excessively agitated.

His announcement stunned them. "There's a slick on the way, Chief."

"Good, Killian. Get 'em ready."

When the insectile object came into view, the Cong began to jabber excitedly among themselves. The thop-thop of the rotor blades drowned out their appeals to reason and mercy. Something had gone terribly wrong. Told by their instructors that the Americans never used torture, they had been trained in interrogation techniques and conditioned to resist them.

When the UH-1A began its final approach, their composure disintegrated totally. Rather than face certain death being thrown from the helicopter, several opted for an attempt to escape.

Three of them broke from the cluster and ran toward the inner fence. One cut himself so badly on a concertina wire that he bled out through a severed artery and dropped to the ground before he could reach the diamond-pattern cyclone fence. Another made it halfway up before a marine guard shot him off with a three-round burst from his M14. The third fell to his knees, sobbing wretchedly.

Even though thoroughly terrorized, the surviving three remained silent on any questions relating to the child bombers. Disgusted, Tonto turned to Anchor

Head. "Send them back to Binh Thuy on the mail chopper. Let the S-Two sweat them a while."

"Aye-aye, Chief. What about the kids?"

Tonto turned to look at the youngsters. They stood in place, wide-eyed and trembling, faces solemn. "What say we give them a try?"

"Good idea."

Anchor Head escorted the boys back to the interrogation room while Tonto headed for the mess. He came back with some cookies and two glasses of milk. "Maybe this will help," he suggested.

Hesitant at first, their resolve crumbled after Tonto took a sip from both glasses and bit into a cookie. Eagerly, they gobbled the cookies and gulped the milk. Then, with slight prodding, they opened up.

The eldest, who identified himself as Hian Lak and gave his age as eleven, spoke in a low intense tone. "There is a hidden training base in the marshlands. It is farther up the river than this place. At the camp, loyal sons of trusted Viet Cong," and there he swelled his chest proudly, "are taught about constructing bombs, how to make their approaches, and the best places to leave the bombs."

"How many boys are there?" Tonto asked.

Lak looked troubled. "I do not know. We were on our way there when you Green Faces captured us."

"Do you know where it is?"

"I am not sure."

Kim Ghea, who said he was ten, tapped his companion on a slender arm. "Comrade Cao Nan said we were within twelve *li* of the camp when we stopped to eat."

Lak brightened, then nodded. "That's right."

Anchor Head produced a map. It took him only a couple of seconds to locate where they had captured the Cong. "Here is where we took you prisoner. Do you think you can show me where the camp is located?"

Lak and Ghea frowned and stared long at the lines and colors on the big square of paper. At last the older boy spoke. "How long is a *li* on here?"

The interpreter told Anchor Head that a *li* was approximately seven-eighths of a kilometer. Anchor Head puzzled that out and then showed the lad with a ruler. Quickly Lak worked it out. His small index finger pointed triumphantly at a spot in a deep valley, surrounded by high, forested hills. Grinning, he turned to Tonto.

"Here. This is where it is."

Tonto patted the youth on his mop of black hair. "We got it, Anchor Head. Now we have to do something about it."

Jason Slater had a glum expression on his long, craggy face as he walked toward the Palace Hotel in My Tho, dressed today in his big white Stetson, cowboy boots, and Western-cut suit. He had lost contact with his counterpart, *Podpolkovnik* Pyotr Rudinov of the KGB. Yes, he knew about the recent promotion. Even the most efficient intelligence service on the planet had its leaks and its moles. Due to his area of operation, Rudinov was given special attention.

Through the cooperation of MI-6, an elderly major in the Asian Affairs Directorate of the KGB who had been doubled by the British provided first-quality product on Rudinov. Through him, a file had been created. It contained every detail of the life of Pyotr Maximovich Rudinov. The schools he had attended as a boy, his military service record, his KGB training, including an intensive three month stay at the Charm School, his matriculation at the *Spetznaz* school, even his political orientation indoctrination prior to service as a *zampolit* in a *Spetznaz* unit, had been meticulously recorded. It had now grown to nearly the size of a Manhattan telephone book. Slater turned to Hank Burroughs, one of the field agents assigned to his My Tho Station.

"Get ahold of Buddha. Have him get some people in and check out Rudinov's Cambodian lair. We need to know where he has gone."

"Right after we eat. I hear the Palace chef is preparing oysters on the half shell, hot and sour giant prawns, and steamed hearts of palm."

Slater made a face. "Your gut is going to get you killed yet, Hank. Me, I'll just settle for a rare steak and French fries."

Burroughs's expression filled with horror. "All that fat? And you say I'm in danger. Didn't you ever hear of heart attacks?"

Laughing, Slater added, "Oh, yeah, and a pint bottle of nut brown ale. Now, do some skull work on finding Rudinov for me."

After the success with the VC kiddies, Tonto Waters and Archie Golden hitched a ride to Binh Thuy for a visit with Dusty Rhodes. They reached the hospital hot, dry, and dust-streaked. Tonto led the way to the head.

Still sweating, Tonto bent over a basin and splashed

water onto his face. "I feel like I've been rolled in mud and deep-fried."

His cammo sleeves hiked up to his elbows, Archie scrubbed energetically. "You got that right, Tonto. You think they'll let us in Dusty's room like this? All the starch in my dungarees has transferred to my body."

Grinning, Tonto pointed to their images in the mirror. "We'll just tell them we came straight in from the field."

Five minutes later, they presented themselves at the nurses' station on Dusty's ward. "Third door down on the port side," a male navy nurse informed them without even looking up.

Dusty had a nice view outside the hospital. The window had been raised two inches at top and bottom to let the humid air circulate. They could smell the jungle. Dusty was seated in a chair, reading a book, when the two SEALs entered the room.

"How're you doin', sir?" greeted Tonto.

Dusty looked up and gave them a huge smile. "Fine as frog hair, guys. Only I wish I could get the hell out of here. What's going on out there?"

"Did Pope tell you about the kiddie bombers?"

"Yeah, he did. Said he was tryin' to get an op laid on to do something about it."

"It's already in the works," Archie said. "We got a break this morning. We found out there's a training school and where it's located."

"Really? Who told you about it?"

Tonto took up the informal briefing. "From a couple of kids on their way there."

"Yeah, Tonto gave them some cookies and milk

and patted them on the head, so they spilled their guts.''

Tonto made little of his part. ''They were ready before any of that. They'd just seen one of the grown-up Cong Anchor Head's Bravos bagged cut to doll rags on the razor wire and another get blown away by a tower guard. Hell, they were only eleven and ten years old.''

His expression grim, Dusty stared at a wall for a moment. ''That young? God, what is it we're fighting here? I still have nightmares about that shock machine General Giap wired me to. Now this. How do we win against that sort of barbarism?''

Archie Golden growled his opinion. ''I say nuke them all and let God sort 'em out.''

They talked a while about life at Tre Noc, and before they knew it another nurse, this one a female in starched white, stepped into the room. Her smile was plastic. ''Sorry. Time is up. You can come back another time.''

Tonto and Archie said their good-byes to Dusty and walked the hall to the exit door for the ward. Outside the hospital, they took a white gravel path that led along the outer wall to Dusty's room.

''I never got the chance to slip him this bottle,'' said Tonto with a wink. From one cargo pocket of his tiger-stripes he produced a half-pint bottle of brandy. ''I'll just slip it through the window.''

Approaching the window from the pathway, Tonto heard the sounds of a scuffle from inside. He quickly motioned to Archie, who came at a trot. ''There's somethin' goin' on in there. Give me a hand.''

Archie cupped his hands and gave Tonto a stirrup

lift until he could see inside the room. What he saw widened Tonto's eyes with shock, though it did not slow his reaction. Two Asian men struggled with Dusty, who did his best to fend them off. One of the men held a knife. The other had a hypodermic needle.

That settled it for Tom Waters. He quickly slung the lower sash upward, drew his 9mm Browning, and fired through the opening. One of the Cambodians dropped with a bullet through his chest. The other bolted. Tonto Waters squeezed through the window and went after the second assailant.

He burst into the hallway, only to find it filled with orderlies wheeling large carts containing the noon meal along from room to room. Panic broke out instantly when the hospital staff observed one man fleeing down the hall, and another in hot pursuit, a pistol in his hand. Unable to fire because of the orderlies, nurses, and patients in the corridor, Tonto poured on the speed.

"Shit!" he spat in frustration as the fugitive rounded a corner and sprinted along a less congested passageway. Tonto gained ground when he, too, rounded the intersection. The fleeing man slammed into a meal cart and rebounded, his speed reduced to zero.

Covering the last six feet between them, Tonto replaced the 9mm in its holster. As the Cambodian started to run again, Tonto launched himself. Arms spread wide, he brought down the man with a flying tackle.

Tonto roughly flipped his prisoner over on his back. He jammed a knee in the man's hard, flat belly and reached out to slap the squirming prisoner in the face.

Then, before he could prevent it, he heard the soft crunch of glass and smelled the bitter almond scent as the wet affairs man swallowed cyanide.

"Awh, shit," Tonto Waters said to the sea of faces as nurses and orderlies gathered around. "This guy was not Cong. He was a professional."

CHAPTER 7 —————————————————

WHEN THE NIS had finished with him, they turned Tonto over to counterintelligence. They asked all the same questions in the same order, then went back and mixed them up a little. It didn't take Tonto long to have all he wanted of this.

"Hey, guys, give me a break. Naval Investigative Services asked me all the same questions half a dozen times. I didn't invite that asshole in here, and I sure didn't provide him with the death pill. I'd say he was connected to some spook operation. Probably Soviet."

A glance passed between his two interrogators. The KGB was using some Laotians and Cambodians in the Asian Wet Affairs directorate, but Need to Know prevented them from telling this cocky chief quartermaster.

"Just bear with us and answer a few more questions, Chief Waters."

Tonto remained surly. "You might try one I haven't already answered."

"How about this? Do you recall seeing either of

the men you killed when you first entered the hospital?''

''I didn't kill but one of them. The other suicided. But, no. Not that I recall.''

''What about when you left Mr. Rhodes's room?''

Tonto considered a moment. ''There was one gook that caught my attention. He was in the hall, near the exit. It coulda been that bright red shirt the one I shot was wearing. Yeah. It just might have been.''

''That's good. What about the other one? The one who swallowed poison?''

''Naw. I would have remembered that Tigers baseball cap. D'you ask Archie any of this?''

''Who is Archie?''

''Machinist's Mate Third Richard Golden. We call him Archie because of his red hair and freckles.''

The stuffier of the two sneered a question. ''What has his appearance to do with the name?''

Tonto eyed him like he had just stepped out of a flying saucer. ''Jeez, ain't you ever read a comic book?''

''Not since I was eleven.''

''Y'know, Archie as in *Archie Andrews*.''

''Remarkable. But, yes, we did ask him. He also noted the red shirt. Had he looked in the room when you discovered the scuffle?''

''No. He was holdin' me up.''

Both CIC agents came to their feet. The friendlier one looked down at Tonto, who remained seated. ''All right, then, that verifies what you said. Also, the shore patrol found your brass outside the window, which fits the rest. I suppose we have to develop anything else from other witnesses. You are free to leave, Chief.''

Tonto showed he understood sarcasm as well. ''Thank you so much.''

''You are welcome. Ah—we may be in touch again.''

Tonto let a grin turn the corners of his mouth. ''If you do, come down to Tre Noc. We'll be sure to show you a good time.''

Early in the afternoon, two high-ranking NVA officers, Lieutenant General Van Vangh and Major General Thrun Diem, arrived from Hanoi at the villa in Vinh Province, used as headquarters by Brigadier General Hoi Pac. With them came a party of five Soviet technicians, led by *Podpolkovnik* Viktor Vassilivich Borkoi. The presence of the six Russians did little to please General Hoi. In fact, Hoi was busy amusing himself with his ''youngest blossom'' when news of their presence was discreetly brought to him.

Complaining over the interruption, he rapidly completed and withdrew from her, then dressed and straightened his uniform. ''May I inquire as to why I was not advised of your visit?'' he demanded when he confronted his unwelcome guests.

Giving a false smile, Major General Thrun, chief of the Directorate of Information, took a deep drag on his black Turkish cigarette in its ivory holder and blew a fat, perfect smoke ring before answering. ''My dear Comrade Hoi, our mission is of the utmost secrecy. We have brought these Soviet gentlemen here to meet with the director of this very important project. When he arrives, we will soon after be gone from your hospitable abode.''

Fornicating politician, Hoi thought with the usual contempt of a military man for civilian authorities. Yet he could not avoid the slight shudder than ran through him, caused by the cold aura that radiated from the overlarge general. At 1.7 meters and nearly ninety kilos, Thrun was indeed much bigger than most Vietnamese. Barely in time did Hoi remember his manners.

''I am honored that you have chosen my head-quarters for this important rendezvous. May I inquire the nature of this project, Comrade General?''

Icily, Thrun Diem informed him, ''You may, but you will not receive an answer. It is an Eyes Only project and you have no need to know.''

Instantly furious at this slighting, it took all Hoi's willpower to prevent him from making an outburst. ''Welcome, then, to all of you. Everyone must be tired from your journey. I will have tea brought, and pastries.''

Thrun eyed him thoughtfully. ''I think . . . some of your famous overproof Chinese wine would be more in order. And some vodka for our Russian friends, if you have some. Oh, permit me to introduce you.''

''Brigadier General Hoi Pac, this is Comrade Lieutenant Colonel Viktor Vassilivich Borkoi, a senior technician of the Soviet Army Rocket Corps.'' He refrained from naming what type of technician. ''*Podpolkovnik* Borkoi, *Brigadirisher* Hoi Pac,'' he continued smoothly in Russian.

Borkoi extended his hand, unaccustomed to the Asian practice of bowing. ''*Ochyeen' preyahtnah.*''

General Hoi studied the sandy-haired young man, with the sea-green eyes and ruddy complexion, then bowed, somewhat stiffly. "*Da, eto preyatnee*," he responded in the same language, mostly to irritate Thrun. This was not going to be a happy visit, Hoi concluded.

Both Alpha and Bravo would go on the mission to take out the terrorist school. They sat hunkered around the interior of one concrete-block barrack room, backs against the walls.

Carl Marino briefed them. "Listen up, guys. We're going to go in on this in a modified parakeet op. One slick, one cobra. A single pass to trash the place, then we drop in before they can recover. I want two XM148s with each squad, one each of our pump forty mike-mikes, and the SAWs. Sixty rounds for each pump-gun tube, the usual six hundred for the Stoners, and two hundred rounds in magazines for all the rest."

He fixed them with a sober, stern look. "Anything adult that moves, take it out. Try not to waste any kids, but don't take any chances. We'll depart here at 1630 hours, fly map of the earth to the valley, then pop up and make the first pass. We'll take fast ropes to the ground with the Cobra covering, then spread out. The idea is to confine the cadre and isolate the kids. All of you have done this often enough it should go smoothly. Now, here are some high altitude shots of the camp. Study them well, then report to the gear locker and armory. Questions?"

Chad Ditto raised his hand. "Yeah, Pope. I understand trying to salvage the kids. But what if some of them resist?'' His expression said he didn't think he would like the answer.

Pope cut not an inch of slack. ''Do what you have to.''

Violent vibrations seeped into the skull of Kent Welby. Why in hell did these choppers have to shake so much? And the way they hedge-hopped over the taller trees and hillocks kept his stomach in a constant state of rebellion. He would have liked to use a barf bag, but he knew the rest of the guys would think him some sort of wimp. Getting out of the aircraft without it landing, even under fire, did not bother him as much as the flight itself.

Kent recalled their long journey across the Pacific to Vietnam. Kerosene odor from the fuel for the turboprop engines of the C-130D seeped into the passenger compartment. In the initial stage, it made nearly everyone airsick. Kent Welby had not been self-conscious about upchucking everything within half an hour after each takeoff. He had plenty of company. Later on, though, it became painfully obvious that Kent was not a great fan of flying.

''You have to get beyond it,'' Kent had been told by one of the instructors in jump school at Fort Benning. ''Your job begins when you get on the ground. Leave the flying to the Air Force dudes. They know what they're doing.''

Even dredging up that memory did not help when the screw gears in the wings whined as the flaps lowered for the last time and the landing gear thumped out of the wheel wells. Kent Welby knew at once that he was in for another of what Tonto Waters called "white knuckle landings." Zipping across the Mekong Delta at over a hundred miles an hour in a craft with an aluminum and magnesium skin and titanium ribs did little to reassure him now. *Would it never end?*

With a sudden, unexpected upward thrust, the chopper began to climb. This was it!

Tom Waters sat next to the open door. A yoke-mounted M-60 machine gun swayed on its tether over his head. It would be used to slash into the terrorist school along with the awesome firepower of the Cobra gunship. The main rotor turned at full revs in order to keep them aloft in the dense air so low to the ground. Every hump and bump as they rose over some obstruction gave Tonto a twinge, though he grinned like a ninny. It was like a roller coaster. And he had loved them as a kid.

Only this would be far more dangerous than anything they had at Jersey Beach or over at Coney Island. From the reconnaissance photos, the interpreters had estimated fully fifty boys, the oldest barely into their teens, and a cadre of twenty. Add to another twenty-four for guards and lesser staff, it made quite a force to engage. *What in hell ever got me here?*

Blame Richard Widmark for that. As a punk kid in high school, Tonto had gone with friends to see *The Frogmen*, and had dreamed of being in UDT for months after. When jobs grew thin—and boring—after graduation from high school, young Tom Waters had recalled his fascination with the exploits of the Under Water Demolitions teams and joined the navy. What the recruiter conveniently failed to tell him was that he had to earn a rating before he could apply for UDT school. That took some time, and when it had been accomplished he was at last off to the goal he coveted. Then came the even more rigorous UDT/R school and he wound up a SEAL.

It didn't seem it had taken so much time, yet the years had gone by and now he sat in a helicopter and waited for a chance to throw himself into harm's way again. Any guy with a room temperature IQ should know better than to ever do what he did on a regular basis. Truth was, Tonto had to admit, he loved it. He had heard the talk, some even from medical officers, about getting addicted to the rush of excitement. Adrenalin junkies, they were called. In his quieter, introspective moments, Tom Waters often wondered if the phrase fit him. Suddenly the UH-1 jinked sharply upward. The red light on the forward bulkhead blinked once, then returned to a steady glow. Next time it would switch to green.

Archie Golden sat with his CAR-15 cradled in his lap. The harness that held him in place against the vibration of the helicopter strained against his shoulders. This was the roughest ride he had ever had in one of these birds. Usually they went in at night. The thermals had subsided somewhat by then. Yeah, he knew the flying lingo. In his carefree days, back before joining the Navy, Archie had toyed with the idea of being a pilot. He had taken ground school and passed the exam, and even gone so far as to solo and log 100 hours. Then the money had run dry and he gave it up. That didn't keep him from imagining his hand on the controls and trying to second guess the pilot. That could be a kick. Choppers were different, though. Sort of tricky.

They had two controls, one for each hand, the cyclic and the collective. Archie thought hard on what he had picked up from yarning sessions with some of the pilots who flew into Tre Noc. The cyclic contained the throttle and was used, along with the rudder peddles, to control pitch and yaw. The collective governed rotor pitch and attitude. It took both hands and both feet to fly a chopper—sort of like patting one's head and rubbing the stomach at the same time. In fact, one Army warrant officer had told him, that was a skill highly looked upon by flight instructors at Fort Rucker. *Give me a nice stick of C-4, a claymore, or a satchel charge any day*, Archie thought with amusement. Right then, the nose went up with a jerk and he knew they were on their way in.

Carl Marino sat with his eyes closed. His head nodded gently with the vibrations of the helicopter. He wasn't exactly asleep. He only let his mind wander and allowed himself to bleed off the tension that always preceded combat. He could not help but think of the small figures in the recon photos. What sort of animals would deliberately train children that young to commit acts of mass murder? Although Pope Marino and his father had not agreed on much while he had been growing, he now had to admit his dad had been right about the Marxist-Socialists. Every day, here in Vietnam, they seemed to prove that they were indeed depraved, morally bankrupt, unprincipled monsters, who would not stop at anything to enforce their will on everyone else.

"The ends justify the means." Marino recalled a poly sci professor in his freshman year who had frequently used the expression, speaking the words lovingly, caressing every word. *"Power comes from the end of a gun."* Mao Tse Tung had said that, and now Mao's army was aiding the North Vietnamese and the Viet Cong in their effort to wrest the government of the south from those who held it. Not that the Southern government had proven any prize specimens, Pope Marino acknowledged. Corruption ranked second only to a military "democracy" that would gag a maggot. Why was it that oppression was seen by so many as the only means of governing people?

Another phrase, from a philosophy course, which had become a cliché, came to Pope's mind. *"All power corrupts. Absolute power corrupts absolutely."* The monolithic structure of the military had certainly given him ample examples of that truth. Lieutenant Marino sensed an increase in the throttle and the chopper began to lift steeply a moment later. Another two minutes and they would be down there among those kids.

Nuong Tri squatted in the river near the bank, splashing soap off his bare shoulders and chest. He wished they had time and a good place to swim. Like his three brothers, he had learned to swim as a baby. He loved the water. But Comrade Phom said that school was more important than recreation. Oh, he liked the lessons on making bombs, and how to decide on the best places to put them. The lessons excited him like nothing else had in his eleven years. Tri's older brother, Cao, came directly at him, showering the air with water as he swam from midstream. Two years junior to him, Tri did not dare defy the orders given them about pleasure swimming. They were to use the river only for bathing, yet Cao gleefully shrugged aside the regulations and enjoyed himself. When he reached Tri, Cao led the way out of the water.

Both boys grabbed towels and began to dry themselves. The air remained muggy, the temperature in the high eighties. The cotton cloth seemed far too little to take away the river's water. Cao and Tri squirmed into short black trousers and yoke-necked, short-sleeved white shirts. They found their thongs among those of the others and slid their feet into them. Laughing, they joined some boys and ran back toward the classroom.

A sudden thunder drew their attention to the sky behind them. As one, fourteen boys turned to stare into the sky. They saw the bug-eyed, insectlike noses of two large, green helicopters. A flicker of orange began from a long, black cylinder on the side of one. A terrible, musical roar smashed into their ears. Screaming, the children scattered in every direction as mushrooms of dust geysered as high as their shoulders.

Swiftly, the impacts tracked toward the building that housed their dormitory and classroom. The structure suddenly bulged, then flew apart in a shower of boards. Black smoke quickly swallowed the bright orange flame inside the destroyed facility. The sound wave hit the boys next, bowling most of them over.

Tri went flying and lost sight of Cao. Acrid fumes from the explosion filled his nose and throat. He coughed frantically. His eyes burned and stung. More loud reports followed. Tri rolled into a ball and tightly clutched his shins with thin arms. He began to sob. *Where was Cao?*

Green light shone from the forward bulkhead as the choppers banked sharply to port and began to circle the compound. One by one the buildings were destroyed. When the Cobra completed its circuit, the Huey broke off and slipped left, hovering over the center of the smoldering, chaotic scene twenty feet below. Ropes spilled from the open doors. Above their heads on the starboard side, the M-60 cut short bursts at any point that showed resistance.

Tonto Waters and Anchor Head Sturgis hit the ground at the same time. Behind them came Archie Golden and Little Pete Peterson. Archie glanced beyond the shoulder of Tonto Waters and saw a small figure rushing directly at them. He held a Type 56 assault rifle, with a yellow-orange flicker at the muzzle.

"Tonto, down!" Archie shouted.

Waters dropped at once and now the screaming little boy faced Archie all alone. The 7.62 chi com bullets that cracked past his head and shoulders made a long, hollow roar. It appeared to him that he moved in glue as Archie raised his Stoner and squeezed the trigger. Then the Stoner opened up with a three-round burst.

One slug struck the magazine of the Type 56 and spun the weapon from small hands. The other two drove puffs of dust from the lad's shirtfront. The boy staggered, bent, and snatched another assault rifle from a dead Cong and then continued to run forward.

He ripped off a long burst of full-auto that snapped above the heads of the Americans with Green Faces.

"No—no!" Archie shouted at him, but he could not hear himself. "Don't make me, kid." Then Archie shot him again.

"Cao! Cao!" another child shrieked as he ran into Archie's field of fire.

In a flash, Archie saw that the kid did not have a weapon. He diverted the muzzle of his Stoner and roughly shoved the boy to the ground. "Stay down," he growled in Vietnamese.

Both squads had moved out by then and begun to engage individual cadre members. Archie looked down at the youth he had manhandled. He looked to be about eight, if he was an American. "Don't move," he added, and started off for his designated objective. On the way, he paused to examine the boy he had killed.

Anguish struck the heart of Archie Golden as he discovered that the youngster could be no older than his son, David. By god, a thirteen-year-old. But so frail and tiny. *Put it behind you*, he admonished. He started on, to find the fighting already diminishing.

Twenty adults had died in the first sweep of the compound. More died rapidly as the SEALs hit the ground. Archie sighted on a VC cadre and cut him down. Half a dozen boys huddled under the guard of Colonel Culpepper of Bravo.

Only one structure remained relatively undamaged. From that structure and a small bunker came the only remaining resistance. Lieutenant Marino studied these strong points a minute then signed to Doc Welby.

He pointed to the bunker. "Put a round from that XM in there."

"Aye aye, sir."

Kent sighted in and fired the blooper. The 40mm grenade sped into the bunker and went off with a muffled thump. White smoke billowed out as the white phosphorous round ignited. Shrieks and screams came from inside. Then the domed roof of the bunker rose a foot as stored ammunition inside went off.

Bravo squad converged on the small shed. The SAW opened up, hosing the side of the maintenance building. Then a couple of grenades sailed through a shattered matting over one window. With their detonation, the fighting ended.

"How many did we take, Chief?" Marino asked Tonto Waters.

Tonto made a quick count. "We've got three adult prisoners and seven kids. Most of the young ones split into the jungle."

"We've got to get out of here. Get them loaded up, fire that building, and we're gone."

CHAPTER 8 ———————————

ABOARD THE slick, the Provencial Recon Unit interpreter questioned the children. They proved more cooperative than expected. Tonto Waters suspected that it might be because they were interrogated separately, using intercom headsets. For one thing, the novelty of it relaxed their wariness. It also allowed them to talk about the school with no one knowing exactly what they said. That held true for all except one of them.

He wept silently and gave his name as Nuong Tri. He asked over and over why they had killed his brother, Cao. From those who did cooperate, they learned that the officer who ran the school had been among the dead. The Kit Carson Scout quickly established that the four men in civilian trousers and guyaberras were explosives technicians. The captured VC sat in surly silence and refused to answer questions. By the time the Huey flared out over the helipad, all of the boys except Tri had been interviewed.

Back at Tre Noc, Doc Welby had a hard time coming to terms with the swift violence of the raid and the deaths of several children. He took his concerns to Pope Marino.

"Pope, what's going to happen to them? The kids, I mean?"

That Marino had been absorbed with the same subject showed in his quick answer. "They'll be questioned again at Binh Thuy, and most likely once more by Jason Slater at My Tho. Then they'll be put into orphanages."

"What if they're not orphans?"

"Don't worry about it, Doc. If their parents are loyal Viet Cong, those kids might as well be dead to them. At least this way they'll have a chance to grow up without being shot by someone on our side or blown up by one of their own bombs."

Pope's assurances helped some. Still, Doc felt he had no one to talk to about his own feelings. He wanted to confide in Francie, but knew he dared not. Besides, he was filled with shame over his reluctance, or more often lately, his inability to perform. Even so, after the debrief, he found himself on the way to meet her.

Her first words acted at once to soothe him. "It was a bad one, Kent Welby?"

"Yes, very bad."

She placed a solicitous hand on one arm and led him to a bar stool in the My Flower Laundry. "I had Momma Troh get some of that strong China wine for you."

"Good, I think I'll need it."

They drank, quietly and away from other patrons. After his second glass of the potent wine, Kent suggested dinner. He and Francie walked hand in hand along the muddy main street of the village and settled for takeout from a corner stall that featured pork ribs, steamed fish, and vegetables.

At the apartment, Francie laid out tableware and called Thran in from play. They ate together silently. When the meal ended, Francie collected the plates and tried to keep her voice casual.

"Thran is going to stay at the Quons, with his friend, Lang. Will you help with the dishes?"

The expression of gratitude and relief that Doc Welby gave her warmed Francie to the core. "I'd be glad to."

Once the chores had been attended to, Francie curled up in the corner of the sagging sofa and Kent joined her. They spoke little, although they touched a lot. Francie's thoughtfulness and tender generosity proved to be all it took to rekindle Doc's passion. After half an hour of intensifying caresses, Doc came to his feet and drew Francie to him. This time, it was he who eagerly led the way to the bedroom. There, they embraced again and eagerly disrobed.

They made fantastic love until half an hour before curfew.

Archie Golden stayed on base. He ignored the platoon bar in favor of his own quarters. He sat at a small, folding table, a steaming mug of coffee close at hand, and wrote a letter to his wife. In it he used a roundabout code they had developed over the years. It would tell her how he truly felt about killing a mere boy.

After the salutation, he wrote several rambling sentences about how he was feeling well and hoped everyone at home had good health, about his brother and his family, about the weather and similar trivialities. Then he inscribed the serious part.

Iris, something is eating at me. It's not being afraid, though I'd be a fool to say I never was. And it's not being seriously wounded, cause I haven't been so far. In fact, it's nothing at all about the job. [Which meant, naturally, that it had everything to do with his job.] It's David. I was glad and relieved to get your letter and the photos and learn that he went ahead and had his bar mitzvah. But, then, that got me to thinking.

David is not really so old. The other side over here has kids his age, and even younger, who are mixed up in the fighting. Sometimes they get shot up pretty bad, or even killed. [Which told his wife that he had encountered such a Vietnamese boy recently.] When I see one of them from a helicopter or on the trail, hauling ammunition, I think of David and wonder if he is really safe. [Which would tell Iris that he had been forced to kill or wound that child.] I mean, with all the demonstrations and violence out there in the world, and the drug thing, what's a father to think or do when he can't hold his son tight and help him understand the dangers? Anyway, give him a big hug for me and a kiss, and tell him how very hard I work at being sure I will see him someday soon.

By the way, has the Haddasah started that

campaign to get care packages of kosher stuff
sent over for the guys who need it at Passover
and the High Holy Days? It would be a good
thing.

Richard and Iris Golden did not keep a strict Kosher kitchen, but they both believed quite strongly in
observing the traditions during the Holy Days. He
scribbled a few more sentences and signed the letter,
''With all my love.''

Archie addressed the envelope, folded his letter and
put it in, unsealed. Pope Marino would have to see
what he had written before it went out. Archie secretly
believed that Pope was aware of his code and, being
the man he was, frankly didn't give a damn. Pope was
a mustang. He had joined the navy after two not-
entirely-brilliant years of college and came up through
the ranks. He had just graduated UDT school and
joined the SEALs when the situation in Vietnam took
a serious turn.

He had been commissioned following an outstand-
ing performance on an operation in Cyprus. But he
still thought about things like a chief petty officer,
which he had become prior to the promotion. Which
led Archie to trust in Pope's discretion in regard to
his code. Iris could and did keep her mouth shut. After
all, she had held a Top Secret clearance when she
worked at the nuclear sub shipyard at Groton, Con-
necticut. He set the letter aside to turn in at first muster in the morning. A knock sounded at the door.

Tonto Waters entered, with Anchor Head Sturgis at
his side. A grinning Tonto invited, ''Hey, let's go get
roaring drunk at My Flower.''

Laughing, Archie Golden came to his feet. "You got that right. I could even drink a *Bahmibah*."

Low combers off the Atlantic washed up on the pristine beach that spread before the rear sundeck of the Reardon family summer home on Hilton Head Island, South Carolina. They had come down a month early to open the house for the Easter holiday. Tall, thick sheets of Plexiglas kept the sharp wind off the two persons seated at a table, fine bone china cups of herbal tea before them. At least the one sipped by Elizabeth Reardon Welby contained tea. Her father's held an inch of Blantons single barrel/small batch bourbon. Betty's agitation could be clearly seen when Norman Reardon raised his cup to his lips.

"Isn't it a bit early for that, Father?"

"Tut-tut, my dear." He actually spoke like that, which irritated his rebellious twenty-three-year-old daughter even more. "This is the finest handmade bourbon in the world. Ninety-three proof, made in Frankfort, Kentucky, and aged twelve years. It goes down like silk and is an excellent aid to digestion."

Youthful scorn colored Betty's words. "But to digest breakfast? I asked you out here to discuss my divorce proceedings."

"And I said before that I am opposed to the idea of you getting a divorce from Kent Welby. Which, by the way, is why the Blantons. If we are to deliberate on an unpleasant subject, a bit of fortification is in order. Generally, I never take a drink before five o'clock, as you well know."

Betty Welby fought back the fury mounting within. "Father, you are avoiding the issue. I already sent

Kent a letter informing him of my intentions. Two, actually. I weakened for a while and sent him notice I did not want a divorce. He answered me by saying, 'Whatever you want.' "

Norman Reardon beamed. "Good for you. And good for him."

"But, then I changed my mind."

Norman took a long pull on the bourbon and signaled a servant, who lingered just out of hearing range, for another. "*That* is not so good. You know the Church's position on divorce."

"I do. And it doesn't matter. I warned Kent when he was preparing to ship out. And now we hear on the news that they are doing such terrible things over there. Our troops are killing innocent women and children, bombing helpless villages."

Norman bristled, as though defending his own son. "I doubt their innocence. And besides, Kent Welby is not in the air force, nor is he a soldier. I'm sure that whatever it is he is doing, it is honorable and just."

"How can you know that? Here you sit, making tons of money off the military-industrial complex, drinking forty-dollar-a-bottle whiskey, and you don't have the first idea what is going on over there. I will not have my—my Kent turned into a monster and condone it by remaining at his side. And, that's another thing. He *is not* at my side. Where he should be."

Norman Reardon shook his head in resignation. "You are not looking at this rationally. It is his duty to serve his country. It is yours to support him at home. That is what your mother did when I was in

Korea, and what you should do now. I'll tell you one thing, which you had better take to heart. If he agrees to this divorce, then he is as big a fool as you are.''

Betty fled to the interior of the house. Her eyes filled with tears and she covered her mouth with one hand to stifle a sob. She found her mother in the solarium.

Painfully she recounted her discussion, or rather the lack of one, with her father. When she finished, her mother faced her, gloved hands on hips, one still holding a trowel. The gray streaks that lanced her still-golden hair gave the senior woman an imperious look.

''Well, Elizabeth, I'll say this. Norman is right. You are a fool to divorce Kent Welby.''

With a final whine and crash of gears, the aging Chinese-made, canvas-topped command car crunched to a stop on the oyster shell drive outside a large French colonial villa. A portico sheltered the car from the light early evening drizzle. Two NVA soldiers at the main entrance snapped to attention when the occupants stepped out onto the paved strip in front of the steps.

Podpolkovnik Pyotr Rudinov looked about him and sniffed the dank odor of rot that came from the abandoned fields surrounding the two-story structure. He followed the lead of the NVA officer who had accompanied him on the final leg of his journey. Major Diem had been delightfully free of the obsessive patriotism that infused most of his colleagues. As such, he had made an excellent traveling companion. After returning the salutes of the guards, Diem opened the door and they entered.

"We are to see General Hoi Pac immediately upon our arrival," Diem informed a uniformed clerk seated at a desk in the foyer.

"Your identity?" the tight-lipped, hard-faced clerk asked officiously.

With a gesture of impatience, Diem produced travel documents and an identity card. "I am Major Diem Gai Vaht, Eighth People's Army, and this is Senior Lieutenant Kovietski of *Spetznaz* from our Sister Republic, the Soviet Union."

Seemingly unimpressed, the clerk eyed them coldly. He took in the Major's trim uniform and holstered Chinese 7.63mm Type 51 pistol. Then he made note of the gray and black jumpsuit worn by Kovietski, the *Spetznaz* dagger on his wide belt, and the 9mm Makarov pistol in its holster. At last he seemed satisfied and stabbed a button on an intercom and spoke briefly. Then he turned to the visitors.

"Second floor, the suite at the rear. General Hoi is entertaining other guests now. He will join you there shortly."

Rudinov started to comment at the rudeness of this underling, then cut it off. He had been advised repeatedly about the excessive xenophobia of most Asians which, when they had power, often expressed itself in arrogance. He climbed the stairs beside Diem in smoldering silence.

His anger at the affront did not prevent him from noting that this had once been a magnificent country home—almost as splendid as those of the Czars, and of the party elite today. Gold leaf had been used in profusion, along with painted frescoes, crystal chandeliers, and rich drapes. Rudinov could appreciate such luxury. His father had been Soviet Army before him, and a member of the *nomenclatura*. Pyotr had always lived in opulent surroundings, at least until his posting to Southeast Asia. A marble statue of a fawn, frozen in the act of bending to take a drink, graced an alcove on the landing. Rudinov paused a moment to admire its excellence. Then he realized that Major Diem had spoken to him.

Diem repeated. "Hoi must be terribly lax to allow such arrogance in his subordinates."

"Or incredibly haughty himself," opined Rudinov.

They found the general's office and adjacent quarters easily. Settled in Louis Quintz chairs before the desk, they waited for their reluctant host.

General Hoi Pac was not pleased with the presence of yet another Russian. He had first encountered this particular *Spetznaz* officer more than a year ago. The man had the same arrogant swagger of any other Russian. Then, when the Americans had destroyed the tons of supplies intended for the projected major offensive in the Delta, the foreign white devil had spoken most rudely to Hoi.

He had treated the general as an inferior. He even blamed failure to protect the food, munitions, and medical supplies on Hoi—as though this senior lieutenant actually outranked him. But then, all Westerners were arrogant and officious barbarians. At the time, his intelligence officer, Colonel Nguyen Dak, had suggested that Senior Lieutenant Kovietski might be much more than he appeared. Then, after the freeing of the prisoners and destruction of the attitude alteration camp, along with the capture of General

Giap, this Kovietski again implied that the responsibility lay with Hoi, and that he and his superiors would not tolerate further failure. That he had come here, no doubt, to meet with these Soviet technicians, supported Dak's theory. Whatever the case, he would have to meet the man.

Rising from the table, he addressed Generals Van and Thrun, and Lieutenant Colonel Borkoi politely. "If you will excuse me, there is a pressing matter I must attend to. It will only take a minute. Please, continue your meal."

Odd, Hoi reflected as he walked from the elaborate dining room on the second floor to his quarters. He had actually come to like this young Russian, Borkoi. The green-eyed technician had an almost Vietnamese sense of humor. His ruddy complexion was not nearly as offensive as the pallid visages of so many Soviets. Borkoi looked almost . . . healthy. Then his thoughts turned to Senior Lieutenant Kovietski and a scowl creased his forehead. This would be, he knew, a stormy meeting.

"Ah! You must be Major Diem," Hoi Pac declared in an affable tone when he entered his office. He pointedly ignored Kovietski until the Russian cleared his throat. "At last we meet in person, my dear Senior Lieutenant. Your communications to me have been, shall we say, most bracing?"

Rudinov let a part of his true self show in the irony of his words. "I trust I have made a modest contribution to your continued successes, General."

Uncertain as to the meaning behind the falsely humble statement, Hoi chose to get right to the point. "May I ask the purpose of the visit?" Rudinov shot a glance at Major Diem, which Hoi read correctly. "I am glad to have you at my headquarters, Major. Now, I am sure you are tired from your journey. My orderly will arrange quarters for you and our Soviet comrade."

Diem excused himself and left. Behind him, the tension between the Russian and Vietnamese increased ever so slightly. "Unfortunately, General Hoi, I am not at liberty to tell you in detail at this time."

Immediate anger flushed the face of General Hoi. "Need I remind you that I am the commander of Vinh Province? I would like an answer, Lieutenant."

Rudinov sensed a crisis in the making and eased off a little. "First, have Lieutenant Colonel Borkoi and the other Soviet technicians arrived as yet?"

Hoi answered testily. "Yes, they have. I was entertaining them at dinner when you arrived. And, they have told me nothing more than you have."

Rudinov forced a smile. "A major operation is to be staged here in Vinh Province. In order for it to succeed, we ask your complete cooperation."

The same damned thing our arrogant senior generals and the Soviet technicians have said. Hoi bit his tongue to keep from snarling as his frustration grew. "I have been told that much. I have been informed that the Soviet head of that project would arrive here shortly."

"It is I," said Kovietski blandly.

"Then I had hopes that you would enlighten me further."

Rudinov gave the perplexed man a breezy smile. "I shall, General Hoi. In due time, I shall."

CHAPTER 9 _____

"WELCOME TO TRE NOC," Carl Marino said to Jason Slater when the CIA station chief stepped off the helicopter at the small naval station.

Slater's lips twisted into a rueful grin when he replied. "You might not say that after you hear what I have brought to you."

Pope Marino cocked an eyebrow. "That bad, is it?"

Slater shook his head and sighed. He pulled his big white Stetson from his head and mopped his brow. "Quite frankly, it couldn't get worse. Let's go inside and I'll tell you about it."

"Step into our headquarters cubicle—I wouldn't grace it with the name office—and give me your tale of woe." Pope led the way.

To his surprised pleasure, the first person Jason Slater saw in the narrow, low-ceilinged room was Cyrus Rhodes. Due to the attempt on his life at Binh Thuy, Dusty had been returned to light duty while he continued as an outpatient at the hospital.

Slater's smile was genuine and warm. "Dusty, it's

good to see you again. How are you doing? How was the hospital?''

"I'm fine, and it was lousy. There was not a nurse there who would spread her fingers for me, let alone her legs. I thought I'd taken vows and become a monk.''

Slater chuckled. "Well, there's always Pope here to ordain you. Uh—by the way, Pope, for the time being, this is for your ears only.''

Dusty had already scrambled to his feet. "I understand. No problem. It's time for tea anyway. Give me a holler when I can come back.''

After Dusty departed, Slater grabbed a metal, battleship gray, straight-backed chair. He reversed it and sat on the thin cushion, his arms folded on the curved top. Without preamble, he launched into his briefing.

"Believe me, this is something I wish I never had to say. Somehow, the NVA have gotten their hands on a nuclear weapon.''

Pope exploded in astonishment. "Jesus, Mary, and Joseph! Did the Chinese give it to them, or the fuckin' Soviets?''

"We're not entirely certain. I should have been more exact in telling you that. We have received a report from a triple-A reliable source that there is a nuclear weapon in North Vietnam. The best analysts in the Company believe that the Soviets brought it there.''

Pope asked the obvious. "One of theirs?''

"No. It's one of ours. One of three, not two as the public was told, that fell from a B-52 into the Atlantic off Spain a while back.''

"I thought our side recovered them," Pope challenged, not wanting to believe it.

"Yeah. Two. But, three fell, and it is believed a Soviet sub picked up the last one. Our call is that the weapon will be detonated somewhere in North Vietnam. We queried our source, and the plan has been verified. International monitors will be able to identify the origin of the device as American."

"They can do that?"

"Yeah. It has to do with the grade, the purity, of the components. Ours are the best in the world. Suffice it to say that the resultant world outcry will force an end to US involvement in Vietnam, if not worse. Our deep-cover agent in Hanoi got out the word that the bomb is believed to be somewhere near the city.

"My superiors suspect that the whole deal is a KGB black bag operation, with sanction from the top. And I do mean Brezhnev, himself. We kicked around ways of handling this and concluded that the best qualified personnel to deal with the bomb are the SEALs. Orders were cut at the highest possible level to use part of your team."

A worried frown bloomed on Marino's forehead. "Does Barry Lailey know anything about this?"

"Nope. The cover story is that the entire First Platoon is going on R and R in Bangkok. Your admiral is aware of this and had the orders cut himself. No one else knows otherwise. Actually, Alpha Squad will not be going with them. They are to be employed in the location and neutralization of our missing weapon. Only three men will go in on the final approach. I'd appreciate it if you would pick them now."

Marino gave it careful consideration. After two minutes he made his reply. "Chief Waters for certain. And a good demolition man should go. That would be Machinist's Mate Third Richard Golden. He's the best I've got. For the third, I suppose Kent Welby. He's one hell of a good long range shot, and good at the sneak and peek stuff, too.''

Slater knew all three well enough to give immediate approval. ''Sounds good. Send for them now, then we'll get down to a few details.''

Both men sat in silence, deep in their private thoughts while the yeoman-clerk went to round up the three petty officers. When they reported in, Jason Slater quickly covered what he had related to Pope Marino. The three NCOs reacted with all the incredulity and shock that Marino had displayed. Tonto Waters expressed it for all of them.

''How in hell could anybody miss something the size of a hydrogen bomb?''

Slater shrugged. ''Maybe the Soviets got there first. The thing is that we know one of our bombs is in North Vietnam. We need to make it useless to them.''

''How do we go about that?'' Archie Golden asked.

''The plan is that the three of you go in and locate the bomb, then render it inactive and slip back out of the North. Not to worry, though. You will be accompanied by an expert in the triggering devices of nuclear weapons.''

Lieutenant Marino looked at him dubiously. ''We've got a SEAL who knows that stuff?''

Slater shook his head. ''No. He's a technician from the Redstone Arsenal, by the name of Alistaire Wordsworth the Third.''

All four SEALs exploded at that. Pope's voice rode over the others. ''No way. Get some rocket scientist out there and we'll all get killed.''

"Nope. Can't do it, Mr. Slater," Tonto Waters added. "The guy is a civilian and a geek. He hasn't had the training and he would be too much of a liability."

Archie concluded for them. "Pope and Tonto are right. He can't operate like us so he can't operate at all."

"No problem, guys. He's okay. Wordsworth is an ex–special forces type, from the old Seventy-seventh. He served with MAAGV-SOG from 'Fifty-nine to 'Sixty-two. He's in excellent condition and is an officer in the army reserve. He serves in a special forces A team. He's already been recalled to active duty for the duration of the mission."

That mollified Tonto some. "So he's a blankethead. We won't hold that against him."

Pope still did not buy it. "When did he make a long swim last? When did he run ten miles? Who says he's in good shape? Some of your senior spooks at Langley?"

"Nope. Admiral Wayland. He interviewed Captain Wordsworth not four days ago."

That had them all changing their minds. Admiral Wayland was OIC of the entire SEAL program.

Pope Marino cut his eyes away from Jason Slater. "All right, so he goes in with us. How do we get there? We don't exactly look like little brown men."

"You will be pleased to know you are going by submarine. Now, let's get to how this is to be carried off. Due to the need for absolute secrecy on this operation, which the Company has named Artful Dodger, your squad will leave Tre Noc with the whole platoon, supposedly to take an R&R liberty in Bang-

kok. Instead, you will break off in Saigon and fly to
the Philippines. There you will be trained for your
mission at a super-secret base in Cagayan Province on
the island of Luzon. You will live in Aparri, under a
cover story of being engineers and geologists for an
oil exploration company. Then you will be taken to
North Vietnam by sub.''

Pope Marino asked the important question.
''When?''

''You will have a week to study the aerial surveil-
lance photos and rehearse.''

It took a second for that to soak in, then Tonto
asked in an incredulous tone, ''You know where it
is?''

That was one question Slater did not want to answer. Yet, he knew he had to level with these men or
lose their support. Not that they would disobey orders,
or refuse to take the mission. But their hearts would
not be in it and that could be dangerous for everyone.
He sighed and then reluctantly gave them the vital
information.

''From the analysis of the arrivals and, more sig-
nificantly, the lack of departures, we think the bomb
is inside, or near to . . . the Hanoi Hilton.''

That set off an explosion among the SEALs.
''Those bastards!'' Archie barked.

Tonto got to the point. ''Why put it there?''

Jason Slater raised his hands, palms out. ''Where
better? They know we never bomb the place. No one
has a burning desire to visit the prison. It is probably
the most secure place to keep a secret in the whole
country.''

Doc had another issue in mind. "Can we take out some of the prisoners when we leave?"

Slater almost shouted. "No! The idea is to get in, screw up the bomb and get out without anyone knowing you had been there. You can make no contact with any of the prisoners at all."

A thin, chill rain lashed against the kitchen window of the Reardon summerhouse. Betty Welby stood frozen in the act of peeling an apple. She *hated* being lectured to. Betty's mother stood beside her, working on the pie crust in a large mixing bowl.

"Mother, I am not a child. I do not need to be preached to."

"No, dear, you are a grown woman. Although, I swear, sometimes it seems like you still are a child. And I don't see what I said as 'preaching.' I simply want to impress on you that marriage is a duty as well as a privilege. Most importantly, it is a Sacrament.

"A wife has the duty to stand beside her husband in his work as well as in the rearing of children or, God forbid, in illness. That duty is embodied in the sacrament of Holy Matrimony."

"What about a man's duty to his wife?" Betty asked.

Sighing, Helen Reardon dropped her blending tool in the orange bowl and turned to face her daughter. "Yes, there is that aspect also. At least of late, since Holy Mother Church, in Her wisdom, has elected to take the term "obey" out of the marriage vow for women. Yet, traditionally, in the eyes of the Church, the wife has given herself to her husband.

"I certainly obeyed your father's wishes while he

was in Korea. We were married on his first leave to
Hawaii a year after the war began.'' Her expression
hardened with the memory. ''I didn't want him there.
I was frightened constantly, but I did what he said
and what a good war wife had to do.''

Betty dropped the apple to rub her hands agitatedly
on her apron. ''But Daddy takes Kent's side,'' she
wailed. ''What can I do, mother?''

Her mother looked at her firmly. ''Do not get this
divorce. I can only believe it will ruin your life. You
admit that you still love Kent. Why don't you write
him and tell him you have changed your mind.''

Betty's face crumpled and tears ran down her
cheeks. ''But I have already written him and said I
did not want a divorce. Then I changed my mind and
wrote him that I did. What can I say now?''

Helen Reardon put one arm around the shoulder of
her daughter and tilted up her chin as she had done
when Betty had been a child. Her expression was
meant to console.

''Write him again, be sweet about it. And tell him
we're making apple pie. He'll love that.''

Betty wavered as she recalled Kent's fondness for
Dutch apple pie. Slowly a tentative smile spread her
lips. ''All right. I will write Kent again and see what
he really wants to do.''

They were picketing the Long Beach debarkation de-
pot today. Petey Danvers saw it as a great opportunity.
He had heard that there were other American protestors in England, on Rhodes scholarships, a couple
hard-core Marxists. Those guys were leading demonstrations against the war at Oxford and in Lon-

don. Cool guys. All of the local TV stations had cameras here. So did the big boys. The networks had turned out in force to cover this demonstration. That was an unusual situation. *Antiwar sentiment must be building, Petey thought.*

Time to turn up the heat, he decided as the first of the homecoming troops appeared at the end of the pier. Petey raised the mouthpiece of the bullhorn to his lips.

"Here come the baby killers. Get those rotten vegetables passed out quick. Block the gate, so they have to come through us. Spit on them and throw that garbage. Remember, the cameras are here. Make lots of noise."

Walking toward the demonstrators in an informal, route-step column of fours, the returning Marines had a furtive, wary air about them. Their weapons secured in gun racks to be offloaded later, they carried only duffel bags and ditty kits. Several faces in the column reflected shock at the angry roar of the picketers. They reached the large gates, which swung open for them, and the first spoiled tomato sailed through the air. It struck a young, boyish-faced sergeant in the chest. The column hesitated a split second before advancing.

At once the demonstrators unleashed their self-righteous wrath. "Baby killers!"

"American assassins!"

"Mother murderers!"

"Fiends! Cowards!"

More garbage hurtled toward the troops. The shouts of the mob grew close to hysterical in nature, as the cameras panned over their actions and the results. The talking heads of the media shouted into their microphones to be heard, singing the praises of these courageous antiwar protestors. A private in the lead platoon was hit in the face by a head of rotten cabbage. He stumbled, but did not go down. An angry mutter rippled through the ranks.

It was immediately answered by the voice of command. "Bat—taaaal—ion—!"

And echoes of, "Com—paneeee! . . . Platoooon!"

"At—tennn-shun! For—waaaard . . . march."

The bullfrog voice of the battalion sergeant major took up the cadence. "Hut . . . two . . . threep . . . fawp!"

Instantly a transformation occurred among the confused, demoralized Marines. Backs straightened and faces molded into expressions of determination and purpose. Then, to the consternation and outrage of Petey Danvers and his willing accomplices in the media, the tremendous *esprit de corps* of the USMC asserted itself.

In full bellow, the BSM commanded, "Sound off!"

A deep, pugnacious roar answered him. "One . . . two."

"Sound off!"

"Three . . . four."

"If it looks and walks like a duck, you can be sure that it's a duck. To burn your draft cards is bad luck, and all you peacenik faggots suck! Sound off!"

Horror seized Petey Danvers. This wasn't going the way it was supposed to. Damn those smug cretins in green and khaki uniforms. Damn them to hell. Suddenly it hit him. The cameras were focused right on the miraculous alteration in the ranks of these warmongers. He raised the megaphone.

His voice broke from anxiety. "Get the cameras off those bastards! Turn 'em off. Cut the film," he shrieked. "Don't show those scum looking good."

Obligingly, most of the cameramen turned their lenses elsewhere. Two of the local outlets continued to cover the swelled chests and pride-filled eyes of the Marines.

"Cadence count!"

"One—two—three—four . . . One, two . . . three, four."

Ruined! It was all falling apart around him. Petey raved as he reached for a tab of LSD.

Considering the high-risk nature of the mission they were going on, Tonto Waters decided to write a letter home. Although he meant his words for his dad, he addressed the missive to his mother. He knew she would read it aloud to everyone gathered on the first Sunday after it arrived.

"Dear Mom," Tonto wrote.

The minor scratches I received a while back have healed. We are kept busy here in the Delta. The wily, little brown men in black pajamas don't seem to like our being here. They are sneaky and cruel and sometimes do a lot of harm. We are constantly on operations, so it may be some time before you hear from me again. Tell Dad that I love him and hope he keeps well. You, too, of course. If I was there, I'd tell Bud to keep his head down when he goes to ball games. That way he won't get konked with a pop fly. Did it really happen that way?

Or did Monica smack him one in the eye?
  It's getting late here, so I had better close.
Yes, I am sleeping well and I watch that I eat
enough vegetables. God bless you both.

Your son

Tonto did not have a premonition; he was merely
being realistic. Most of the Americans who entered
North Vietnam were not there voluntarily and usually
wound up prisoners of war. All of them tried to get
out fast. Now he, Archie, and Doc would not only be
going in there voluntarily, they would actually be entering the most infamous POW camp on either side.
For a moment, he stared blankly at the words he had
written. The thought of what they were going to do
made Tonto's gut churn.

CHAPTER 10 _____

GUARDS PEERED suspiciously into the command car that idled in front of the high, wooden gates. *Podpolkovnik* Rudinov gazed back with all the cold indifference he could muster. Such a place would wait for him, were he to fail in this mission. *Welcome to Thran Lon Dong Prison*, he thought, acutely conscious of the irony. The yellow-painted walls soared twelve meters above him, the top crowned with five strands of barbed wire, strung on insulators that indicated they were electrified. There would be no escape from this place—nor any successful frontal assault to free the inmates.

Built more like a fortress than a POW compound, the place the Americans called the Hanoi Hilton would keep its secrets forever. Beside him, General Thrun reached out for his papers. One of the guards handed them over with seeming reluctance. From the seat in front of them, Lieutenant Colonel Borkoi turned an anxious glance back at Rudinov. Borkoi was not KGB. The lax discipline of the Soviet air force was well known to GRU and KGB alike. Borkoi should have remained frozen in place.

These men would confine them both on the least excuse. Being foreigners, they were naturally suspect in a nation fast gaining the reputation of being paranoid. At last one of the ponderous gates swung inward. The engine of the Chinese command car groaned in protest as it delivered power to the rear wheels. They rolled in past other guards.

Although an exercise yard existed, no one was using it at the time. Following directions from Thrun, the driver aimed them toward the cell block on the west side of the prison. There he halted the vehicle and the passengers disgorged. ''Remain here, Comrade Sergeant,'' General Thrun instructed.

No doubt, Rudinov thought as he stooped slightly to enter a low doorway, *General Hoi sees his exlusion from this visit as more reason to sit and stew, and to plot with Colonel Dak.* Dak reminded Rudinov of— of what? Out of his memories of charm school, *Padpolkovnik* Rudinov dredged up the American idiom and expression *used car salesman*. Yes, that was it. Dak would make the perfect used car salesman. That brought a smile to his lips. Rudinov could imagine Dak saying, ''It was owned by a little old lady from Pasadena, who only drove it Sundays to church.'' The KGB *residentura* turned left to follow General Thrun down a corridor that fronted a cell block.

Suddenly the smile left his face as the deathly silence that permeated the walkway registered on him. How oppressive. He knew that the prisoners were forbidden to communicate with one another, yet, he had expected some sound—a cough, someone humming, the scrape of a shoe sole, anything but this ominous quiet. Worse even, than the gulag. Their party stopped before a door not unlike any of the others.

Beyond it, Rudinov saw over the shoulder of Borkoi a large, thick-walled room with what appeared to be an overhead door in the outer wall. Then his eyes focused on a medium-sized, rubber-tired, metal rack. The object that rested on it had been concealed by a draped tarpaulin. At Thrun's direction, they walked to it.

Rudinov's astonishment showed clearly on his face when the tarpaulin was pulled back by two workers and he looked at a sleek, torpedolike object. The American hydrogen bomb's dull, smoke-gray outer casing glistened, denoting the care and attention it had received since being recovered from the floor of the Atlantic.

"It's . . . not what I expected," he said softly.

Lieutenant Colonel Borkoi took up the explanation. "Their technology has come a long way since Nineteen-forty-five. You expected to see a fat, cumbersome object like the first atomic bomb?"

"No. I knew they were streamlined long ago. Only . . . the lethal menace this exudes. Amazing. What about the radiation?"

Borkoi hastened to reassure him. "There is no danger. So long as the device maintains its integrity, the emissions are so small as to barely register on the most sensitive detector."

"Then the Americans cannot find it here?" General Thrun asked bluntly.

"Not unless they suspected that it was here in the

first place,'' Rudinov said. "They do not have enough highly receptive sensors to sniff out every corner of the world. If I understand what Colonel Borkoi has said,'' he quickly added, aware that he had let slip knowledge that a senior lieutenant in *Spetznaz* would not be expected to have, "they would have to aim a satellite directly at the prison to detect any radiation. Is that right?''

Borkoi gave him a curious look before answering. "That is quite correct. But, then, I suppose one learns quite a lot about the Americans and nuclear weapons in *Spetznaz*.''

At least Borkoi will not give away my true rank and position, Rudinov thought with relief. "Yes, we do. They are, after all, the enemy. Now, shall we discuss the procedure for moving this device to the place it will be employed? I am quite concerned about security.''

General Thrun turned icy black eyes on Rudinov. "*You* are concerned? I thought this was *my* project, *Lieutenant*.'' He made the rank sound like something lower than a recruit.

That decided Rudinov. He had been given a free hand on the matter and decided that with little love lost between this bureaucrat from Hanoi and General Hoi, his true station would be safely kept secret by General Thrun. Accordingly, he stepped closer to the Vietnamese officer and drew from an inside pocket his identity card.

Facing it, one saw on the left side the crest of the KGB, placed off-center to the right, with a department number in the upper right-hand corner and the expiration date written vertically along the right margin.

Written from the lower left margin was his service number. On the facing side, the plastic-encased ID that assured anyone who saw it that the bearer, Pyotr Maximovich Rudinov was a lieutenant colonel in the Committee for State Security.

Rudinov spoke quietly, so as not to make the workmen aware of what he said. "You are aware, of course, General, that this is a KGB operation. It is entirely under our jurisdiction. I am the one in charge."

For a moment, Thrun bristled. "But it is in our country that the bomb is going to be set off."

"Your army deputy chief of staff, General Tran Van Quang, endorsed this enthusiastically. You, yourself, as chief of the Directorate of Information, wrote the endorsement that stated that your government and its people were willing to make the patriotic sacrifice represented by the project. That you believed it would result in expulsion of the Americans, if not actually bring an immediate end to the war and reunite your country."

"I agree, Comrade Colonel. But you must realize that there is a war going on around us. Equipment and men are at a premium. You must take into account the effect of the American bombing. Our bridges are destroyed, our roads all but impassable, live ordnance is lying around everywhere. We can move only so fast. When do you want the bomb moved? And where?"

"The where comes later. I want it ready to transport within the next fifteen days."

*   *   *

Doc Welby sat on his bunk, head bowed, eyes staring at nothing. In one hand he held the lastest letter from his wife. In it, she said that she had changed her mind again. She wanted the divorce after all. Numbed by that, he found it impossible to move for a while. At last he roused himself and stepped to the small table in one corner. Grunting with great effort, he seated himself and drew close a pen and paper. *Only two days before we leave*, he thought as he began to write.

"My dearest Betty," he wrote. "Although it pains me to tell you this . . ." Did it really? Doc asked himself, his mind occupied by the lovely figure of Francie Song. Then he put pen to paper again. "I will not contest the divorce. I am not angry with you, only disappointed. But I have come to see that if it is over, it's over. I am in good health and safe. Give my best to your parents."

He signed it simply, *Kent*. Then, surrendering to the jubilation that surged through him, he went off to share the good news with Francie Song.

Dusty Rhodes sat at his desk in the Tre Noc headquarters and shuffled papers. He did not mind being out of the loop on whatever Jason Slater had brought to them. Secret operations were a part of life for every SEAL. He quickly came to the conclusion that something incredibly big was being laid on when the orders came down for the platoon to take two weeks R&R in Bangkok. It all added up with Slater's visit.

"We didn't even request it," he muttered aloud.

"Sir?" asked the yeoman at his desk.

"These leave papers. I've never known the navy to be this generous with long-term liberty."

Every bit as curious as Dusty, Yeoman Evans raised an eyebrow. "D'you think there's a catch, sir?"

"By me, Evans. I just got back here. What do I know?" *Besides Jason Slater coming here looking like a man who has just been told he is to be the father of quintuplets and left seeming mightily relieved.*

"You must know something, sir, you're the AOIC."

Dusty pulled a face. "That and a dime will buy me a cup of coffee."

Evans looked surprised. "Haven't you heard, sir? Back in the world it's up to a quarter now."

Pope Marino entered then. "Dusty, you and Evans here will be the station party while we're gone. This is just a suggestion, but don't cut out on your outpatient calls to Binh Thuy and use that as the excuse. Anything important comes in, buck it over to Second Platoon."

"Yeah, I follow you." Dusty gave him a calculating gaze. "Do you expect anything important happening?"

"You never know, Dusty."

Dusty resigned his curiosity. "All right, I can live with that. Pat a few bottoms for me, will you? Oh! And, don't get wrapped up with one of those streetcorner trollops. I hear they're all fireships."

"Not to worry. Hey, where'd you get that antique expression? I haven't heard it outside an old pirate movie for years."

A grin blossomed on Dusty's face. "I had an old uncle who had been to sea once. He used it all the time. Trollops and fireships. They just sort of go together. And—ah—good luck out there.''

Pope Marino bent close and spoke in a low whisper. "Keep that under your flying saucer, buddy."

Lieutenant Commander Barry Lailey could not believe the orders he stared at as he paced the floor of his office. It was a pass-along FYI copy to inform the S-2 that First Platoon of Team 2 would be taking two weeks R&R in Bangkok. Who had come up with this? And how had they gotten it past him? Mr. Ott's platoon had received replacements only a week ago.

To make it worse, the platoon was scheduled for an interdiction sweep along the Mekong River in another week. Lailey turned to the last page of the orders. The annex was an endorsement, reassigning the search and destroy mission to Second Platoon. Damn! Somehow they had gotten around him. Leave it to Marino to do that.

Darkly, Lailey recalled his first encounter with Carl Marino. The young Ensign had just "appropriated" a case of new Israeli gas masks for his platoon. The protective gear was generally considered far superior to American-made masks. Ensign Marino had flashed a boyish smile when called to task for squirreling away another unit's issue equipment. He seemed to consider it some sort of game.

"Why, I don't know what you're talking about, sir," he had blandly told then LCDR Lailey. "We have used the masks my men have been issued twice in training exercises. They're almost due new filter cartridges."

Lailey had narrowed his eyes. "You are sure these masks have been used."

"Oh, aye aye, sir. Granted we may have rushed the exercises, held them pretty close together, but there is that platoon proficiency competition. My men are highly motivated, sir."

Lailey nailed him with a cold, hard gaze. "If I had any solid proof that it was you who walked off with those Israeli masks, you'd put in your twenty and never make j.g. Be assured, Mr. Marino, that I will be keeping an eye on you. We do not tolerate scroungers in this team."

Marino had stiffened to a position of attention. "Aye aye, sir. And I have every confidence my men will place first in overall efficiency. Is that all, sir?"

Lailey dismissed him with an angry wave. "Yes, get out of here."

That had been a long while ago and Marino remained a fixer and a hustler. Somehow he had gone around the chain of command and arranged for this little end run. Well, before they sat down to their first beer in Bangkok, the secret would be found out. Barry Lailey had every confidence in his ability to ferret out the how and what lay behind it.

Sergeant First Class Elmore Yates cleared his throat nervously and kept glancing left and right and beyond the man facing him. He considered them to be dangerously exposed in this clearing only a klick from the base at Tre Noc. *Arrogant bastard*, he thought for the thousandth time. It bothered him mightily to have to take orders from this oversized gook. But it paid well.

Since he worked in the Plans and Operations section, part of his duties being to secure the mail pouch for Saigon, he had been able to insert, without detection, the envelopes containing the money orders, made in Swiss francs, that he had received in payment for his information. They were addressed to the *La Borsa Suisse Nationale* in Lausanne, where he had a secret, numbered account.

From there he could send bank drafts to his daddy. Momma was slowly dying of cancer. Her hospital bills had become enormous. Daddy had already lost the farm. Yet, Elmore had his duty and he knew it. His efforts to help cover them had brought him to stealing and black marketeering. When he had been caught, it had not been by the American CID. Which put him in a far deeper trap than the one he had dug for himself. They made an offer with an attractive price attached, which he accepted; after all he needed the money. And that brought him to where he was at the mercy of the hulking, hard-faced man who insolently sneered at him now.

"Never take anything at face value," the man he believed to be a Cambodian named Phon Caliphong, lectured him. "From now on, you are to keep closer account on the activities of these SEALs. I do not believe that they are going to Bangkok. They have just received replacements. Those men need training. It is unlikely that any request for leave would be approved under these circumstances. You will step up your reports to three a week."

"Do you expect me to go AWOL and follow them to Bangkok?"

Caliphong scowled. "Do not waste my time with your Western rudeness. Use your assets. Threaten them, hurt them if you must, to get quality product from them.''

Yates tried to put steel in his voice. ''Even if the result is that I am compromised?''

Caliphong gave him a nasty smile. ''You are compromised already. *We* know about you. We have photographs of you stealing your government's property and later turning it over to black market dealers. Medicine, food, even weapons. Your greed knows no bounds and you are our . . . creature.''

Phon Caliphong was in reality *Starshii Serzhant* Feodor Dudov of the KGB. He watched with detached amusement as this redheaded Marine sergeant absorbed what he had said and tried unsuccessfully to conceal his reaction. He decided not to give the man any time to rally his defenses. ''Something earth-shakingly important is about to happen and our superior wants you to keep constant surveillance on the SEALs until it is over.''

CHAPTER 11 ─────────────

COLORFUL CHINESE lanterns made flying saucerlike gyrations in the stiff breeze that blew up the Bassiac River. On the night before the SEALs of First Platoon moved out, a party had been given for them at the Phon Bai restaurant. It had been the idea of Francie Song and some of the other local girls who had boyfriends among the sailors. The rock music that came from the live musicians had a distinctly Asian flavor to it, yet no one minded.

Francie Song danced with Doc Welby, blissful to be held close and tight to his muscular frame. Only a single worry line showed on her forehead. "You look like you are going on a mission, rather than rest and recreation, Kent Welby."

Doc turned icy at that. He had come to the party directly from the final briefing on their quick shuffle plan to get on a plane to the Philippines. The thought of going into North Vietnam to disable a hydrogen bomb left him with more trepidation than all the previous missions combined. What if they screwed up and it went off? It haunted him, but he could say nothing.

"It's the thought of being separated from you," he exaggerated smoothly.

"That's sweet. I'll miss you terribly, too."

Doc gave her a serious look. "Francie, I swear that I will not even look at another girl. Not one. I'll sit alone in my room if I have to."

Francie looked pained. "No. Enjoy your time. Go out, eat good food, drink beer, dance with the girls. Ah—at least, dance *upright* with them."

Doc faked a shocked expression. "Where did you learn such a naughty expression?"

With a shrug, Francie dismissed it. "I hear other sailors talking. I pick it up. Now, Kent Welby," she changed subjects, growing somber. "I have a secret I must share with you." There could not be a better time, she decided, seeing him in the golden glow of the lanterns.

"What secrets do you have, honey?"

"I—we—that is Kent Welby, I am carrying your baby." It came out in a rush and for a moment, Francie feared that his reaction would be negative.

Doc stopped dead still on the dance floor and stared at her, then crushed her close to him. "You are? Really, my kid? Francie . . . that's—that's *wonderful*." He wanted to shout it out to the others, but held his tongue. "We'll—we'll leave early, go to your place and talk about it. Now that you know the good news, that Betty has asked for a divorce again, is that why you chose tonight to tell me?"

Francie nodded. "Yes, partly, and because you vowed to stay away from other women. Now I know that I have all of you. It makes me so happy.''

''Me, too.'' Kent kissed her lightly on the lips and swung the slight, young Vietnamese woman around in a jubilant fling.

Tonto Waters sat alone in the platoon bar. He had not gone to the party at Phon Bai. He looked again at the creased sheet of creamy, thick paper he held between a thumb and forefinger. It had come only that day from Eloise Deladier. There had been no return address. Slowly he reread the words she had written.

My darling, darling, Tom,
You will have noticed that there is no return ad-
dress. I am sorry, my love, but I cannot provide
you with one. To reach me, you must send it care
of the French Consulate in Macao. I regret to
say that I will not be able to see you again for
a long time.

It all has to do with my work. Journalists must
go when and where their editors tell them to go.
Right now I am in an uninteresting place, with
no name, and boring people. I will be here a
while. Perhaps in a month or two I will return
to Saigon. I hope you are taking care of yourself
and keeping out of the way of unfriendly bullets.
Good health continues to bless me and I long to
be at your side. Write me when you can. I re-
main in love with you.

She had signed it simply with her first name.

Dusty Rhodes entered the platoon bar and stood watching Tonto several minutes. At last he spoke up.

"Your absence was immediately noted, Chief. Something biting your tail?"

"Eloise. Not her, exactly. Her bosses have sent her off to Bum Fuck, Egypt, or some such, and I can't even write her directly."

Dusty cocked an eyebrow. "This is *Le Monde* we're talking, right?"

Tonto grunted. "You know better."

"Well, what say you come over to the party, Tonto. I gather it's the last good time some of you will be having for a while."

Tonto eyed Dusty levelly. "Yeah, well, there is that. Okay. So, let's go eat, drink and make merry."

"You've got that right. Tomorrow she may die."

"Who?"

"Mary. Get off your duff, Chief, and paste a smile on that mug of yours. That's an order."

"Gotcha, Mr. Rhodes."

With an amused, knowing twinkle in his eyes, Thran went off agreeably to the Quons. Once the little imp had departed, Doc waltzed Francie around the tiny living room of her apartment and they opened a bottle of wine. Doc lifted his glass and peered at Francie over the rim.

"To the new mother."

"Ah—but I have Thran already. To the new father. He is your first?"

"Yes. Uh—Francie, how do you know it is a he?"

"I am carrying him . . . high." She made gestures. "Like I did Thran. It will be a boy."

Doc thought of something else. "We have to get a

crib for him. And clothes. Lots of clothes. And—er—diapers, of course.''

Francie laughed lightly. ''Mrs. Quon is making a lace gown for him.''

Doc grew instantly indignant. ''A *gown*? No son of mine is going to wear dresses.''

Francie laughed at his lack of knowledge about babies. ''All babies wear gowns. It makes it easier to change their diapers that way. Call it a nightshirt if you want. Even little boys do not have regular clothes until they are six months old. Do you not know anything about babies?''

A puzzled frown creased Doc's high brow. ''No. I really don't.''

Another tinkle of laughter escaped Francie. ''You will learn fast enough. Oh, it will be so wonderful.''

Her confidence and joy set Doc on fire. He set aside his glass and reached for hers. ''Let's save the wine for later.''

''What will we have in its place?''

Doc took Francie by the hand. ''Love, my dearest. Long, slow, delicious love.''

Pope Marino sat closeted with Jason Slater. The OIC's desk was covered with maps and papers. They had been going over the final details of the operation for half an hour. Slater tapped the map at the mouth of the Hong River with the eraser end of his pencil.

''Your idea of having them approach Hanoi in an underwater swim up the Red River is great, Carl. Will your gear sustain the trip both directions?''

''It should. Just in case, I'll see that they have replacement cartridges. They can recharge the Draeger rebreather units and bury them, to retrieve after the job is finished.''

Jason Slater made ready to leave. He stuffed all the materials from the desk into his attaché case and locked it securely. ''Fine. I'm going on ahead to set up the training area. Wordsworth is already in Aparri. He's getting a kick out of going out to the oil platform every day. He says there's nothing for him to do out there but fish. A couple of times he's caught enough to feed the whole crew lunch. They enjoyed the change in diet. Say, you're missing a party, aren't you?''

''Yeah. Big bash at Phon Bai. I'll drop by after we finish here.''

''We're done as far as I'm concerned. What worries me is that whoever is in charge of that damned bomb hasn't got all the time in the world to set up their 'American war criminals' nuclear attack.' I would guess they plan to use it within the next two weeks.''

Pope Marino made a face. ''Now tell me the good news.''

Slater looked at him levelly. ''That *was* the good news. Well, I'm out of here.''

Why a party for guys goin' on R&R? SFC Elmore Yates wondered as he stood in the shadows. He had learned of it from Francie Song. It piqued his curiosity. As a result, he once again stalked the lovers. He had watched them in the backyard garden of the Phon Bai and followed when they left for the apartment. Yates stood in the darkness of an alley now and added up all he had.

Answer to question number one. Yes, something

had to be up. What was it? Set number two aside for a while. Guys going on liberty did not have parties. Guys being rotated back to the world or being transferred did. So that left him what? Sure as hell not Bangkok. And they hadn't been in-country long enough to be going back to the East Coast. Up north? If so, how far? The Highlands? The Plain of Jars? Maybe the DMZ. Elmore still did not have enough of the pieces yet for the puzzle to make sense. With a snort of impatience Yates dismissed it.

Whatever, he would not have a chance to get revenge on Welby again. He might as well act tonight. Maybe he could beat the information out of the little punk before he killed him.

"I'll go with you to the gate," Francie Song announced as she slipped into a silk blouse. "I can pick up Thran on the way back."

Kent Welby pulled up his skivvy shorts, very pleased with his performance tonight. "There'll be a mortar attack again," he cautioned.

"We'll be careful."

Unmoved by her assurance, Doc admonished, "You'd better. There's three of you now."

Francie patted her belly. "That sounds nice. Soon you will get to see your son."

"When?"

Calculating, Francie smiled when she told him. "Four months. Maybe a week or two more."

Doc beamed as he pulled on his cammo T-shirt. "I can hardly wait. I'm ready," he added, "except for my boondockers." He would get them at the door.

Outside, the wind had increased. It drove a thin rain

into their faces, so many needles. The gusts proved too strong for Francie's umbrella. Heads down, they walked hand-in-hand along the main street. For three blocks they remained alone. Then, as they passed an alley, a blur of motion drew Doc's attention.

He reacted too slowly, having to push Francie aside before he could face their unknown assailant. Elmore Yates crashed into Doc Welby chest-to-chest. The burly Marine sergeant wore a watch cap over his face, with eyeholes cut in it. He tried to land a wild blow, to be caught with a solid right to the gut. Wheezing, he backpedaled.

"Kent Welby, be careful," Francie cautioned.

Yates turned his face her direction. "Shut up, bitch. You'll get yours later."

That cost him what little remained of his surprise advantage. Kent Welby dropped into the T-dachi stance and lashed a front kick at his attacker's left kneecap. His ankle-high Navy utility boot smacked solidly into its target. Groaning, Yates sank to his good knee. Doc did a 360 spin and snapped another blow with the foot, this time to the chest of Elmore Yates.

Yates slammed back against the wall of the green grocery. More a street brawler than a martial artist, the Marine had experience and intelligence enough to realize he was far outclassed. When he sprang to his feet, the keen edge of a knife glinted in the faint street light.

Francie Song saw it and screamed. Doc Welby got a quick view of the blade and moved accordingly. Setting himself, he gave a high, piercing *ki-yi* and sprang into the air, his right leg cocked at the hip and knee. The eyes of Elmore Yates followed him uncomprehendingly.

That nearly proved to be fatal. At the apex of his leap, laid out flat, Doc snapped out his leg and drove the edge of his boondocker into the bridge of his assailant's nose. Blood spurted, to be quickly absorbed by the watch cap. Yates's head jerked back and he went rubber-legged. The knife momentarily forgotten, Yates clawed at his obstructed breathing passage. Doc came right after him.

Using *shuto* strokes, he hammered Yates back against the wall and chopped the knife from his hand. Moaning softly, the Marine saw the initiative of the battle flee him. He struck out blindly, whirled, and ran off down the alley. His footsteps swiftly faded in the wind. In spite of his defeat, Elmore Yates took with him the conviction that the SEALs were up to something, based on the party and Francie accompanying Welby to the gate. He silently vowed to find out all about it.

"Who was that?" Francie asked fearfully, sure that she already knew.

Doc Welby panted lightly. "I don't know. I never saw his face. He was in good shape, though he did have some gut on him. I'll walk you back."

"No, Kent Welby, I can go home in safety. You go on, get to the base. Good night, my dear, I love you."

"I love you, too, Francie." After she had gone, Doc Welby made a vow of his own. "Some day I'll find out who that bastard is and fix his clock."

*   *   *

With infinite care, Lieutenant Colonel Borkoi removed the last screw on the service plate above the triggering mechanism of the American hydrogen bomb. His hands, encased in surgical gloves, assured not the least chance of a slip. His eyes stung and burned. He was tired after the journey to Hanoi that morning, and a full day of work on the bomb. It was after twenty-three hours, the blurred face of his watch told him. He should quit, save this test for the next day.

Podpolkovnik Rudinov might have been reading his mind. "You looked fatigued. Why not stop for the night, drink some vodka, and come back tomorrow?"

Borkoi sighed. "Another round trip in that command car would ruin me."

"The Hotel Patriot is three blocks from here. I'll have our driver go book us rooms."

"That sounds good. What about the vodka?"

Smiling, Rudinov bent and opened the lid of a small insulated box. White smoke boiled out. "Fortunately, I have provided for that need in advance. Dry ice keeps it cold."

"Where did you . . . ?"

"Our embassy. The *residentura* there is an old friend of mine. He knows I cannot bear warm vodka. He also had dispatches for me. Everything is still on schedule."

Borkoi ran the back of his hand over his forehead. "While the driver goes for the rooms, I'll have a vodka and then test these circuits. I'm . . . really not that tired."

He climbed from the bomb rack and accepted a tall,

narrow glass of the clear liquor. " *'Nastrovia, tovarish Pyotr.*"

"To your health, too, Comrade Viktor."

Borkoi drank deeply of his vodka and smacked his lips. "That saved my life. Another swallow and I'll go back." He finished off the glass in three gulps and handed it to Rudinov. Then he returned to his labors while the KGB agent went to find their driver.

Borkoi carefully lifted off the metal access panel and peered through the clear partition beyond. With carefully controlled hands, he raised one edge of the Lexan and then the entire end. Cautiously he laid that aside and studied the wiring harness beyond. Satisfied as to what he wanted, he lifted an instrument and turned it on. Then he inserted a probe into the harness. The gauge swung up only thirty percent. He touched another spot with the same result.

"As I thought," he said aloud to himself. "The batteries have weakened over time. They will have to be replaced."

When told of that, Rudinov scowled. "Where do we find batteries of that quality, size, and voltage in this benighted country?"

Borkoi thought a moment. "From your friend with the dry ice at the embassy?"

A warm smile lighted the face of Pyotr Rudinov. "You are a sheer genius. Of course. First thing in the morning. For now, I am ready for a late supper and bed."

With genuine relief, Borkoi agreed. "I'll gladly second that. And don't worry. With the proper batteries, the weapon will be ready when you want it."

Rudinov produced an anticipatory smile. "And that will be precisely eight days from now."

CHAPTER 12 _____

DAWN ARRIVED in pink and gray at Tre Noc, a bloated orange ball hanging low in the east. Mist rose thickly from the river. The twelve SEALs of First Platoon, Team 2 boarded the helicopter that had landed only minutes before. Their main rotors still spun lazily as the liberty-bound sailors climbed aboard. A second after the last man entered, the engines spooled up and the birds lifted ungainfully off the tarmac.

Once airborne, the SEALs pulled civilian clothes from their ditty bags and began to change. With three squads totally in the dark as to the mission of Alpha Squad, their surprise could be understood when they landed at Ton Son Nhut and, after deplaning near three aircraft ready for boarding, Chief Waters spoke out in the sudden silence.

"You know, I'm not so hot for Bangkok."

"Me, neither," Chad Ditto added. "The Philippines sounds like the place for me. I hear Manila is boss this time of the year."

Grinning, Lieutenant Marino contributed his part to

the farce. "You've got that right, Repeat. How many of you feel the same way?"

All of Alpha raised their hands. The remainder had been SEALs a sufficient amount of time and knew enough about covert operations not to offer a like opinion. Something was going down and they had no need to know. Pope Marino spoke again.

"Matter of fact, I had a second set of liberty papers prepared. You guys who want to go to the Philippines come with me. There's a plane over there headed that way. The rest of you, good luck, we'll see you in two weeks."

With that, Alpha Squad picked up their liberty bags and walked away. Dressed as they were, they blended right in with the troops bound for the Philippines. Five minutes later, a youthful air force corporal appeared in the doorway of the Gulfstream and motioned for the men to board.

"This is more like it," Archie Golden declared when he saw the plush interior of the large business jet.

Compared to their usual mode of travel, luxury abounded. The bulkheads were insulated and paneled like an airliner, with rows of upholstered seats and soft overhead lighting. The leave-bound troops filled every seat. By preference, the SEALs sat in a group, on one side in the rear. A common belief had it that in a crash, the fuel in the wings flashed forward and those seated behind the wing root had the best chance for survival. When the last man entered, a gawky soldier in a loud Hawaiian print shirt and chinos, the door closed behind him and the starboard engine spooled up. The port engine fired a moment later. The

Gulfstream lumbered off the ramp and along the taxiway.

Speakers crackled to life above each pair of seats. "Good morning, gentlemen. Welcome aboard Flight Delta Foxtrot Two-seven-niner to Manila. Our first stop will be at Caviete Naval Air Station to let our swabbie friends off with their own people. Then it is on to our final destination. This is your captain, Major Mannering. We will be airborne momentarily. Our flight will have a duration of two hours and twenty-five minutes. We will arrive in time for noon chow. Once we're in the air, the cabin crew will be distributing light refreshments. If you are wondering about this little speech of mine, I would like to explain that this is my last flight. Five months from now I will be driving a Boeing Seven-oh-seven for Pan American Airways."

That was followed by brief applause from some of the passengers. The speakers went silent as the Gulfstream turned sharply at an intersection and then again onto the apron of the active runway. The engines ran up to full and the brakes came off. With that, the aircraft began its takeoff roll. Doc Welby, in the aisle seat next to Chad Ditto, went ghostly white. His hands gripped the armrests.

"It still gets to you, doesn't it?" Repeat badgered.

"Actually, it's not the takeoff that bothers me. I'm anticipating the landing," Doc told him calmly.

Chad did not laugh. He was only a little better at concealing his misgivings than Kent Welby. Chad had never flown before he became a SEAL. The small town in Kansas from which he had come did not even have a working airport. He had quickly found out that military aircraft were far from soothing vehicles for the passengers. Noise and vibrations were the norm. The bent metal–framed web seats offered little comfort. And the meals sucked—C-Rations or worse.

Now Chad could smell the aroma of fresh-brewed coffee. There was a pull-down tray on the seat in front of him and he had visions of real food coming from the tiny galley in the narrow tail of the plane.

The hydraulics groaned and the wheels came up. Ahead, the nose rose sharply. The hatch to the flight deck had been secured in the open position and Chad could see the pilot and copilot going through the take-off routine as they climbed to turn out of the pattern. Beside him, Kent Welby kept his eyes fixed on the headrest in front of him.

Doc silently recited the Hail Mary as the starboard wing tip dipped sharply and their climb ended. His reflex jump strained the seat belt as he heard a clatter behind him. Was the plane falling apart? Then from the corner of his eye he caught sight of a service cart. An airman first class pushed it forward and set the brake.

"Coffee, milk or juice?" he asked.

"What kind of juice?"

"Fresh squeezed orange, grapefruit, or pineapple."

Such temptation stifled the queasiness in the stomach of Doc Welby. "How about all three?" he asked.

"No problem." The mess steward poured from metal pitchers and handed the plastic glasses to Doc one at a time. Then he offered Doc a cello-covered tray.

It held a large cinnamon roll, a square of cream cheese, and a package of nuts. "Compliments of Major Mannering. Because of his retirement.''

"That's great, but where did he get the stuff?''

"Some airline that flies into Saigon. Air America it's called.''

Ahead of them, Pope Marino groaned. "Damn spooks are everywhere.''

Apparently Major Mannering was an easy man to work for, because the airman had no hesitation to ask Pope a question. "What do you mean, 'spooks,' sir?''

"Air America is a CIA operation, airman.''

Tonto Waters joined the fun. "Yeah, they probably have bugs planted in the food trays.''

A puzzled expression washed over the young airman's face. "Bugs? Like cockroaches?''

Tonto covered his eyes with one hand. "Nevermind.''

In the office that had been grudgingly provided for him by General Hoi, *Podpolkovnik* Rudinov opened the folder that contained the orders governing the deployment of Operation Night Fire. Moscow Central had designated the target to be in Vinh Province, yet they had left the choice of the exact location to him. He considered that for the tenth time and a cold, mirthless smile spread on his face.

"Yes, I know exactly where I'll put it,'' he declared aloud in soft, satisfied tones.

It still jolted him to read that the bomb would be detonated in exactly ten days. *General Hoi will be frantic when he learns. That disgusting little pedophile*, Rudinov thought. *In the* Rodina *we put people like that in institutions, not in charge of a brigade.* Rudinov looked again at the date. He would have to make arrangements at once for the covert movement of the bomb to the south.

Welby's stomach lurched only once when the main gear went down. They landed at Caviete Naval Air Station and the SEALs deplaned. The eight men were immediately bused to a transient mess hall, where the food proved to be fantastic—thick, juicy hamburger steaks, grilled on an outside barbecue, French fries made from real potatoes not frozen, fresh corn, and a mound of tropical fruit.

"Fleet sailors eat like this?" Archie Golden spoke his disbelief.

Pope Marino answered him. "No. It's only Airdales that get this kind of chow. Fleet sailors get real steaks and ice cream."

Archie whooped at that. "Poor babies. What a sacrifice. They wouldn't last a week out in the bush."

Repeat Ditto delivered his judgment with a straight face. "Who'd want them there?"

They got in line and took up trays. A burly man, also in civvies, joined the group. He looked them over, then spoke softly. "You the guys headed north?"

"That's us," Pope Marino allowed.

"Right. I'm one of your drivers. Chief Signalman Reno Jenkins."

"A pleasure, Chief. I'm Lieutenant Marino."

"We've got three Philippine jitneys outside for the ride. The other guys will chow down and we'll meet you there. You got a lot of stuff along?"

Pope shook his head. "Nope. Just what you see stacked by the door." All of their gear for the mission would be at the secret base outside Aparri or on board the sub.

Jenkins cut his gaze to the stack of ditty bags. He put on a relieved expression. "Good. Maybe we won't attract too much attention."

He did not expand on his cryptic remark and turned to the servers on the line. "Make mine rare."

Tonto Waters halted abruptly and did a double take when he caught sight of the "jitneys." They were modified jeeps, with extended beds in the back to allow for up to ten passengers. Uprights had been extended from the tops of the front fenders, behind the front seats, and at the rear corners to accommodate a stretched canvas cover, which had been painted with bright lacquer. A fringe of white crocheted balls dangled from the edge. One jeep had been painted a bright yellow, with a green top. Another was metallic purple, with a yellow cover. The third screamed at them in brilliant Chinese red, the roof a bilious chartreuse. Tonto pointed at them.

"What in God's name are those?"

Reno Jenkins came from around one of the vehicles. "Your ride to Aparri, Chief. Military equipment would only point a finger at you. I understood this was to be a—ah—covert operation."

Pope Marino recovered enough to quip, "Yeah, like '*The Purloined Letter*'?"

"You got it, sir. If you want to hide something important, put it in plain sight."

"Are you a Poe fan, Chief?" asked Marino.

"Yes, sir. I've read everything I know of that he

wrote. I memorized "The Raven" when I was a kid of ten."

Pope did not skimp on a compliment. "Quite an accomplishment. I never did get it right."

"Thank you, sir. Now, since there's only the eight of you, we only need two vehicles. Stow your gear and climb aboard. It's gonna be a long ride, so I arranged for chow. It's in those boxes behind the front seats."

Surprise registered on the face of Tonto Waters when a second sailor climbed into the right-hand front seat with a shotgun in hand. Tonto figured he would hear about it eventually. Chief Jenkins drove the jitney in which Tonto rode in the style of a Filipino driver, which turned out to be only a slight bit less crazy than a kamikazi taxi in Tokyo.

Tropical forest closed in around them the minute they left the base. The two jeeps whizzed along the two-lane, macadam highway, past rice paddies, cane fields, and banana plantations. They zigged and zagged around water buffalo and the small boys who tended them, motor-scooter powered rickshaws, and other impediments to safe travel. Shortly after passing the outskirts of Manila, the ground began to quickly rise.

Before long, mountains surrounded them and the highway had become a narrow dirt road. The vegetation around them had grown thick and wild. Chief Jenkins looked back at Tonto, which made the SEAL wince. "This is Huk country," he stated casually.

Tonto did not in the least want a conversation with a driver who wasn't watching where he was going, but he had to ask. "The guerrillas fighting the government?"

"Yeah. They're Marxists now, or claim to be, but the Huks have been fighting the government since Christ was a seaman third. Bob, here, is along as shotgun guard because they sometimes attack vehicles on the road."

"That's why we have these wild buses?"

Jenkins shrugged and glanced back at the road. "Partly, Waters, but those bastards ambush anything that rolls. If it's military, the Filipinos or ours, they have a special hard-on for them."

Tonto grimaced. "Cheery."

An hour went by with Jenkins steering the car. By then, the peaks towered, green and lush, above what had become a mere rutted trail. Chief Jenkins rounded a curve and braked sharply. A large tree had been felled across the road.

"Goddamn, it's them!" Jenkins shouted as he dived out of the driver's seat.

A fraction of a second later, a spiderwebbed hole appeared in the windshield and the bullet cracked past the nose of Tonto Waters.

Small bowlegged men in cammo boonie hats and diaperlike loincloths fired at the two-vehicle convoy from the sides of the road. Bob, the shotgun guard, took out two with his 12 gauge, while the SEALs jolted into action. Tonto Waters had already retrieved his 9mm Browning from his ditty bag.

He raised it up in time to blast the life out of a screaming Huk wielding an AK-47 on full rock and roll. The man flew backward, as though propelled by the expanding gases in the muzzle bloom. Finger on the trigger, he expended the entire magazine into the air. Tonto turned to his right to find that the squad members with him had piled out of the exposed vehicle.

Accustomed to being the ambushers, rather than the ambushees, the SEALs swung into action smoothly. The Huks quickly learned that there were jungle fighters fiercer than themselves. The volume of return fire increased as the SEALs spread out. Back at the second jitney, the driver had been able to turn sideways. Tonto saw Pope Marino firing over the top of the seats toward the right side of the road.

A clump of fern exploded, showering needles everywhere, and a Huk fell forward out of the middle. A three-round burst from ahead of the lead jeep clanged into the radiator. Steam geysered and Tonto wrote off the vehicle. He steadied his grip and took aim a little to the left and above the muzzle bloom.

Silenced by a bullet through the head, the Huk died twitching in the thick carpet of rotting vegetation. *Geez, he was actually shooting more accurately*, Tonto thought with wonder. Two meaty smacks drew Tonto's attention to Bob.

He had taken a round high in the chest and another in the throat, which had torn through his carotid artery. Bob died where he squatted beside the front fender. *Never waste anything*, Tonto thought as he reached forward and relieved the dead man of his shotgun. Now things could really start to happen. Firing his Browning to keep down the heads of the enemy, Tonto struggled to slide the bandolier of number 4 buckshot cartridges over the head and shoulder of the dead sailor. It came free as the Browning ran dry. Tonto stuck the pistol behind his belt and opened the action of the Ithaca to make sure a round had been chambered.

Encouraged by the death of Bob, the Huks shrieked insults in their mountain dialect and renewed their efforts to wipe out the intruders. What they got for their efforts was a hailstorm of buckshot as Tonto Waters opened up with the shotgun.

From the second jeep, Pope Marino called out to the SEALs. "Take 'em now."

To a man, the SEALs came out from their cover, weapons blazing. Tonto shoved fresh cartridges into the tube as he advanced, firing at hip level. Three Huks went down. Without grenades for once, the SEALs went forward at a steady run. Accuracy went out the window, of course, but it unnerved the remaining Huks. People usually ran from them. A quick head count informed them that only eleven out of the twenty who had manned this ambush had survived.

Doc Welby downed one of those with a high hold on his Browning. Zoro Agilar ran right into another of the squatty, muscular Huks, before he rammed the muzzle of his pistol against the bare chest of the guerrilla and blasted a fist-sized hole in him.

Repeat Ditto dropped a fat Huk in a cammo jacket and short pants. Thinking fast, he scooped up the dead man's AK-47 and used it to kill another of the terrorists. To his right, Tonto Waters tipped the apple cart of an ugly Huk who grew uglier when the .24 caliber balls pushed in his face. Behind him, one hardly more than a kid turned to flee, only to catch a 9mm slug in the back from Randy Andy Holt.

In less than two minutes, silence returned to the trail. Only three of the Huks had escaped into the jungle.

Walking with a jaunty roll, Chief Reno Jenkins appeared in front of the jeep he had been driving.

"Well, that settles that. We all ride in one jitney from here on. Too bad about Bob. He was a good man."

Pope Marino helped lay out the dead guard on the floor of the jitney. "Think we'll run into any more?"

Chief Jenkins studied their surroundings for a moment. "You never know."

CHAPTER 13 _____

"YOU GUYS is SEALs, ain't'cha?" Chief Jenkins asked Tonto Waters when he stopped at the last of four small villas on the edge of Aparri.

Tonto opted for caution. "Now, what would make you think that?"

Jenkins canted his head to one side. "Nobody else could have gone through those Huks and kicked so much ass like that. And you've got those non-reg pistols. What are they? Brownings?"

"Yep."

"Made in Belgium, right?"

Tonto gave Jenkins a level, deadpan gaze. "Sometimes it pays not to know as much as you want to know."

Reno Jenkins nodded solemnly, then muttered to himself as Tonto headed for the door, "Yeah, covert operation all right." Then he put the jitney in gear and drove away.

Behind him, Tonto Waters went through the door into a parquet-floored hallway. Its arched ceiling led to a set of French doors. Those gave way to a Spanish

Colonial courtyard, lush with palm and banana trees, bougainvillea and tiny orchids. The soles of Tonto's shoes clicked as he proceeded along the passageway. A doorway on his left led into a small dining room.

A large, round table almost filled the space. On it, someone had propped a note. Tonto sat down the canvas bag and crossed to retrieve it. The words were in neat, block print.

GULAGONG'S ON THE MELICON IS THE IN PLACE. HAPPY HOUR FROM 1700 TO 1900.

It was signed, AW, III.

Tonto looked at his watch. It showed 1550. Just time enough to rig the lights and TV on timers like they had been told. He found the bedroom and put away his bag, stuck the reloaded Browning in the small of his back, and covered it with his shirt. Then he went in search of a cab.

Gulagong's turned out to be built of salt-grayed, weathered wood, with the prow of a fishing boat sticking out of the roof, and fishnet draped over the low, two-story structure. It faced the bay on a wide boulevard. Tonto's cab was powered by one of the ubiquitous motor scooter engines, this one noisy and smoky. He stepped out and handed the driver some peso bills, then headed for the entrance.

What's this rocket scientist guy's name? Tonto asked himself. *Wadsworth? No, Wordsworth.* He entered and crossed to the reservations desk. "Do you have a reservation for a Mr. Wordsworth?"

The pretty young Filipina checked the sheet under the portrait light, running a slim, rose-tipped finger along the penciled-in names. "Yes, sir. Upstairs in the Mindanao Room. There are some gentlemen already there."

"Thank you."

On the second floor, Tonto found the Mindanao room by the sounds of laughter and clinking glasses. He stepped through the open doorway to be greeted by a trim, hard-muscled man about two inches taller than himself, which made him five-eleven.

"Alistaire Wordsworth," he announced from above a small, straight nose and gray eyes.

"Tom Waters."

"There are only two of you yet to arrive." Wordsworth ran long, strong fingers through a pronounced widow's peak in his light brown hair.

Tonto looked around and took in the faces. "Yeah. Our two kid SEALs: Repeat Ditto and Zoro Agilar."

"Get you a drink?"

"I'll go for that." They started toward the bar as Tonto continued. "We had a little run-in with some Huks on the way down. Got myself a bit of the old cotton mouth." Compared to Wordsworth, Tonto suddenly realized, he absolutely babbled.

Repeat and Zoro entered the room. At once, Alistaire Wordsworth turned their direction and stepped away from Tonto Waters. "The other two. Excuse me."

If brevity is the soul of wit, Tonto considered, *this guy must be a genius*. Wordsworth quickly brought Chad and Porfirio over to join Tonto at the bar. The three SEALs ordered San Miguel beer.

"The Jamaican rum," said Wordsworth. "Rocks. Two squeezes lime, please."

When everyone had a drink in hand, Captain Wordsworth led a procession across the room to a table beside floor-to-ceiling windows. He spoke loudly for the benefit of the restaurant employees within hearing. Obviously it came from a prepared script, based on his sudden verbosity. "I'm glad you're all here at last. We'll begin the oil field surveys tomorrow morning." Then, in a lowered tone, "We'll eat dinner here. I've already ordered. Then Lieutenant Marino and the three who are going in with me will meet Mr. Slater at the facility at twenty-thirty."

"Not that we aren't used to night operations," Archie Golden complained good-naturedly.

When the food came, it was ample and delicious— exotic Philippine vegetables, a whole roast suckling pig, and rice. They all ate heartily. When the last of the dessert had been consumed, Pope Marino stood, stretched and looked toward the door.

"Well, Wordy, we had better get out there."

Bingo! Tonto Waters thought. *That name is for sure going to stick.*

Inside a low building built half underground, Jason Slater greeted the four SEALs warmly as they arrived separately. When all were accounted for, he waved an arm around the large interior. "Welcome to Camp Nowhere. I trust you all put on your timers? Good. Now, let's get to it."

Enlarged photomosaic layouts had been spread on a long table in the middle of the metal-walled building. Vertical renderings, had been taped to three walls. Marino and his men stared with fascination at the edifice depicted by the spy plane pictures.

"My God, what an obscene place," Archie Golden said at last. He stepped closer and peered at one in detail. "The walls look sickly and they've got scabs."

"They are painted yellow. An ugly, Oriental yellow that seems to be the only paint chosen for government buildings in North Vietnam. We'll get to the Hilton in due time. Here's where we start.

"You'll exit the sub underwater some ten klicks offshore. Then use one of your inflatable STABs to get within two and a half klicks. From there, your pathfinders will swim in to do a survey of the mouth of the Hong River. If all's clear, the rest of the squad will come in to cover your departure, then return to the sub. From here it is seventy-nine kilometers up-river to Hanoi. For the first seventy-five klicks you will alternately swim underwater, using your Draeger rebreathers, and use your Slider units to power you along on surface swims. It will be a neap tide, so you'll have a tidal bore of about four to six knots. Neither the sleds nor your rebreather units will leave telltale strings of bubbles."

Tonto Waters spoke the thought that he had held since he first learned of the mission. "Kinda shaky goin' in there. Those folks aren't exactly our greatest fans."

"That's why you'll not exit the water directly at Hanoi. You'll swim a little beyond and hold over for the day, then return to a small village called Ha Dong. There you will find suitable transportation, preferably a closed van of some sort."

"Yeah, we just rent it from Hertz?" Archie asked.

"Not exactly. You'll learn about it later. Now, let's get to the Hanoi Hilton. Prisons are made to keep people in, not keep them out. You will have to recon in the van to find the best way in and use it.''

For the next half hour, Jason Slater went over the details of what the four men would do inside the POW compound, how to find the bomb, and how to get out again. Using copies of photos taken by Hanoi Jane for propaganda purposes, he showed them the layout of the interior: where the prisoners were housed, the cell blocks and catwalks, inside corridors, and the doors to the cells. He concluded with an admonition. ''Leave the deactivated bomb behind, get out of there ASAP, and head for the river.

''You will return to the mouth of the Hong River and radio for the pickup. You will be supplied with low-level radiation detectors to help locate the bomb. But I am trying for an overflight, using a supersecret, supersensitive detection equipment to verify the bomb's location inside the prison.'' Slater raised a hand to stave off the obvious question. ''If it's not there, we'll find it.''

Tonto raised a hand. ''How do we keep all those guards from tripping over us while we're inside?''

''This is going to be a joint operation. Some Naval Air will conduct a bombing raid while you go in. Since the Hilton is never bombed, the guards are reported to have become complacent. They usually sleep through them. Our sources tell us that since the inmates are under permanent lockdown, the warden has relaxed the regulations on internal patrols.

''If there are no more questions, we'll call it for tonight. Tomorrow night, Wordsworth Three will give you the first run-through on the bomb itself. Then we start the rehearsals on entering the prison and dealing with the physical plant.''

She almost stayed away. Francie Song had found another note from Yates in her time-card rack. The Pagoda again. The moment he saw her, he came quickly to her side. Yates took her roughly by one elbow and steered her away from a trio of youngsters who chattered and giggled at the carp pool. He started in on her at once.

"I want to know, and I want it fast. Where have the missing SEALs gone, how long will they be there, and when will they return.''

Francie twisted away. "That's simple. I already told you. They are on two weeks liberty in Bangkok.''

"I know that not all of them went there, including your paramour, Kent Welby. The whole of Alpha Squad, and the OIC, did not get off the plane in Bangkok. They went somewhere else. Find out where that is.''

Elmore Yates nearly shook with the intensity of his demand. He remembered the threats of the big Cambodian, Calaphong, when the KGB operative had informed him that not all of the SEALs went to Bangkok and demanded to know where they had gone. The eyes of Yates's control had flashed a cold, black fury as he suggested that failure to perform might get copies of the compromising photographs sent to the NIS. That set off visions of a court-martial and the cold stone walls of Portsmouth Naval Prison. This damned girl represented his best source for what he must have. She would give it to him . . . or else.

Impetuously he grabbed her left arm and squeezed hard. Francie winced.

"Come on, quit evading me. Tell me where they have gone? And, be quick about it."

"I can't tell you what I don't know. And—and, I—I won't tell you if I do find out."

Something inside Elmore Yates snapped. His balled fist crashed into Francie's high cheekbone. Pain shot through her head and her vision blurred. She brought her hands to her face, which made her chest and belly vulnerable. Yates lowered his hands to the open target and began to pound her.

Francie screamed in pain and horror. The baby! She staggered back and covered her stomach as best she could. Yates used a one-two punch to hit her in the left eye, then the right.

"Stop it! Stop it," she pleaded. "You hurting my—" Desperately she gulped back the word. "Hurting me."

Yates shoved his face close to hers and snarled at her. "You'll hurt a hell of a lot more if you don't tell me everything you know." He punched her abdomen with a solid blow that took the last of her strength and she dropped painfully to her knees. The flesh around her eyes burned and swelled and tears ran in steady streams. Feebly, she raised her hands to try to fend him off. At the pond, the children stood silent, faces blank with horror.

"I tell you, I don't know where they are. I thought he . . . he said . . . he was going to—to Bangkok. That's all." Yates hit her again.

"You work in plans and operations. Check the op order."

"I have. There was none. Only a copy of the leave papers. Please, please, don't hurt me any more."

With a final clip to the jaw, Yates left her to fall into unconsciousness. Her last thought was of the baby.

Elizabeth Welby sat in the right-hand seat of her father's Beech Baron as the elder Reardon flew the family to their home in Chattanooga, Tennessee. She had told her father about her decision to not seek a divorce and her letter to ask Kent what he really wanted to do just before Norman had started the starboard engine. Now he reached out to the autopilot and set it, then keyed the boom mike before his lips, the radio knob set on intercom.

"I'm proud of my girl, Betty. You made the right decision. Once he's had a taste of combat and served his tour in Vietnam, I'm sure Kent will find my offer of medical school much more attractive than the SEALs. When he is home and settled down at the university, he'll put the navy behind him. Sometimes I think we are asking too much of the boys we send over there."

"Why is that, Father?"

Norman Reardon considered it a moment. "There hasn't been a real war since Korea, and not enough preparation for this one. What concerns me most is motivation and a clear-cut enemy defined. Also, those clowns in Washington don't seem to see eye-to-eye on what our clearly defined national interest is. Who is the enemy? Little brown men in black pajamas? Or the political ideology they claim to espouse? If it is the latter, are our men prepared to take on the Viet-

namese communists' big brothers in China and the
Soviet Union?'' He frowned. ''If hostilities are
opened with either of them, I am afraid of what might
happen to this country.''

''What? *That* coming from my dear, sweet, hawk-
ish father? I never thought I'd live to see the day.''

''Tut-tut, my dear. Even if I seem to love my country to an inordinate degree; I willingly served her in
time of need; and I thoroughly hate those cowards
who are burning their draft cards and running off to
Canada to avoid serving. I am not blind to the very
real dangers that we might face, should the Soviets
become too riled.'' He laughed, a short, hard bark.
''Not that I've joined the 'Better Red than dead'
crowd of hankie-stompers and handwringers. I'm still
your old dad.''

Impulsively, Betty Welby reached across the small
space that separated them and squeezed his forearm.
''And I love you for it, Father.''

Tonto Waters slipped out the back door of the villa
at 2005 hours the next night. He walked alone out of
the town of Aparri to a thicket of cabbage palm,
where he located a moped that had been deposited
there for his use. Unlocking it from the deeply buried
steel post, he straddled the bicycle and began to pedal.
Slowly he gained speed to the point where he could
engage the lever that let the tiny gasoline engine sputter to life.

Chief Waters rode out to the hidden camp and
joined the others who had come by different routes.
Together, they went with Alistaire Wordsworth to an
isolated portion of the ''Vil Range''. There they en-

tered a concrete bunker and stared in fascination at what rested on a bomb rack in the center of the floor.

Overhead lights gave a soft glow to the slate—nearly charcoal—gray cylinder. Wonder tinted the words of Archie Golden. "That's some baby. Is it real?"

"No. It's a mockup. Gather around it and I'll go over the basics." When the three who were going in on the mission complied, Wordy methodically pointed out the features of the hydrogen bomb, urging each man to repeat the nomenclature after him.

"The fins are driven by an electric motor the size of a travel alarm. It is directed by an inertial guidance system. That has been preprogrammed by the bombardier. The casing is of lead-lined titanium with a nonreflective coating of paint.

"Up here, right behind the nose, is where the initiator is installed." When speaking on his favorite subject, Wordy could be quite verbose, the SEALs soon found out. "It is activated by a radio-altimeter. It has a proximity backup that works like a barometer."

"What's the initiator for?" asked Doc Welby.

"It is what sets off the detonating charges behind each hemisphere of plutonium—to drive them together and reach critical mass."

Archie grew more fascinated by the second. "How critical is the machining on those hemispheres?"

Wordsworth considered a second. "To within plus or minus point zero-one-zero-niner margin of error."

Archie whistled through his teeth. As a machinist's mate, he could well appreciate the degree of accuracy required. It left him envious of the men who had done it. "How many pass final inspection?"

"Two-point-five of every hundred. One reason it is so expensive to make nuclear weapons.

Archie figured out the reason at once. "If they're not that perfect, they won't go off?"

"That's right. This, the Mark Four, is not MIRVed into several smaller-yield warheads. We will want to dent one or both of the hemispheres, or jimmy the rails. Every system has double or triple redundancy. Like the initiator. Now, this . . ." He pointed to a round-edged rectangle, precisely fitted to the curve of the casing . . . "is not an inspection hatch. It gives access to the wiring harness for the bomb. I will demonstrate," Wordsworth concluded.

He took up a battery-powered screwdriver and removed the eight phillips-head screws. Then he lifted off the metal plate. Inside was another of clear acrylic. It was imbedded in a material like that which holds a windshield, only much more pliable. Using a slot-blade tool, he removed the transparent cover. Archie's eyes glowed as he gazed into the guts of the mockup bomb.

"We're going to cut these wires," Wordsworth indicated them with the tool, "in two places, and remove what we take out. It's done in this order; white, green, red, black. Then I am going to paint the white one black beyond the cuts, and the red one white. But the main thing to remember is . . . We have to damage the hemispheres. And we have to do that without achieving critical mass. Otherwise we'll end up being just a few more radioactive atoms over Hanoi."

CHAPTER 14 _____

ALISTAIRE WORDSWORTH III thought that the training was going well. He remained amused at how the SEAL called Archie had fallen in love with the nuke mockup. Each evening's training session began with a run-through on sabotaging the bomb. The reason everyone had to know how to do it was chillingly pragmatic. Wordsworth might get wasted. He didn't mind that, he decided, as he watched Archie bend over the mockup.

Archie spoke as he clipped wires. "Man, I'm droolin' over the thought of having a couple of these babies to play with. I could really kick Charlie's butt."

"Nuclear weapons do not discriminate," Wordy reminded him. "Collateral damage would be astronomical."

Archie sounded disappointed. "Yeah, there is that. The kinda war we're fightin', the mamasan who mops your bunk area in the morning may be shootin' a Type Fifty-six at you that night. Some Blanketheads I know have got the idea that we oughta kill 'em all and let God sort them out.''

"A bit extreme.''

"Aye, sir. That it is.'' Archie made an impish expression. "But it sure would be effective.''

Wordsworth put a hand to the small of his back. "I'm still sore from climbing that wall three times last night.''

Tonto Waters laughed softly. "It helps if you don't fall one of those times. Speakin' of which, it's about time to get out there.''

"You still have your run-through on the bomb,'' Wordsworth reminded Tonto.

Tonto cut him a sideways glance and suppressed a shudder. "That thing makes me nervous.'' He sighed heavily. "Okay, I had better get at it.''

"Talk your way through it, for a check. After all, this is the last night,'' Wordsworth suggested.

Tonto Waters did his turn on the bomb and then climbed down from the rack. "We had better get out there.''

When the four men reached the wall that represented the outer perimeter of the Hanoi Hilton, they had a surprise waiting. Lieutenant Marino, who supervised this aspect of their training, and marine Gunnery Sergeant Graham, head of the guard force, held a prisoner. He was obviously a Huk and most likely not alone.

Pope Marino turned him over to the marine sergeant who operated the base, then made silent signs to indicate that the SEALs sweep the area. Tonto,

Doc, and Archie spread out and disappeared into the darkness. Pope and Wordy went in the opposite direction.

It did not take the two officers long to come upon another Huk. He squatted in a clump of brush, looking off to the west. Wordsworth leaned close to Marino and whispered in his ear.

"We can't let any of them get out of here."

Cold as that sounded, Pope agreed. "My thought exactly."

Before Marino could act on the decision, Wordy raised his Browning and shot the Huk through the head. The shot made a muffled sound, above the cycling of the action. The Huk guerrilla slumped forward and twitched violently for a while, then went still.

"We'll swing around toward the others," Pope mouthed softly. "I've got a hunch there are more."

Separated by a hundred meters, Tonto, Doc, and Archie walked low and slow, took advantage of every shadow, their eyes always alert for the slightest movement. Tonto spotted them first. Five Huks, not fifty meters ahead, had settled into an ambush position across the road. He silently wished for his shotgun. Thirteen rounds in the Hi-Power did not seem like much when up against nearly two-to-one odds. He glanced to his right and saw Archie freeze in midstride.

Good, he had seen them, too. Tonto looked left as Doc melted into the tough saw grass. At least the suppressors gave them an advantage. The Huks would never know where the initial shots came from. He raised his and sighted on the broad chest of one Huk.

A brief *phutt!* came from the end wipe of the hush-puppy and the man uttered a harsh gasp before he fell to one side. At once, his comrades reacted noisily, jabbering in their own language what sounded to Tonto like questions. The stuttering report of several AK-47 assault rifles accompanied the demands to know what had happened. Two more took hits, by which time the SEALs were on the move again.

Doc Welby nearly stepped on one Huk lying prone behind a bipod mounted light machine gun. The enemy turned at the sound of footsteps and Doc fired hastily. He blasted through both jaw hinges. Shrieking hysterically, the Huk gagged on his own blood. Doc shot him again, this time in the chest. Suddenly the air near his head whistled with the sound of a machete wielded by a squatty, pinched-faced Huk.

Doc dropped to one knee and turned in the direction of his assailant. He saw only a darker blob against the starry sky. That proved enough. Once more the silent Browning spat a slug that punched a neat hole in the meaty side of the Huk. It made a much larger exit wound. Groaning, the man dropped his machete and went down.

From a short distance away, Doc heard the sound of Archie finishing off another. *Good, that should account for all of them*, he thought.

Pope and Wordy reached the ambush site five minutes later. They found Archie tending the wound of the sole surviving Huk. Marino shrugged and reached for the small mobile radio clipped to his belt.

"Sergeant Graham, we have another one for you to transport. And we've got six bodies to clean up. Better bring a truck." He turned to the others. "At least we have two to interrogate. Maybe we can find out who sent them and how they knew we were here."

Tonto stood up for the absent men in the squad. "It can't be any of the guys, Pope. They know better than to run their mouths. I'd say the Huks, or some-one, has this place under nearly constant surveil-lance."

Pope Marino considered that. "You might be right. Hell of a thing if it's true. No one is supposed to know about this place. But, you know how that works everywhere else. Well, there's work to be done in the 'prison.' We'll leave our living pair to the tender mercies of Jason Slater and the Marine complement."

Jason Slater paced in front of the chair occupied by the unwounded Huk. The man was short, squat, and ugly. His face held a perpetual snarl. So far, the CIA station chief had made no progress. The Filipino interpreter for the Marines did not speak the Huk dialect, and the prisoner refused to speak Tagalog. In mounting exasperation, Slater turned to the interpreter and spoke in Spanish.

"This is getting us nowhere. Take him out and shoot him." An instant later, a shark smile spread on his face when he saw the captive's eyes widen in alarm. "So, we have a common language after all. Who sent you here? Who are you working for?"

Only silence followed. In three fast strides, Jason Slater closed on the bound man. He stepped behind and placed the Huk in a sleeper hold. In seconds, the man blacked out. Slater walked to a table and poured himself a cup of coffee from a pot on a hot plate.

"This may take some time," he observed to the others in the room.

Gunny Graham exchanged looks with his assistant. "Did you kill him, sir?"

"Nooo. Just put him to sleep for a while."

Graham eyed the slumped man thoughtfully. "D'you think we should run the other one in here while he's still out? Might scare the scumbag into talking."

Slater brightened. "Brilliant, Gunny. You do that."

He took a deep swig of coffee and grimaced. The marines made mud, the navy battery acid. He longed for his Colombian Supremo, fresh ground and brewed in a Melitta.

Graham returned shortly. Supported by two Marine PFCs, the wounded Huk took one look at what appeared to be his dead comrade and sagged in resignation. Through the interpreter, Jason Slater began his questioning.

"Who is your leader and why did he send you here?"

Weakened by blood loss and pain, certain he would be next to die if he held back, the Huk answered hesitantly. "No. It is not a Huk operation. We were contacted by a white man. He would pay us to find out about you. What you do. The money offered must have been good. Our leader sent us here tonight. That is all I know."

Slater nodded. "It's a good start." To the Marines, "Take him back."

At the doorway, the injured Huk stiffened in anger

when his comrade groaned and muttered softly. The Marines whisked their captive away. Slater turned back to the man in the chair.

"Refuse to answer another question and next time you won't wake up. Now, who sent you?"

Swallowing hard, and wanting to massage his sore throat, the Huk made a low, husky reply in Spanish. "There is a man. A white man. We were sent to him tonight by our leader."

That suited Slater fine. Spanish he knew. "For what purpose?"

"To find out what you . . . do here."

"He paid you?"

An affirmative nod. Then, "No, he paid our leader."

"In pesos?"

"No. American dollars. A lot of them."

Jason Slater could hardly contain his pleasure at the results. "Where is this man?"

"In Aparri."

Slater turned to Gunnery Sergeant Graham. "Gunny, go get Chief Waters and Machinist's Mate Golden."

When Tonto and Archie reported to the CIA agent, Slater made a quick explanation of what he had learned. Then he added, "The whole thing stinks to me. When you finish your rehearsal for tonight, I want you two to come with me. We'll pay a little visit on this so-called white man."

A stillness lay over Aparri at 0320 hours when Jason Slater, along with Tonto Waters and Archie Golden, silently approached a house set apart from its neighbors by a vacant lot on one side, and by an inlet of the sea on the other. Untended trees hung their branches close to the ground and the scant front yard was hard-packed dirt, completely devoid of grass. The dwelling looked deserted. Slater spoke in Spanish to the Huk, who accompanied them.

"Are you sure this is the place?"

Nodding in a surly manner, the Huk answered. "He is there, inside. We come here before to get orders, a picture box."

Picture box? "Do you mean, camera?

"That is same."

Slater pointed to a tree on the opposite side of the street. "Over there. Hands behind your back."

From the small guardhouse at the base, Slater had taken a pair of handcuffs. With them, he secured the guerrilla. He took a length of rope from a small bag, along with a roll of duct tape. He tied the Huk to the tree and tore off a strip of the silver-backed adhesive. That, he placed over the man's mouth.

"Stay here," Slater told the Huk.

Quietly the CIA operative and the two SEALs moved off toward the target.

Not a light showed from the interior of the house. A quick pass around the building revealed three entrances: front and rear, and a sliding glass door that opened onto a sun deck. Ideal for their purposes.

Slater laid out a quick plan. "We'll go in all three doors at the same time. Check your watches."

Big, waterproof divers' watches on the wrists of the SEALs could be read easily. Slater pulled a round case watch from a small pocket in his jeans and opened the gold cover. All three timepieces were within twenty seconds of one another. "We'll go in exactly five minutes from now, Mark."

Quickly they went to their chosen doors. Tonto reached out and tried the knob. *Naw, that would be too easy.* To his surprise it turned freely. One eye on his watch, he waited out the time in silence. Not a sound came from beyond the portal.

At the front door, Archie Golden eased up on the porch steps, walking close to the edge of the treads to decrease the chance of any telltale squeaks. Stealthily he glided across the small stoop and flattened himself beside the door, Browning out and ready.

He tried the knob and found it locked. *Damn, now I'll have to kick it in.* Checking the area around him, Archie braced himself and checked his watch.

Jason Slater skirted the steps to the sundeck and vaulted the banister to land cat-light on the two-by-six planking. In equal silence he crossed to the sliding panel and tested it. It had been locked. Slater reached into an inside coat pocket and produced a set of lock-picks. He selected one, inserted it and a tension bar, and began to wiggle. Abruptly the lock turned. He put away the small kit and checked his watch. Time to go.

Vladimir Gorodov lay in heavy slumber. He did not expect the Huks to return before daylight. Accordingly, he had drunk vodka freely. He had been fuzzy-brained when he stumbled into his room and pulled off his shirt. He lay awake for a while, wondering if he had locked all of the doors. Then it didn't matter, for he fell into deep, alcohol-induced sleep.

He did not suspect an intruder when a loud, gun-

shotlike sound dragged him up to almost full wake-
fulness. Tinkling glass followed. Seconds later,
footfalls pounded through the hallways. That jerked
Gorodov wide awake. A flat crack from a Tokarev
7.63mm pistol froze him in place. Oddly, nothing followed. His first coherent thought was that the Huks
had come back for him. They knew he had money
somewhere and they probably did not know about
banks. So the thing to do was hide.

Gorodov grabbed up his Makarov pistol and swung
his legs out of the bed. The two men sent with him
by the Manila *residentura* could take care of those
mountain peasants. He had only a short way to go to
the small closet and the access hatch to the attic
within. Unfortunately, the vodka got in his way. His
head swam the moment he stood.

Groaning through closed lips, Gorodov wavered his
way toward his sanctuary. His bare toe found a leg of
the chair where he had dumped his shirt. Pain shot up
to his groin. Before he could stifle it, his mouth
opened and a cry came out. Limping, he tried unsteadily to cover the last few feet to the door.

With a lurch, Gorodov reached the closet. Two
more shots sounded from the opposite direction as the
inebriated Russian closed the door behind himself. He
faintly heard voices from the front and rear.

''Clear.''

''Clear.''

''Good here.''

Three of them and they were speaking English.
Alarm and confusion spread through him. Had the
Huks been caught? Unable to use the light, Gorodov
fumbled to find the pull cord to the foldout stair to

the attic. The intruders would find the room any second.

More silence followed. Gorodov's fingers brushed the cord. He grabbed for it. Perversely it eluded him. He tried again, sweat beading on his forehead.

"In here," Tonto Waters spoke softly to the other two. "I think this is the room. I heard someone yell like he'd been hurt."

He had flattened himself to one side of the door, with Archie Golden and Jason Slater opposite him. At Tonto's nod, Archie stepped in front of the closed partition, Browning 9mm at the ready. He reared back, leg cocked, and kicked the panel beside the knob. It flew open and Archie used his momentum to drop down low to the floor. Tonto jumped over the right shoulder and extended arm of the prone Archie and rushed the interior at an oblique angle.

To their surprise, no shots had been fired. A quick check of the room revealed no one there. Jason Slater motioned for another examination. The window was closed and latched. Tonto was first to find the closet door.

If someone had shouted in this room, he had to be in there. Tonto pointed to Archie, then the knob, made turning and pulling motions, and stepped in front of the partition. At his nod, Archie reached out, twisted the knob and yanked the door open.

Faint light from a setting quarter moon filtered through the window and allowed Tonto Waters to see a darker mass against the blackness in the closet. In the slowed down time sequence of combat, Tonto realized that the figure was moving upward. He fired his Browning hastily and the fugitive fell, screaming, to the floor.

Archie and Jason closed in to secure the captive. Using a flashlight provided by Slater, Tonto began to toss the room. He found nothing that would reveal the identity of the "white man." Then he put the light on the moaning, retched figure of Vladimir Gorodov. Limned in the circle of brightness, beside the fallen man's shoulder, Tonto saw a Makarov pistol.

"Hey, Cowboy, this guy has a Soviet pistol."

Jason Slater looked at it and nodded. "You're right, Tonto." To Gorodov he snapped, "*Choom vey?*"

Gorodov's eyes widened, then he responded in rapid Russian. "I demand immediate medical treatment, and to be taken to the Soviet Embassy in Manila. I have diplomatic immunity."

Slater repeated his question. "Who are you?"

Gorodov grimaced in pain. "I am Arkady Frodor, cultural attaché to the Soviet ambassador."

With another flashlight, Archie searched the pockets of a suit coat hanging in the closet. He came up with a leather folder. "Lookie here."

Slater examined the contents and grinned nastily. "Kay-Gay-Bay, right?"

"*Yeb vas!*"

Slater put on his Duke Wayne drawl. "Well, pilgrim, I'd say you weren't in any condition to tell anyone to fuck himself." To the others, "Put a field dressing on him and we'll take him out to the base. I'll have to get the station chief down here to take care of him."

"What about the two we wasted?"

"Leave 'em, Tonto. Someone can come along and clean up later. I'd say we made a pretty good haul here. Though I do wonder why the KGB wanted to know all about us."

CHAPTER 15 _____

EARLY THE next morning, dressed in civvies, Alpha Squad flew by civilian helicopter to 135-B, an oil rig off the coast of Luzon. Outwardly it was the same routine they had followed the three previous days. This time they would not be coming back. Tonto Waters gazed out across the South China Sea and summed up the thoughts of all the SEALs.

"Do we go fishing, or take a swim?"

Jason Slater reached the top of the ladder that led to the launch he had come out on in time to hear that. "You'll get all the fishing you want tonight," he declared, establishing their cover story. "I've arranged for a charter boat to take us out." Then, quietly, he told them. "For now, we've got the engineering section room all to ourselves to go over the photos once more and verbally rehearse the mission. The rest of the squad can do as they wish."

Eyes widened by the reality of this, Archie Golden asked, "Then this is not some sort of operational exercise?"

"Artful Dodger is for real, and it's definitely on. I

received confirmation before I left for the platform.''

Archie beamed. ''What a hoot. I'm gonna get my hands on a real...'' Abruptly he cut it off before saying more than he should.

Slater and Lieutenant Marino exchanged significant glances. Slater spoke to the three SEALs who comprised Operation Artful Dodger. ''Shall we arm ourselves with coffee and go up? Wordsworth should already be there.''

Green, purple, and yellow still colored the face of Francie Song as she lay with her feet in the stirrups of the examination table. The doctor stepped away from her now and spoke with a cool detachment.

''You may get up now. It has been a week since the attack? There has been no bleeding? No indication of premature labor?''

''No, Doctor,'' Francie replied. ''Although at first, it hurt terribly. The baby seemed to shift.''

Changing subjects, the doctor asked, ''This man who hit you? You say he was Viet Cong?''

Francie avoided his direct stare. ''Yes. Viet Cong. He was angry that I work for the Americans.''

''Would you recognize him if you saw him again?''

''No. He just came at me and ... beat me. Why are you asking this? I came about the baby, not to discuss my assault. I just want to forget that.''

The doctor gave it up. ''Very well, I can understand feeling that way.'' He took a deep breath and sighed before continuing. ''There is a strong fetal heartbeat and normal movement. I think we can at last say that everything is as it should be. Although I wish you would have followed the advice I gave when you first came to me. A trauma like you suffered might still have unpleasant consequences for you or the child.''

Francie gave the doctor a hot glare. ''Aborting him would be even more unpleasant. Thank you, Doctor, and good day.'' With that, she left, her mind on Kent Welby and what he might be doing.

After an intense morning of verbal walkthroughs of the mission, Tonto got to go fishing after all. He went at it diligently from the landing platform. He caught one big grouper and a dozen smaller, rainbow-colored fish, which he turned over to the oil rig crew's cook to prepare for dinner. An hour later, they boarded a fishing boat that came alongside and sailed out into the South China Sea.

Darkness fell with the usual swiftness out on the water. An instant after the upper crescent of bloated orange dropped below the glassy surface, Repeat Ditto shouted excitedly to the others.

''There it is! D'ya see it?''

''See what?'' Zoro Agilar asked.

Chad Ditto eagerly explained. ''The green flash. Sometimes, when conditions are just right, there's a quick flash of green when the sun sets over water. I saw it just now. I swear.''

''*Ay mierda!* There ain't no green flash. I never saw one.''

''Yeah, Zoro, but you're from New Mexico. There's no ocean there.''

Aguilar responded defensively. ''Yeah, but I been to Padre Island.''

Repeat thought a moment. ''The sun sets over land that's behind you there.''

Looking sheepish, Zoro allowed that. "You've got a point, *amigo*."

An hour after sunset, a soft flash of red light came from off the port bow. The charter boat changed course and ran in along the hull of a low, sleek submarine. Skilled hands made fast the lines thrown from the CIA-owned fishing boat and a narrow gangplank was lowered to the craft.

To show that he could be as good a sailor as any of them, Alistaire Wordsworth scampered up the incline and performed a crisp salute to the fantail, where the flag normally flew, then another to the boyish-faced ensign who had officer of the deck duty. "Permission to come aboard, sir."

Ensign Rogers replied gravely, "Permission granted."

Lieutenant Carl Marino came next, followed the same formula, and then added, "Permission to board my men."

"Granted. Welcome to the USS *Sunperch*. We'll go below and let your transportation cast off."

Down in the red-lit interior of the Perch-class submarine, Wordy Wordsworth and Pope Marino introduced themselves by name only. Then Pope indicated Alpha Squad. "These are my crew."

Commander Stanley McDade, the captain of the *Sunperch*, did not miss the omission of names. "I'll have you shown to your quarters. All of your gear is stowed in the aft torpedo room. My navigator, Mr. Jiles, tells me it will take us three days to reach your AO."

*   *   *

Gripped by desperation, Francie Song approached her meeting with Elmore Yates with halting steps. He had not selected the pagoda garden this time. Instead he named an isolated bamboo pole dock where local fishermen tied up their sampans. To Francie, that meant that if she failed him this time, at the least, she would receive another beating.

She wished fiercely to get her hands on a gun, or even a long, sharp knife. Then she could protect herself and the baby. Her footsteps rustled on the woven palm matting that formed the dock as she approached the solitary figure at the far end.

Elmore Yates glowered at her as she stopped in front of him. "You're late again."

"We are busy, as you know."

SSG Yates shook his head. "Francie—Francie, what am I to do with you?"

"You could . . . let me go."

Elmore Yates surprised her with his next words. "After you help me with this we'll consider it."

Hope flared and died as quickly. Unable to concentrate, Francie realized that she had to tell him something. He would not believe the truth; that she did not know where the missing SEALs went. Born of her turmoil, a possible solution revealed itself. She would have to be careful not to give too many details. And she must be convincing. Abruptly she realized that Yates had been talking to her.

"I'm sorry, what did you say?"

"I asked you what you had for me."

"I could find nothing in Operations. No, wait, here what I have to say. I have a friend in Binh Thuy. She also works for the Americans. This is a very secret mission. Only verbal orders came to Tre Noc. That is why there was nothing to find in the files.''

Impatient, now that it appeared he had what he wanted, Yates snapped at her. ''Get to the point.''

''They—Alpha Squad—have gone on a covert mission in the mountains of Cambodia.''

''Where in the mountains?''

Francie shrugged. ''I do not know. There is supposed to be—to be a large training base there, run by the NVA.''

''When are they to hit it?''

''I don't know. That is all my friend told me.'' Her blush came naturally. ''She only told me that because she knows how much I love Kent Welby.''

That much he could believe. Maybe the bitch was telling the truth. ''All right, I'll accept that. Find out more before we meet two days from now.''

''But, I cannot. My friend . . . is worried about telling me what she already did.''

''You can figure a way to pry more out of her, Francie. If you need inspiration for doing so, consider this. The life of your son Thran depends upon it. You're doing this for your little boy.''

Captain McDade spoke to his XO. ''Take her down.''

''Aye aye. All hands to diving stations. Prepare to dive.'' In what seemed an incredibly short time to the SEALs, the klaxon whooped and Lieutenant Commander Hobbs called out the chilling words. ''Dive! Dive! Dive!''

Water gushed into the ballast tanks with a solid roar. The *Sunperch* sank, rather than making a running dive, so the decks remained almost level. Once the dive had been executed, the chief of the boat, Jeff Connors, escorted the SEALs to their quarters.

Unlike the World War II boats and earlier models, the crew and any passengers were not obliged to sleep atop loaded torpedoes. Neat little compartments along the length of the sub housed six men each. Not a lot of effort was wasted on making the bunks spacious. Chief Connors distributed the SEALs and then nodded aft.

"When you are settled in, I'll show you where your gear is stowed."

He returned in twenty minutes, time enough for everyone to change into tiger-stripes of French origin and put up their personal items. Connors spoke cheerily. "We're level at six hundred feet, speed seventeen knots, on a heading of two-seven-zero. Now, let's go to your toy locker."

In the aft torpedo room, everything gleamed from constant wiping and polishing—except for a mound of equipment covered by a large, green tarpaulin. It looked as out of place as a wart on the face of the *Mona Lisa*. Randy Andy and Zoro Agilar pulled it back to reveal the Draeger rebreather units and the Sliders—handheld, electric-powered personal sleds. Archie Golden went at once to a separate backpack rig.

He opened it and examined the contents. He lifted one of the four M18 claymore mines and looked appealingly at Lieutenant Marino. "Tell me what use we're going to have for these. I like 'em well enough, as you guys know, but to go where we're going doesn't make much sense."

"Take a couple anyway, Archie," suggested Marino.

Archie dug deeper and came out with four quarter-pound blocks of C-4. "Now that's more like it."

By then, a number of off-watch sailors had gathered around to get a look at the SEAL equipment. To them, it looked exotic. Marino had a reminder for the four who would go to Hanoi. "You know that you won't have any shoulder-fired weapons along, just your suppressed pistols. So any support fire will have to come from the rest of the squad. And then only to get your butts out of there. If it becomes absolutely necessary for one or all of you to have a rifle, waste some NVA guys and use theirs."

After the equipment had been taken by the SEALs to where it would be close at hand, Archie Golden took a look around the interior of the sub and sniffed deeply. Fists on hips, he addressed his remark to Zoro Agilar.

"Now I know why they call 'em Pig Boats."

A chorus of jeers answered him from the submariners and his fellow SEALs. Chief Connors turned to Archie. "First time I heard that one I laughed so hard I kicked the slats outta my cradle. You're gonna have to come up with something more original than that, Red."

Archie glowered. "The name's Archie . . . to my friends." Then he brightened. "Though I suppose that includes you for the duration of the trip."

Grinning, Connors extended a hand. "Yeah, I guess it does. C'mon, I'll buy you a cup of joe down on the mess deck."

Marino spoke up. "Just a reminder. There'll be

lockout drill for the four of you at zero-eight-hundred tomorrow. I expect you to be bright-eyed and bushy-tailed.''

Although Elmore Yates suspected that Francie Song had lied to him about the SEALs, he also knew he had to tell Caliphong something. They met in a tea house frequented exclusively by Asians, located in a small village five klicks from Tre Noc.

From the outside it looked like the ordinary Vietnamese hooch, if a little larger, with a veranda around three sides. Inside, Yates found most of the woven palm mat walls had been cleared out to form a large common room, with sliding screens at several places that could be used to form private space. A counter ran along one wall, with backless stools for the customers. Behind it, charcoal fires smoked in brick stoves. One held a large pot of rice, another noodles in a thin pork broth. Metal pots of tea clustered on the third. A backbar held quarts of LeRoux and twelve-ounce bottles of Bahmibah beer. One of the screens slid back and Caliphong gestured for the Marine to join him.

Inside the small cubical they sat on cushions and Caliphong poured tea. Caliphong noted the strain lines at the corners of the American's mouth, the tightness at the edges of the eyes. *He is either going to lie, or he does not trust the source of his information*, Caliphong/Dudov marked.

''You have something for me?''

''Yes. I have been told by one of my contacts that the SEALs are on some sort of secret mission in your country.''

"In . . ." Stunned, Dudov almost said "the Rodina?" but checked himself and completed the sentence. "Cambodia?"

"That's what I was told." Yates did not look Dudov directly in the eyes.

"Where?"

"I don't have that yet. I will, though. You were right, the liberty papers were cut as a cover, so we can figure the mission will last at least ten days."

"When is it to begin?"

"My source said she did not know. I doubt that."

"So do I. It is vital that you find out." Hard, black eyes narrowed as Dudov leaned toward Yates. "Are you sleeping with her?"

That question startled Yates. It was the last thing he expected to be asked. "No! No, I'm not sleeping with her." *Damn it*, he added in his mind.

"Perhaps you should try it. Loosen her up a little."

"She won't have anything to do with me." Yates looked away, ashamed of his admission.

Dudov put a nasty sneer on his face. "Why is that the case? I thought you were quite the ladies' man. Remember that two-on-one session you had with those Vietnamese girls at the home of the Saigon black marketeer?"

He referred to one of the incriminating photographs the KGB owned. Yates could only sit and squirm at Caliphong's taunt.

Caliphong/Dudov made a curt, cutting motion with the blade of one hand. "I want an answer in two days. Bed her, torture her, do whatever is necessary."

"I have already threatened harm to her only child, a boy of seven."

Eyes flew wide in surprise. "That, my friend, might prove to be a very fatal mistake."

CHAPTER 16 _____

THREE DAYS later, the SEALs were jarred awake by the whoop of the klaxon as it blared out General Quarters shortly after noon. With nothing to do, the SEALs had languished for the past two days. They did their daily dozen rigorously, of course, and ran in place. Two sessions of lockout drill added spice to their lives, but failed to entirely banish boredom. Now they found themselves in the way. When the klaxon silenced, Captain McDade's voice followed.

"Now hear this. This is the captain. We have entered North Vietnamese waters. Sonar has made contact with one target with twin, fast running screws. Two more single screws, doing slow turns. Rig for silent running."

Soon, the weird swishing sound of a surface vessel passing close along the side of a submarine could be heard by crew and passengers. It tightened guts throughout the *Sunperch*. The screws made an even louder resonance as they churned the water, approaching from stern to bow. The ping of an obsolete sonar lanced past the hovering sub without making contact.

However, these pulses did raise the hairs on the back of the neck of Tonto Waters.

What was he *doing* down here? He didn't even like swimming. But he had to do that to be a SEAL, so he did. Now, they were sitting ducks. Visions of the Soviet version of a SUBROK missile belching from a tube and surging toward them played behind Tonto's eyes. He edged toward the open hatch that led to the bridge one deck above. *Why doesn't the captain do something?*

"Negative buoyancy. Thirty degrees down bubble," McDade's calm voice came to Tonto. "There's a thermal layer down there twenty fathoms. We get under that and we've got it dicked," he opined.

Screws turning on electric motors, the *Sunperch* left almost no cavitation image. Obviously the ultra high frequency narrow beam transducer being used by the North Vietnamese did not pick it up. The onboard sonar spiked the surface ship and the operator turned to the captain.

"He's turning, sir. Making another pass. Bearing now two-seven-niner and opening."

Relief brought a sigh to the lips of McDade. "He missed us when he was that close, and now he'll never find us. Steady on the angle on the bow. There's still two others out there."

Thanks, I needed that, Tonto Waters thought.

"Contact! Bearing zero-one-five. Single screw, doing slow turns," sang out the sonar operator. "There's a splash. Sonodrogue in the water. He's gonna quarter our bow. He's increasing turns now."

McDade spoke his mind. "What got them all riled up in the first place?"

Lieutenant Commander Hobbs turned to the CO. "Who knows with them? Maybe they're running a training exercise."

"That's all we need, Gordie."

Lieutenant Commander Barry Lailey looked up over the rims of his spectacles. Damn, how he hated bifocals. He constantly had to throw his head back to read titles on a bookshelf or the features of someone standing close. Like now, with this stranger standing beside him at the bar of the officers' mess.

Lailey spoke from his disappointment. "I was expecting Jason Slater. I owe him a drink or two."

Bobby Noonan, Slater's number two, kept a reassuring blank expression when he replied. "He's back at Langley for a briefing. The brass hats want to know firsthand what is going on in the Delta."

Lailey raised the scotch-rocks to his lips, sipped, and sat it on the napkin. "Hmmm. I really needed to talk to him about something."

"Maybe I can help."

Lailey considered Noonan a moment. "We seem to have misplaced six SEALs and the OIC of Team Two."

Noonan flashed a brief smile. "Really? How did you manage that?"

Lailey frowned. "I don't know. The whole of First Platoon received orders for liberty in Bangkok. I learned recently that only one squad arrived there."

"And?" prompted Noonan.

Now came the hard part. "I thought maybe Jase might know something about it. It's really rather embarrassing that Operations and Intelligence know nothing about this.''

Bobby Noonan fought to keep the grin from showing. He knew all about Barry Lailey and his vendetta against Carl Marino. He also knew all about Operation Artful Dodger. In his present attempt to find fault with Marino, Lailey had hung himself way out there. Bobby enjoyed watching him twist in the wind.

Noonan knocked off the last of his Tom Collins and signaled the bartender for another. Then he arranged a solicitous expression. ''I'm sorry this isn't pleasant news. But rest assured, we know nothing about it either.''

Quite to the contrary Lailey's spirits rose with that. ''Oh. Then that would indicate that they are absent without leave. Or they've deserted. Thank you, Mr. Noonan, you've really made my day.''

''Glad to oblige.''

''I had better get paperwork in motion on this. Finish your drink. Have another. I'll take care of the tab.''

After Lailey's departure, Noonan thought to himself, *When this is all over, that one is going to look the right proper idiot, as the Limeys would say.*

Ping . . . bong! Ping . . . bong! The chilling sound of sonar contact could be heard all over the *Sunperch.* The sonar operator turned to Lieutenant Commander Hobbs, who had the con, and spoke the obvious.

''They've got us.''

Hobbs nodded and touched a finger to the hailer. ''Captain to the bridge. We've been picked up by enemy sonar.''

McDade reached the bridge in under a minute and immediately ordered evasive maneuvers. He put the bow down, laid a zigzag course, and dived for the thermal layer. He turned to Hobbs.

"The thermal is thinner here. If that muther sticks with us for long, we might not be able to shake free."

"Then what?"

"According to orders, we withdraw and try again tomorrow night. Which won't make our passengers all that happy."

Pingggg! . . . Pinggg!

"He's off us now, sir."

Stan McDade shot a glance at the sonar operator. "For now. I'll still not lay any odds."

Sonar sang out a steady call. "I have contact with two more single-screw vessels, sir. They're making high turns and heading our way."

Again the ultrahigh frequency of the enemy sonar echoed along the side of *Sunperch.* "I read surface craft closing at flank speed." Another pulse came from the North Vietnamese. No return.

Then, *Pinggg . . . bonggg!*

"Damn! He's got us again," McDade muttered.

"That's a different one, sir," the sonarman said. "Our first contact has carried beyond our course."

Captain McDade made a quick decision. "Hard right rudder."

"Right rudder, aye."

Thirty seconds passed, then, "Rudder amidship."

"Amidship, aye." The pings stubbornly persisted.

After a minute crept by, McDade snapped, "Hard right rudder."

*Pinggg . . . bonggg! Pinggg . . . bonggg! Pinggg!
Pinnggg!* McDade breathed softly. "He's off us."

"As you said, 'for now,'" Hobbs offered.

Ten minutes later, the *Sunperch* received simultaneous pings from opposite sides of the sub. "Engine turns increasing, sir," reported the sonarman. "Now at flank speed."

McDade turned to the boat's talker system. "Now hear this. All hands prepare for a depth charge run."

Hollow booms echoed through the pressurized tube as hatches began being slammed closed. The regular lighting flickered and went to battle red. The SEALs had already changed to wetsuits and waited in their quarters for the summons to the lockout tube. At the captain's announcement, Archie Golden did a double take and spoke to a sailor whose battle station was manning the aft hatch to their compartment.

"*Ashcans?*" Archie's confusion rang in his voice.

"You can count on it."

"I thought every navy in the world had gone to missiles or hunter-killer torpedoes."

Shaking his head, the sailor enlightened Archie. "The North Vietnamese navy's technology is still in the dark ages. Sort of around World War One. They don't have any ship of the line bigger than a frigate, and only one of those. Most of their stuff is obsolete Soviet or Chinese patrol boats, and a lot of motorized junks."

Archie grinned with relief. "Interesting. That don't sound too risky for us, then."

"Wrong. Every patrol boat has a launching rack for depth charges. The frigate has two and torpedo tubes as well.'' His news did not endear him to Archie.

Two minutes later, the word passed from compartment to compartment. The submariner enjoyed giving the information to the SEALs. ''Ears says the first depth charges are in the water. Any time now.''

Betty Welby could not take the lonely feeling that shrouded her whenever she remained alone all day at her parents' home in Chattanooga. This afternoon had been no exception. She had finally shrugged into a thick, cable-knit sweater and form-fitting slacks, put on her walking shoes, and left the house. Her aimless meander took her to a small park on the west side of town. There she was struck deep to the heart by a touching scene.

A young woman, near her own age, laughed and played with three small children, bundled up as though for February, rather than March. They waddled when they ran at one another. Like balloons in the Macy's parade, they bounded off at acute angles when they bumped together.

''Brian, Eric, you watch out for your sister, y'hear?'' The mother's voice was sweet and melodious.

Seated on a bench near her was a man, obviously her husband, who looked on with total adoration. With a terrible pang, Betty recognized the uniform he wore. He was in a blue naval officer's uniform. Among the decortions in neat rows on his chest, he wore the yellow ribbon with red and green vertical bars that denoted service in Vietnam. Above them, he wore a set of naval jump wings, a sure bet he was a SEAL.

"Tom," the wife said, her voice heavy with regret. "I wish this liberty could last forever."

Tom shook his head. "You know it can't. I have to report back to Coronado three days from now."

"Will you be staying there a while? I mean, we could come out, rent an apartment."

"No. We're shipping out in a week."

A sob caught in the young woman's throat. "Where?"

"Vietnam."

"Again?"

Sighing, he patted her hand. "Yes. Two tours is average for SEALs, darling. It's just . . . something I have to do."

Sudden tears welled in the eyes of Betty Welby. Her cheeks flushed with shame for her selfishness as she turned away. Weeping freely, she began a stumbling, blinded run toward her parents' home.

The pucker factor increased dramatically for the SEALs while they waited for the depth charges to descend. Due to the superior insulation of the modern sub, they did not hear the double click of the explosive canisters' arming devices. The roar of the first charge detonating caught them by surprise. One more quickly followed.

Tonto Waters fought to control his jumpy nerves. "Damn, that was close."

The sailor who had enjoyed ragging Archie a few minutes ago grinned and shook his head. "Nope. Not close by more than three hundred meters. Wait'll one pops thirty meters from the hull.''

Tonto looked unbelieving. ''You've done this before?''

''Yeah. Last patrol off Haiphong. The skipper outsmarted them—like he's trying to do now.''

''I wish him all the luck.''

''We all do. Look, we've been trained for this, but it's not a walk through a rose garden. It scares the crap out of every one of us. Every time.''

''Once is enough for me, thanks.'' Tonto sat silent and studied his clenched fists.

Two more depth charges went off. The sailor turned to the unnerved SEALs. ''Let me tell you what I know about these things. Right now, the slopes are settin' their charges too shallow. They're going off above us and behind. He's working from the last course and depth readings on his sonar.''

There had been depth charge racks on the surface ship on which Tonto had earned his quartermaster's rating, but he knew nothing at all about how they worked. ''You mean they can set those things to go off at different depths?''

''Sure. They gotta. Otherwise they'd have misses ninety-nine percent of the time. These jerk-offs usually do.''

''Comforting,'' Tonto agreed, not yet convinced.

The whisper of screws overhead began to diminish. They faded to nothingness quite rapidly. Five minutes went by in blessed silence. Then the sound began to grow from another angle.

The depth charge went off with a terrible *WHAM!* So close had it come to *Sunperch* that it jarred dinner plates and mugs out of their storage racks in the galley. The sub wallowed and dipped, then turned sharply to the right. When the second one detonated, a loud crash of shattering crockery filled the mess compartment.

On the bridge, Captain McDade handed a reel of magnetic recording tape to the signals rating at the radio console. "Sparks, thread this up and pipe it through the external speaker on my command."

"Aye, sir." The radio operator went to his task. The old man was going to try that again.

Two minutes later, the *Sunperch* turned to port on command from McDade. Another explosion came from outside the hull. They had the depth right, but the range was off. Then, sudden and unexpected all aboard heard a loud *BANG!*

In the compartment occupied by Tonto and Archie, a steam line broke. At once the submariner leaped to contain the damage. He swiftly turned a valve until it shut off the scalding vapor. Everyone showed cautious relief.

Tonto studied the faces of his fellow SEALs. *For all their guts*, he thought, *they are looking a little green around their mouths. I probably look worse*.

"Captain, enemy vessels are on diverging courses. They are making all good turns away from us."

"Thank you, Ears." After waiting ten minutes for clearance from his sonarman, McDade took up the mike for the speaker system and keyed it. "Now hear this. Stand down from general quarters. Our little ruse seems to have worked again."

Pope Marino hastened to express his gratitude to

the captain and inform him all was in readiness. "Permission to come on the bridge, sir."

"Come on up, Lieutenant."

Pope climbed the ladder and faced the older man. He liked what he saw. McDade seemed to be in his late thirties, of medium, stocky build, with twinkling blue eyes and a square face. Pope had earlier seen photographs of a woman and three small children in the captain's quarters. McDade had a leonine mane of black hair, already shot through the sides with gray.

"Sir, we're ready for the final run-in. And we're grateful for getting out of that mess. Only, what did you mean about a ruse? Was it the zigzagging and going under the thermal layer?"

McDade smiled and rubbed absently at his bare chin in remembrance of the Van Dyke beard he usually grew when on long leave. "No. Neither of those. Right now, I have reason to believe they think they were depth charging a cetacean. The only thing those jokers topside heard for the last five minutes they were over us was a recording of the distress calls of a panicked whale." Pope Marino joined his laughter. Then McDade turned away to his helm. "Helmsman, steer course two-seven-three. It's time to take our passengers to their bus stop."

CHAPTER 17 ───────────────

CAPTAIN MCDADE'S voice blared from the speakers throughout the *Sunperch* shortly after midnight. "Now hear this. Will the passengers lay forward to the escape trunk."

"This is it, guys," Marino addressed Alpha Squad when they assembled. "Just like every one before. Buddy system and check each other's breathing apparatus."

By twos, the SEALs entered the tube, and a submariner closed the hatch and spun the watertight wheel. At the control panel a young petty officer activated the flooding control. Water rushed in to replace the air being drawn off into a pressure tank in the sub. It made a low hissing roar as the volume of water increased.

When water covered the first pair, Richard Golden and Chad Ditto, they became slightly buoyant. This buoyancy increased as the topside hatch opened and the pressurization process reversed. They rose on an elevator of water up out of sight and clear of the sub. They continued to the surface, breathing out all the

195

while. Both SEALs kept their eyes on their depth gauges, controlling the ascent to avoid nitrogen compression problems.

When they reached the surface, Archie lit a hooded flashlight. Attached to him by a thin, nylon line, he let it drop down out of sight. Eight minutes passed and four more heads popped up. They brought with them the deflated IBS, which they had taken from a canister on the aft deck of the sub. Archie and Repeat joined them and they quickly inflated the IBS. Last to surface came Pope Marino and Alistaire Wordsworth III.

With all of their gear stowed, the SEALs slithered up over the sides of the vessel and Doc Welby took the helm. The electric motor made only a soft whine and produced such a small propeller wake that it could not be picked up by ordinary listening devices. They headed west.

Tonto Waters, in his usual position as point man, would go in with one other SEAL to do a quick evaluation of their landing site. Already he was sweating under his wetsuit. Warm, humid air brushed his face as the small boat made way. Everyone kept watch in all directions. Those with the most vivid imaginations visualized the sudden lance of bright white as a North Vietnamese patrol boat detected them and put on its searchlight. They would be pinned to the black water like a specimen in a biology lab.

To Tonto it might have been another night training exercise. He thought of the many they had run back at Little Creek. Most vivid, of course, was the first one . . .

They did not have to surface from a sub. Nor did

they have to inflate the STAB. All that they were re-quired was to get aboard and steer to shore. The whole experience rapidly became a Chinese fire drill.

Noise discipline was not enforced at this early stage of training due to the many instructions that had to be given. So, it wasn't surprising when Archie Golden complained loudly to True Blue Oakes. "Get yer elbow outta my eye."

"I'll give you elbow, white bread."

"Yo' momma," Archie came back in good humor.

One could easily tell when the stress of their train-ing got to True Blue. He always spoke softly, in ex-cellent, precise English. Not so when strain and fatigue dragged at him. Where he had picked up the ghetto patois no one ever knew, and True Blue never told. He had been raised in Shaker Heights, Long Is-land, the second son of a successful lawyer, attended good schools and even two years of college—like Doc Welby—before he became bored and joined the Navy.

True Blue had difficulty with the swimming re-quirements for SEAL qualification, but so did Tonto Waters. True Blue liked the water well enough, Tom Waters did not. The problem lay in fatigue after even the moderate length swims. Long swims simply wore out True Blue. Now aboard the boat, Tonto noticed it was going in circles. He turned to the stern to ask, "Who's steering this thing?"

Surprise nearly knocked Tonto out of the boat when he recognized CDR Preston, head of the boat school. "Stow it, sailor. How do you expect us to pick up the rest of those three-thumbed idiots?"

"Aye aye, sir. Pardon me, sir," Tonto blurted.

It all went downhill from there. The exercise took

four times as long as expected. The next time they did better, though only by a hair. Three days of going at it produced satisfactory improvement, although they were also burdened by their usual load of classes, PT, and the required swim. Eventually they were ready for a night exercise. Which brought them back to the beginning. That being a disaster.

. . . Which this would become if the enemy spotted them. The mild vibrations lessened even more, and Tonto Waters knew they had reached the area of the coastal shelf. He and Zoro Agilar adjusted their face-plates and put their mouthpieces in. With a nod, and a thumbs up, they went over the sides.

Podpolkovnik Rudinov stepped from the aged, worn command car and surveyed the grim walls of the Hanoi Hilton. Time and familiarity did not flatter the prison. The yellow paint on the walls still had a sickly hue. The electrified barbed wire strands atop the walls still looked threatening. He walked into the cellblock where the hydrogen bomb was housed and strode directly to the door.

When it opened for him, he passed through the room to the large overhead door in the outer wall. "Raise this," he commanded one of the Soviet technicians, who punched a button on a receptacle box and the motor engaged. With a loud grind, the door slid up to reveal a small convoy outside.

Rudinov gestured for the vehicles to enter. Among them, a lowboy tractor-trailer rolled past the KGB man. He nodded his satisfaction. When the last vehicle entered and the door closed, he turned to the technicians and spoke in Russian.

"Good news, Comrades. Two days from now we will be moving the bomb to its detonation site. Then, during the next American bombing raid, it will be set off."

Their swim seemed endless, even though it was made on the neap tide. After what seemed hours to Tonto Waters, although it was only forty minutes, he could hear the wash of surf. As he rose on a swell, he saw a thin line of white. He tapped Zoro on one shoulder and motioned downward.

They submerged and did the final run-in underwater. When Tonto detected the swirl of sand, riled by his flippers, he stopped and signaled to Zoro, who joined him. Cautiously, Tonto grounded himself and raised his head above water. Beside him, Zoro did likewise. They took a good look around, then raised their faceplates.

Surprisingly, the beach was deserted. Tonto studied every detail; the shadows formed by trees and hummocks of drifted sand, the wreck of an old fishing boat, the mound of rocks that marked the mouth of the Red River. Nothing seemed changed from the photos and handmade maps that came from a routine coastal survey conducted a month ago. Tonto led the way to the narrow strip of beach, then turned and signaled with a red filtered flashlight for the squad to come on in. He and Zoro spread out to cover the landing.

Fluttering eerily overhead, the mortar bombs began to fall inside the Tre Noc compound. They went off with sharp explosions that caused Francie Song to jerk in-

voluntarily each time. She lay alone in her bed and
wondered every night where her Kent Welby had really gone and how long he would be away. He *said*
two weeks. But he had also said they were going to
Bangkok. A short round burst with stunning violence
over the rooftops of the small village. Francie could
hear the shrapnel slashing at the walls of the buildings. She also heard a sniffling from the doorway to
her bedroom.

Young Thran, clad only in his diaperlike loincloth,
trudged into the room. He dug at one eye socket with
the knuckle of an index finger. Tears ran from the
other eye.

"I'm afraid, Momma. I'm really afraid."

Francie held out her arms to him and Thran rushed
to be embraced. Francie held him to her breast while
he sobbed silently. His trembling became more pronounced as the mortar shells warbled down. Moved
by his terror and the very real threat that another short
round would pick their building to go off above, she
tried to comfort the boy.

"It will be all right, Thran. They are falling away
from us."

"Not that last one," Thran gulped.

"Yes, but that was a mistake."

Francie loosened her hold on Thran and he climbed
up on the bed to snuggle against her. He twitched
violently every time a round went off. When the last
shell detonated, Thran looked up at his mother and
asked in childish innocence, "Momma, are you going
to make Kent Welby my poppa?"

She had asked herself that so many times that the
boy's query jolted her. Francie hugged Thran to her

tightly, uncertain what to say. Then the answer came, clear and honest. "I hope so, Thran. Oh, I surely do."

Tonto Waters and Archie Golden joined Doc Welby and Wordy Wordsworth while the rest of the squad landed and took up positions to cover their departure up the Red River. The river ran slow and deep. Their one-man Slider sleds were taken to the riverbank. Pope Marino joined them there.

He extended his hand and shook with each man. "Good luck. We'll be waiting for your radio signal."

Wordsworth grinned. "Thanks, Pope. You can expect to hear from us in about thirty-six hours."

With a final, curt nod, Lieutenant Marino stepped away and the four eased into the water. They buddy-checked one another's rebreather units, then lifted the faceplates up on their foreheads and gave thumbs up. Then they received the sleds and tested the motors. The screws turned silently at once. They exchanged a last thumbs up with those on the bank and pushed out into the brown water.

Quickly, they cut the surface in smooth arrowhead shapes. Aided by the tidal bore in the river they rapidly picked up speed. They would submerge after an hour, Tonto had decided. Marino looked after them for a long minute, drew a deep breath, and spoke to Chad Ditto.

"Round 'em up. Let's get back to the sub."

With all aboard, Zoro Agilar pointed the nose of the STAB out into the Gulf of Tonkin. As it ghosted across the low swells, an ominous rumble of thunder rolled down out of the jungle hills beyond the beach.

*   *   *

Alone in the isolated world of translucent tan water, Tonto Waters constantly reminded himself to breathe deeply and slowly. He also kept his eye on the compass. At their speed and position on the water, the small light of the glow-painted binnacle light on the sleds could not be seen from the banks of the river. Tonto checked the location of the other three SEALS and eased into his familiar point position.

Steady as she goes, he told himself.

Although they made a remarkable six knots with the aid of the tidal bore, the journey upriver seemed endless. After the hour had passed, Tonto released one of the handholds to look at his watch. It agreed with the one on the tiny instrument console on the rounded back of the sled. *My God, another ten or eleven hours of this*, Tonto thought.

From above he heard a faint rumble. It came again a few seconds later. Then again, louder now. In a flickering millisecond, the air and water around Tonto strobed whitely. He bobbed up and down immediately after and heard crackling roar. The surface of the river became pockmarked and a sound not unlike mud balls dropped on sheetmetal could be heard.

It was raining. A full-blown thunderstorm. They would be smart to get beyond this. If not, they might wind up back at the mouth of the Red River. He increased the throttle two notches and signaled the others to do the same.

After being informed that everything was in readiness, *Podpolkovnik* Rudinov declared an early end to the evening's work. Now, near midnight, he sat at his ease in the best restaurant in Hanoi. With him was

Viktor Borkoi. On the table that separated them rested the many small plates that had held their appetizers and an ice bucket with a bottle of Russian vodka. The liquor container tipped at a drunken angle. A lot had been consumed so far. Borkoi belched softly and nodded toward the scraps that remained.

"I like the cabbage rolls," he remarked.

"Here it is *bok choi*, Comrade. The content is pork, rather than lamb, and seasoned with the hottest damned peppers I have ever tasted. *Slava vory!* for vodka."

" 'Thank God?' "

Rudinov made a dismissive gesture. "A figure of speech. Nothing meant by it." He changed the subject. "So, everything is ready, comrade?"

"*Da*, Pyotr Maximovich. I have three initiators, crafted from the original by our scientists. They differ from the original only in that they are activated by timer, not altitude. Surely one of the three will work."

Rudinov suddenly grew serious. "And if they do not?"

Borkoi shrugged, the question simple enough to answer. "Then we do not get an explosion."

A frown creased the forehead of Rudinov. "That would be most unfortunate." He paused then and looked up as a waiter, carrying a huge tray, approached their table. After he had set out the six dishes of their main meal and left, Rudinov continued.

"Is there any way the device can be set off in the event of the failure of all of your initiators?"

Borkoi nodded grimly. "There is, provided one is willing to go along with the bomb."

"Not to my liking. Pass the tea, will you?"

Only half in jest, Borkoi suggested, "You could always get General Hoi to volunteer to make the ultimate sacrifice for his country."

Rudinov's eyes glowed. "That sounds like a marvelous idea. I must give it some serious thought."

Beyond the thunderstorm, the SEALs saw the distant lights of a small village and submerged. They went on their rebreather units, but they still made good time. With frequent brief rest stops, they maintained their strength to swim. According to the plan, they alternated surface and underwater swims until they had gone beyond Hanoi, before cautiously surfacing for the last time. Tonto Waters saw at once that they had picked the wrong side of a highway bridge that spanned the Red River. Streams of dimly lit trucks whizzed past, going north and south.

"Damn, now don't that beat all?" Tonto said to himself. He tapped the others lightly as their heads broke the surface. "We have to go a little farther. We're on the wrong side of that bridge."

"It will be light soon," Wordsworth reminded them.

Tonto looked at his diver's watch. "We can make it." He peered into the darkness beyond the bridge. "Looks like there is some real thick growth the other side. It will give us the chance to bury our gear and head for the ROD site."

At once the SEALs sank below the surface of the river and started west again. It took only six minutes to clear the bridge. Another ten and Tonto figured they had traveled beyond the sight of the passing vehicles. Cautiously the SEALs surfaced and climbed from the water.

Using entrenching tools fastened to the sleds, they carefully removed the top layer of soil, grass, and leaves of an area large enough to conceal all their swim gear. Then they dug the pit, put in the sleds, rebreathers, and wetsuits, all wrapped in protective plastic. This they covered with dirt, well tamped, and finally with the surface inch or two. Their tampering became effectively invisible. They took the leftover dirt to the river and poured it in. Lastly they cloaked their faces and hands with the green-black-and-brown camouflage grease paint that gave them their justly feared reputation among the Viet Cong. Tonto Waters checked the map, oriented himself, and set out at the point.

Although confident of the security this deep in their country, the North Vietnamese government remained a police state, and as such, maintained abundant military patrols through the area. One of these patrols, led by Sergeant Dien Voh, had been assigned to cover the bank of the Hong River, east and west of the bridge, on the Hanoi side. Sergeant Dien led his men along a much-used trail that meandered parallel to the water course.

He did not expect to see anyone or anything out of order, although he might have had Tonto Waters not been so good as point man. Tonto spotted Dien's point man a comfortable five minutes before they would have made contact.

Immediately, he turned and raised his Browning above his head, turned sideways, in an improvised

signal for *enemy in sight*. At once, the four men
melted into the jungle undergrowth. The two parties
were roughly at right angles to one another. Still following the trail, that put the NVA unit obliquely
across the front of the SEALs. Under more normal
conditions, the NVA soldiers would have soon become history. This time, though, the SEALs dared not
reveal their presence. They crouched and watched the
troops advance through slitted eyes.

Tonto quickly identified the senior man. He walked
in the middle with an RTO at his side. The big, cumbersome radio backpack and long whip antenna
marked it as a near antique. *Something Chinese, no
doubt*, Tonto reckoned. *Made for the Korean War*.
The point man walked past Tonto's position without
even a glance in that direction.

Another one did the same. From behind the patrol
leader, a soldier said something in Vietnamese that
sounded urgent. The sergeant replied and kept walking. He and his radio-telephone operator came abreast
of Archie Golden's position and he called a halt.

With a sigh of contentment, the trooper who had
spoken before hurried to the side of the trail. He unzipped his fly and prepared to relieve himself. He
stood directly opposite Tonto Waters.

That son of a bitch is going to see me, Tonto
thought, readying his suppressed Browning. Instead of
giving an alarm, the man let go a golden stream that
splattered on a bed of leaves. While he did, he stared
directly at Tonto. Chief Waters froze. Done up in his
green face, Tonto knew he would be invisible so long
as he kept his eyes and mouth shut. A sudden urge to
sneeze threatened Tonto's security.

His nose itched and tingled. His diaphragm heaved with the effort to contain it. The palms of Tonto's hands grew wet and his ears sweaty. Gradually he fought down the demand. The NVA soldier finished his business and hurried off to join his comrades.

Gray light hovered on the eastern horizon when another patrol suddenly appeared. It happened so fast that all the SEALs could do was sink down out of sight in the tulie weeds and low fan palms. Time proved an ally. Obviously on their way home, the NVA soldiers were not at the peak of their alertness. All the SEALs could do was wait and hope they were not seen.

Nerves stretched taut as the NVA soldiers ambled slowly toward the hidden SEALs. Doc Welby grew convinced that they would, when they neared, hear his heartbeat. All four Americans heaved silent sighs of relief when the patrol cut directly across their route of march and disappeared into the bush.

CHAPTER 18 _____

IT TOOK only ten minutes walk for Tonto Waters to find the Rest Over Day site. Thick brush ringed them and there was no sign of human presence for a long distance. Gratefully, Tonto removed the Alice pack that contained a radiation detector, C-Rations for four meals, spare loaded magazines for the Browning, and a tough, thin, space blanket. He stretched to ease the ache in his shoulders and settled with the others to fix chow.

"What pleasant surprise does Momma Cee have for us today?" he asked as he hefted a green box of C-Rations. Then he read the label. "Oh, joy. Salisbury steak." He pulled out the can to display and sat the accessory pack aside. "One of the better gourmet treats provided by a loving government."

"Don't wimp out on us, Tonto. I got those wonderful sausage patties."

Archie Golden affected a solemn expression. "May the Lord have mercy on your soul, Doc." He looked at the label on the carton he had selected and grimaced. "And mine, too. I got ham and beans in tomato sauce."

They opened cans and heated what required it over Sterno, then set a canteen cup to boil water for their coffee powder. All the while, Wordy Wordsworth looked perplexed, worry lines deep on his forehead. When the unpalatable powdered coffee made the rounds, he spoke his mind.

"I don't know if it's such a good idea to heat our food out here. The odor of cooking carries a long way."

Tonto readily agreed. "You're right, Wordy. Bad as these C-Rats are, they're not a whole lot worse cold."

After twenty minutes of concentrated chewing, the four men made ready to roll up and sleep through the day. When they had their space blankets deployed, Wordy motioned for Tonto and the others to join him.

"I want to go over what is to be done when we locate the bomb. The sensors indicate that it is inside the west wall. If it is, we have no problem. If it's not, we've all been over the contingency plan. After we rehearse the destruction sequence, we'll go through that again, too."

Step by step Wordsworth took them through the procedure for rendering the bomb inoperative. Then they discussed the contingency plan. Afterward, he concluded, "Last, and most important, we must avoid detonating the weapon at all costs."

"Amen to that," Tonto added, his mind only vaguely haunted by the image of a mushroom cloud.

*   *   *

It would have been a beautiful day for an escape attempt at the Hanoi Hilton. With the exception of a single guard in two of the towers, all of the guard force had been positioned on the west wall, and out in the cleared ground beyond. Today was the day that the shrouded secret within the palisade would be loaded on a lowboy trailer for transportation.

Not even the warden knew the nature of the secret cargo aboard that trailer. Professionally paranoid, though totally unaware of the pending attack, *Podpolkovnik* Rudinov nevertheless urged the utmost speed.

"We must have everything prepared for tomorrow morning. The convoy will move quite slowly. It must be in place by tomorrow night. Watch out what you are doing with that hoist!" he shouted suddenly.

A commotion at the inner door drew his attention. He turned to see General Hoi advancing toward him, Viktor Borkoi and General Thrun in his wake. The short, rotund North Vietnamese general could barely contain his umbrage. By the time he reached Rudinov, who had moved to cut him off, he all but frothed at the mouth.

"Why was I brought here? And who are you to order me to be brought here?"

Rudinov first tried diplomacy. "First of all, General, since Operation Night Fire is to be conducted in your province, it was done as a courtesy to you."

Hoi spat. "Spare me the courtesy. I want to know what gives you the authority to bring the two most powerful generals in the People's Army, along with myself, to this prisoner of war facility? And, I repeat, what is it that brought us here?"

Disgusted with such arrogance, and knowing that Hoi would have to learn sooner or later, Rudinov stepped to the side and made a sweeping gesture, pointing at the shrouded bomb in its loading harness. "Why, this is what brought us all here."

Shrouded in tarpaulin, Hoi could not recognize the shape for what it was. He forgot his dudgeon. "Exactly what is it?"

A cold, nasty smile spread the lips of Rudinov. "It is an American hydrogen bomb."

When he grasped the reality of that, horror flooded the face of General Hoi. "That—*that* is what you are going to bring into my province?"

"Yes it is. It will be detonated there at a location of my choice."

Hoi's face flushed red. He blew up like a puffer fish and his words rang off the stone walls. "That—that is—is *monstrous*. I will not allow it. I will have troops block the road, deny you entry. My government cannot possibly be aware of this hideous plan to poison a large portion of our country."

Rudinov could endure no more. He reached out, took Hoi by an elbow, and steered him away from the bystanders. Once they were alone, Rudinov dropped all pretense of subservience.

"Remember back when your plans for an offensive were destroyed by the American SEALs? Remember what I told you at the time. It is we, the Soviet Union, who decide major policy. Yours is a client state. This decision has been made at the highest levels.

"Technically, in the eyes of the heads of the Politburo, the Soviet Army, and the Committee for State

Security, I outrank you. I even outrank Generals Thrun and Van in this matter.''

General Hoi's close-set eyes glittered with repressed rage. "Who, exactly, are you?"

"Some while ago, I made General Thrun aware of this. The time has come, regrettably, to make you aware also." Rudinov produced his ID folder. "If you cannot read Russian, I will gladly translate for you. It identifies me as Pyotr Maximovich Rudinov, a lieutenant colonel in the *Komitet Gosudarstvennoi Bezopasnosti*. The KGB."

In less time than seemed possible, General Hoi turned deathly white. He began to tremble when Rudinov went on. "Operation Night Fire is a project of the *Komitet*, and as such, is untouchable by any of your compatriots. Once permission was granted by your government, neither you, nor any other Vietnamese has a say in how we carry it off." Dismissing Hoi with his coldest gaze, Rudinov turned and stalked off to where Borkoi stood with the NVA generals.

Murphy's Law caught up to Betty Welby. She sat at the Queen Anne desk in her room and sobbed wretchedly. This morning's mail brought a letter from Kent.

To her horror, Kent had written that he would not contest a divorce. That he was not angry at her, only disappointed, and that if it was over, it was over.

"How could he be so cruel?" she wailed.

Her mother entered the room. She quickly hid her shock at the appearance of her daughter. "Why, what's the matter, dear? You seem so upset."

"Oh, Mother, everything is ruined. Kent wrote me back and said he would not contest a divorce. After I listened to you and Daddy, and changed my mind, he writes back to me to say that it is over.''

Helen Reardon reached for the crumpled letter in Betty's hand. ''May I read that, dear?''

Betty's desolation put enough force in her remonstration that her long, golden hair swayed in agitation. ''What good will it do?''

Helen remained steadfast. ''Let me see it, please.''

Quickly, Helen perused the handwritten lines. When she finished, she looked up at Betty. ''Think, dear. When did you last write Kent to tell him you were not going to seek a divorce? That you wanted to know how he truly thought?''

Betty wrinkled her brow. ''You know as well as I, Mother. It was five days ago.''

Helen Reardon nodded. ''And this letter was written to you eight days ago. At least, that is the date Kent inscribed on it.''

Betty managed to look both relieved and wretched at the same time. ''Oh, Mother, I feel so awful. Why didn't I see that? Do you think . . . when he gets my new letter . . . it will make a difference?''

Putting her arms around her daughter's shoulders, Helen spoke softly from her love. ''I'm sure it will, dear.''

''Oh, Mother,'' Betty stifled a sob. ''I—I hope so.''

Tonto Waters slept only four hours. He rarely needed more, unless he had gone for two or three nights without any sleep. He stayed low, under a camouflage cover, and went over his equipment. He knew that Archie had brought along four captured Soviet RGD-5 hand grenades, along with two claymores. Doc had some Mk 5 British grenades. Privately, Tonto doubted that they would need them.

Golden had been pragmatic about it. "Better to have 'em and not need 'em, than to need 'em and not have 'em."

Tonto field-stripped his Browning and cleaned it yet again. He checked all the spare magazines to see that they would feed freely, lightly oiled the outer surfaces, and replaced them in his pack. His mind drifted to where they were going.

The Hanoi Hilton. Made famous by the televised visit of Hanoi Jane—who interviewed some of the emaciated, demoralized prisoners—and spouted pro-Northern propaganda. An ugly structure for an ugly purpose. The special overflight requested by Jason Slater had been approved. The result had been given to them on the morning they departed for the submarine.

A low level of radiation had been detected in the thick west wall of the prison. All of the experts had agreed that it had to be the missing bomb. Further, the deep-cover agent in Hanoi had reported that a thick steel overhead door had recently been installed at a point thirty meters from the northwest corner of the wall. What bothered Tonto the most was that the message also indicated a considerable increase in activity around the prison.

Good that they had found the bomb. Bad news about the activity. Chief Waters suspected that it indicated that whoever was in charge was about to move the weapon elsewhere. That could certainly complicate matters. *No sense worrying about it*, he chided himself. Tonto shifted mental gears and reflected on his last, brief liberty before leaving for Vietnam. He had gone to New Jersey to visit his parents. . . .

"You are definitely going to Vietnam?" his father had said to him, more a statement than a question.

Tonto looked at the tall, spare man who had provided for his large family without complaint, and even with a touch of good humor. "No doubt," Tonto had answered him. "The orders came down a month ago. We'll be there a year or eighteen months, then rotate back to Little Creek. Most of the teams have done two tours so far. It won't be bad."

"I don't like it, Tom."

"Why, Dad?"

The elder Waters looked thoughtfully at his son. "From what we hear, one cannot tell the good guys from the bad. They say every Vietnamese is a Viet Cong at night."

Tonto grinned. "We do our best work in the dark."

"I'm proud of you, son. You know that. Only . . . you don't mind if I worry a little?"

"If it makes you feel better, Dad. But little Tommy Waters can look out for himself. Besides, I've got all my buds to take care of."

They had ended the day with boilermakers at a local tavern and weaved their way home in the warmest camaraderie Tonto ever recalled between himself and his father . . .

"Can't sleep either, eh?" Alistaire Wordsworth whispered in Tonto's ear.

Tonto studied Wordsworth for a brief moment. A shock of light brown hair hung down from his prominent widow's peak, and he had tight little squint lines around his gray eyes. Usually, Tonto could read a man from his face, yet he knew little or nothing about this bomb builder.

"You got that right. I usually only hit the bunk for around four hours or so." Then, in a different tone, "Tell me about yourself, Wordy."

Wordsworth shrugged. "What's to tell? I was born into a family of lawyers and politicians. Attended the right prep school, and then Harvard. I really wanted MIT. I had fallen in love with chemistry and physics in the eighth grade at Groton. My father and grandfather expected me to go to Harvard Law and come into the firm. I rebelled. When they saw that pleading would not get them their way, they threatened to cut off my tuition money. I quit Harvard in my junior year and joined the army."

"Yeah, and became a Blankethead. How'd that get you to being a rocket scientist?"

"Long story. As part of my crap—Career Rotation Program—I did a stint at the tactical nuke school. I learned a lot about detonating devices for obsolete weapons. While I was there I put in for Special Forces and was accepted. When I completed my tour here, I went back and completed my studies and did two years of graduate work at MIT. When the job opening came up, I turned out to be the lucky one—with veterans' points and a glowing recommendation from the case officer who worked with us in Special Operations. I've been doing detonating devices ever since."

Tonto still felt he did not have enough. "Are you married?"

"Yep. Wife and two kids. The oldest, my daughter, is eight. Jimmy is six."

"Then why in hell are you over here running

around in the bush when you could be home with your family?''

Wordsworth looked Tonto straight in the eye. ''That glowing praise from the Company came with a price. A month ago, two suits from the CIA showed up and made me an offer I could not refuse. They didn't tell me everything, only said they wanted me to go back to Vietnam. They said I owed them. And I did, I suppose.''

Waters chuckled softly. ''You and Pope must see eye-to-eye on the spooks.''

Wordy shook his head. ''No. I'm not bitter. They have their job and I have mine. As it happens, I get a high off of this sort of thing.''

''What's your wife think?''

Wordy cut his gaze away. ''Next topic, please.''

Aware he had stepped on a tender spot, Tonto slacked off. ''Nothin' much. I was married once. Got a kid, too.''

''But not again?''

''Naw, Wordy, not while I'm doin' this. You ought to talk with Doc. He's got him a wife who wants to divorce him because he obeyed orders and came to 'Nam.''

''Maybe some time. Now, I think I'll clean my pistol.''

At nightfall the SEALs made ready to move out again. They returned to the riverbank and dug up their gear. Everyone maintained silence throughout. Not until he had stepped into the water did Tonto Waters speak in a low whisper.

''It is only two klicks down to Ha Dong, which is

right across the river from Hanoi. Goin' downstream, we'll make it in about twelve minutes. Check your time on your watch. Okay, let's move out.''

At five minutes to midnight, Tonto Waters swam to the bank and cautiously raised his head above the surface. Cleared, cultivated fields stretched in both directions along the river. A long, five-minute check showed no sign of life. Tonto submerged again and tapped Archie on the shoulder.

Archie relayed the all clear down the line. With great care, they rose and waded close in on the bank. Immediately, they removed their rebreathers. At points along the shore above the high-water mark, they dug holes horizontally into the soft earth. Into these, they stuffed their sleds and the self-contained breathing apparatus. Next came their wetsuits. Tonto sweated freely as he used his hands to plug the hole with dirt. When the last man finished, the SEALs crawled up into the nearest field.

Wordy motioned them to him. ''Now,'' he whispered, ''here's a little part Jason Slater asked me to keep quiet until we got here. You know that covered van? We've got one. It is in the village over there.''

''How do you know that?'' Doc Welby asked.

A white smile flashed in the starlight. ''One of Slater's people is waiting for us. He is a baker and delivers all around Hanoi. He even drops off bread and pastries at places close to the Hilton. He'll take us there and bring us back to Ha Dong. Then he wants to come out with us.''

Tonto put a hand on Wordy's wrist. ''No. That's

not possible. We don't have the gear or a spare sled, even if he could use the stuff.''

''He has something, Slater assured me of that. It's probably Chinese made. Not as efficient or as comfortable as what we have. But he is willing to take the risk. His cover will be blown once they discover the bomb has been gimmicked. So it's worth the danger involved.''

''I'm not even warm for this, but if it means the guy gets thrown to the wolves otherwise, I'll go along.''

''Big of you, Chief.'' So far, Wordy had played down his rank as a captain, the Army equivalent to Pope Marino's Navy lieutenant. It was by way of a gentle reminder that he was the senior man on the mission.

''Aye aye, sir,'' Tonto said soberly.

Keeping low, the four men crossed the field toward the distant village. No lights showed, not even street lamps. Each of them carried his gear in an Alice pack that rode his back. At fifty meters they melted into the ground as a dog began to yap questioningly. Tonto gritted his teeth, certain they would be discovered at any second. The barking ended abruptly in a soulful yowl as the thin crescent moon rose above the horizon.

Tonto decided he could breathe again. When he drew in a deep draft, it came filled with the heady, yeasty aroma of baking bread. Wordy touched him on the arm. Taking care to keep the volume low, he spoke close to Tonto's ear.

''It is the third building from the south. Slide up there and knock on the door three times, wait a three-count, knock once, wait a two-count, then knock twice. If it is clear, you will be let in. If not . . . we're all in deep shit. We'll cover you.''

It suddenly occurred to Tonto Waters that this Captain Wordy Wordsworth had a good deal more connection to the Company than he let on. Tonto had his gut tied in two knots by the time he reached the back door of the bakery. He went through the knock routine. With growing trepidation, he waited out a count of thirty. Suddenly a lemon slice of light appeared around the doorjamb. A smiling Chinese stood inside, only partly visible. He gestured urgently.

''Y'all come on in. I've been waiting for you.'' It came out in a perfect Texas drawl.

CHAPTER 19 ————————————

THEIR HOST introduced himself to the SEALs as Johnny Yu. They gathered in the spacious pantry, amid stacks of flour bags, sugar bins and tubs of shortening. Johnny Yu was large for a Chinese, having been born and raised in San Angelo, Texas. His perpetually smiling face topped a square, linebacker's body, and he constantly made gestures as big as his native state. He used a wide-flung arm to indicate the door to his small loading dock.

"The truck is waiting, gentlemen. We'll load in a minute. Oh, and I have AKs for y'all. I will follow my usual delivery rounds, including a stop at a restaurant across from the prison. There's where you will unass the bird, so to speak." He paused, noting their puzzlement. "Oh, I was born and grew up in Texas, attended A and M and went airborne as a second lieutenant out of ROTC, Eighty-deuce an' proud of it. From there, I joined the Company and have been here ever since I learned Vietnamese. That's the story of Johnny Yu. I'd love to swap life stories with all of you, but we have a job to do."

With that, he led the way to the loading dock. As they stepped down to enter the closed van, Archie Golden muttered softly to Tonto Waters. "Shit. Wordy don't say anything, and this guy never shuts up. Is it like that with all these spooks?" His low snicker followed.

Secure in the van, Johnny Yu at the wheel, they rode along a narrow dirt road and across a bridge into Hanoi. Tension hung, a palpable thing, among the loaves, croissant rolls, and boxed pastries as the van neared a checkpoint. Wordsworth and the SEALs drew sheets of white canvas over them as Yu slowed to a stop.

"Good morning, Comrade Sergeant," Yu said cheerily.

"It would be if I were home with my wife, Comrade Bakeryman."

"Yes, there is that. My wife works the same hours as I. When we are finished, and the sun is high, there's no energy for . . . that."

A snort of laughter answered Yu, and the NVA sentry said, "There's always energy for that."

To Tonto, it sounded threatening. His hand hovered over the grip of his suppressed Browning. Yu took the words in stride.

"Perhaps I am growing old."

Continuing his heckling, the guard bragged, "I am forty years old, and I manage to keep it up most of the time."

Yu waggled a finger in the soldier's face. "Too much ginseng. But, watch out, one day it will catch up to you. I am yet to see forty, and my wand rarely stirs, even in the presence of a lotus blossom."

"Then I pity you, Comrade. Now—ah—do you happen to have any spare sweets?"

"Oh, yes, as a matter of fact, I do." Yu reached across the front seat and came back with a square, white box. "Some cheese-filled crescent rolls. Enough for your whole squad, I imagine."

"You are most generous. Pass on, Comrade."

Well beyond the sentry post, Wordsworth gave the SEALs a digest of what had been said. That brought a raised eyebrow from Archie Golden. "So, you speak Vietnamese?"

"Yes. Not perfectly, but enough to make out simple conversation."

Tonto had a question, too. "And Yu here has been bribing that dork for some time, eh?"

Yu answered for himself. "Oh, yes. From the first day, partner. He—ah—made clear that it was expected. Ancient Oriental custom. Uh—we're comin' up on my first delivery. Lay low while I take in their rack of goods."

Two hours later, the van reached the final delivery place, a restaurant across a narrow street from the Hanoi Hilton. Since the eatery was not yet open, Yu let himself in with a key and unloaded the last of the baked goods. While he did, the SEALs left the rear of the vehicle. When he completed his task, Yu joined them.

"The rest is up to you guys, whatever it is you are up to. I'll wait here for when you come back. I've been doing that for the last two weeks. Some of the prison guards, who eat here, think I have something on the side with one of the girls who works here, so nothing will seem out of order. Good luck.''

"Thanks, Johnny, we're gonna need it," Tonto replied.

One by one, they crossed the street and disappeared into the deep shadows thrown by the low buildings. Fresh on each of their minds was the thought of just how blind was the blind spot they had figured existed. Careful examination, with measurements and sightings, in all conditions of lighting, indicated that one particular spot on the north wall, a space of barely six feet, could not be seen from any of the guard towers in total darkness. A flaw in construction put the jutting corner of a tower in such a place that it covered the spot in deep shadow.

Their task would be to scale the wall, slide under the lowest electrified wire and fade into the interior of the prison. It was not a job any of them looked forward to, yet it had worked repeatedly on the mockup.

Use of the blind spot depended upon perfect timing. It also depended upon the planned air strike. Among the targets selected for this night's raid was the electric power substation that served the Hanoi Hilton. Stealthily, the three SEALs and Wordy Wordsworth approached the intimidating wall, two blocks from where Johnny Yu waited. Dressed all in black, their faces done in green, they blended into the shadows perfectly. Tonto checked his diver's watch and noted they had five minutes to wait.

Each long sixty seconds dragged past. The second hand of Tonto's watch had ticked off to ten past the appointed time when the utter silence shattered with the abrupt, eerie wail of air raid sirens. Flashes appeared in the sky on the far side of the city of Hanoi, followed by soft pops of the detonating antiaircraft shells. Rapidly, the noises grew in intensity. With a gut-wrenching whoosh and roar, a SAM missile took flight. Tonto whispered a reminder to the others.

"We will have exactly three minutes to scale the wall and *di-di* the hell down to that covered catwalk. No room for errors, so keep a Tee-Ay, guys."

Bombs began to walk across the rail yards. As they grew closer, their detonations could be felt through the soles of the boots worn by the SEALs. They turned away from the source and shielded their eyes to preserve their night vision.

A gap in the carpet of bombs encased the four square blocks around the Hanoi Hilton. Then an ear-shattering explosion staggered the SEALs with its shockwave and plunged the area into darkness. None of the team needed prompting. At once, they fired the launch tubes containing grapnel spikes upward to imbed in the wall a foot below the top.

After checking to make sure the hooks were secure, the three SEALs and Wordy went hand-over-hand up the lines attached. Tonto Waters reached the top first and eased under the inoperative electric wire. Doc Welby came next, followed closely by Wordy Wordsworth and Archie Golden. Swiftly, they freed the grapnels and coiled the lines, to ensure there would be no trace of their entrance. It proved a short, four-foot drop to the open catwalk. Shouts came from below in Vietnamese—not of alarm, only of complaint over the extinguished lights and the inoperative barbed wire. Quickly, they moved in utter darkness to the steps that led to the covered catwalk. As usual, Tonto had the point.

They cat-footed down the metal treads to the lower parapet and began their circuit of the prison to the west wall. All the while their consciousness remained divided between the mission and the pitiful captives below them. Tension mounted as they reached the interior walkway directly over the cells containing American prisoners. Tonto's gut tightened as he thought of how close they were to their comrades.

Blackout lights casting narrow, yellow ribbons on the road ahead, the scout car rumbled along a pothole-riddled strip of concrete toward Hanoi. Seated in the rear, Generals Thrun and Van conversed with one another, completely ignoring General Hoi Pac, who sat facing them. In the front, right seat, *Podpolkovnik* Rudinov sat in silent amusement at the snub. When the malevolent blossoms of antiaircraft fire erupted in the sky over the distant city and the glow of streetlights faded to darkness, he sat up and took closer notice.

"The Americans are bombing again," he observed to the others. "We should pull to the side of the road until it is over."

Still smarting from the arrogant, preemptive manner of this Russian barbarian when he had announced that Hoi was wanted in Hanoi, General Hoi spoke testily. "Whatever you want. This is your expedition, comrade."

"Thank you, General, for noticing that. Yes, I think we shall wait."

Moments later, the bombs began to fall.

*   *   *

Dammit, Tonto thought. Their proximity to the prisoners, and their inability to do anything to help the forlorn men, made him ache. It would be so easy to slip down there and free them. *But where would they go?* his mind taunted him. Weakened and starved, they could not go out with the SEALs. Turned loose in Hanoi, they would be gunned down like dogs.

Made miserable by such contemplations, Tonto turned his mind to the mission. *Remember the sequence for cutting the wires, establish security so Wordy could do his thing. Exfiltrate somehow and join up with Johnny Yu. Then back to the river. Yeah, that's it*, he urged himself on. *Just how do we get out of here?* Their original plan did not sound so good. *Maybe that door that had been put in the wall recently? Open it and everybody out, then reach in and hit the close button. Might work. Provided the electricity was back on again.*

Not a sound came from the cells directly below their feet. Alistaire Wordsworth focused on the part he would play in disarming the bomb. He would need enough time to not only remove the service hatch and cut the wires, but also to disable the electronic sequencer and the hemispheres of plutonium, then replace everything like it had been before.

No small task. He could damn near do it with his eyes closed. And, if the backup generator did not kick in soon, he might have to. He brushed away that line of thought and tried to visualize the men living in degradation and misery below them. If only they knew fellow Americans were inside the prison, armed and able. . . . *Better let that slide*, Wordy reminded himself. If only they could get them all out—yeah, a damn big IF, taller than the Empire State Building. Somewhere in the complex below, a diesel engine coughed and came to life.

Archie Golden looked through the open spaces between the platform of the catwalk. Below in the dark, locked cells, lay men like himself. They made no sound. Not even breathing could be heard. It set his nerves on edge. Was this the sound of defeated, hopeless men? Had they given up on any chance for release? Clearly he saw the cruelty in the idea of taking a few out with them and leaving the rest behind. Abruptly, he dropped his speculations as he came to a stairway leading down.

A quick glance below and Archie began to descend. Tonto was just ahead of him, Doc and Wordy behind. One more tier and they would be on the ground level. The engine powering the generator wound up to speed and a dim, yellow light began to glow from what must be forty-watt bulbs strung along the passageway. Archie hastened his pace.

Kee-rist! What are we doing here? Surrounded by at least a hundred decidedly hostile North Vietnamese soldiers, in the bowels of the world's most infamous prison, what chance do we have? Odd that none of the guards seems to be up and around, Kent Welby thought to himself. Not that he longed for their company. Then he became conscious of the unnatural stillness of the place.

Estimates had it that fully two hundred Americans were being detained in this wretched place. What was it like to be a prisoner? Hell, it had to be even worse than being shot. Doc Welby grew goosebumps at the thought. For all he or any of the others knew, they could be shot *and* made prisoners in the next second. Images of never seeing Francie again flashed through his head. Then Betty's face crowded his mind. The palms of his hands felt wet and sticky at the same time. *Please God, let us find the bomb and get this over with*, he prayed fervently.

Moving with caution, the three SEALs and Wordy found their way down to the first level of the westernmost cell block. An eerie silence hung over the passageway and behind the closed doors. Tonto Waters raised a cautioning hand when he reached an intersection. Everyone froze in place.

Tonto made a quick look around the corner. *All clear*. Consulting memory, he turned into the next corridor and headed for where the new door had been cut into the wall. Followed by Archie and Doc, he proceeded toward where an inner door had to be. He had almost reached it when a roving guard appeared behind them.

CHAPTER 20 _____

STARTLED BY the appearance of these strangers in black, the guard remained alert enough to attempt to call out a challenge to them. He opened his mouth to speak when Wordy, who had lagged behind, moved with lightning speed. He closed on the NVA soldier and snaked an arm around the man's throat. Swiftly, he jammed the needle of a syringe into the exposed side of the guard's neck and injected a fast-acting sedative.

By that time Archie Golden had reached the struggling sentry, who went rigid, then relaxed into limp unconsciousness. Archie caught him as Wordy let go. Quickly, Tonto searched for and found what he hoped would be there. Three paces along the corridor an unlocked door gave way to a room filled with brooms, mops, and buckets. While Archie and Wordy dragged the comatose North Vietnamese to it and bundled him inside, Tonto looked at the nuclear expert with new eyes. Wordy was just too damn good with the spook stuff. He had to be more than they had been told.

"That was close," Tonto mouthed silently to them

as they joined him. Then he added in a whisper to Wordsworth's ear, "You done good work, Wordy."

"Thanks," came a breathy reply. "The place we're looking for should be around that next passageway."

None of them expected what Tonto discovered when he peeked around the corner. Four men in Russian uniforms, a corporal and three privates, stood on guard outside their objective. Moving slowly, so as not to attract attention, Tonto turned back to the others. Thinking quickly, he raised one hand to indicate four of the enemy, then mouthed his words without sound. "*Hushpuppies.*"

After a quick count of three, they rounded the corner in a rush and took out all four guards before even one could react. Tonto led the way to the dead Soviet soldiers and relieved the corporal of a ring of keys. With it he unlocked the door and opened it. Beyond it lay a room as sterile as an operating theater. In the next instant, the SEALs found themselves in for more surprises.

Three technicians in white lab coats worked over the bomb. One looked up and over his shoulder. His mouth formed a surprised O a moment before Archie Golden shot him between the eyes with his suppressed Browning. The 9mm slug took off a large portion of the back of the man's head.

Another Soviet tech dropped the instrument he held and made a dive for an AK-47 resting against a bomb rack. He never made it. Doc Welby put two fast rounds through his chest and dumped him in a heap on a pile of tarpaulin.

His sole living companion tried to hide behind the bomb. Tonto Waters ducked low, trusted to luck, and tried for a leg shot. His bullet went true and smashed a kneecap. Screaming, the technician fell on his side. Tonto stepped over and finished him with a shot behind the left ear. Behind them, Wordy Wordsworth secured and locked the door. He looked at the coldly efficient killing machines and shook his head.

"What do we do now?" he asked, as though confused.

Tonto Waters made it short and sweet. "What we came here for. First let's get rid of these bodies."

Together, the three SEALs and Wordsworth stuffed the corpses into packing crates. At that point, Tonto realized that the hydrogen bomb was loaded on a lowboy trailer.

He pointed it out to the others. "Hey, guys, dig this. Someone's gettin' ready to move this thing."

Wordy went directly to the nuclear weapon and set to work opening the access panel. "All the more reason we have to act fast. Give me a hand, will you, Archie?"

Gleefully rubbing his hands together in anticipation Archie spoke through a grin. "Man-oh-man, you don't have to ask twice."

Precisely on time, at 0130, the second wave of bombers swept over Hanoi. Sirens wailed and those in the suspected target areas scrambled for shelters. Although they knew that the prison had never been bombed, pandemonium broke out in the Hanoi Hilton. Already restive as a result of the strange goings on in the west wall, the guard force reacted with confusion and fear. Unable to power their searchlights, they could only make a physical inspection of the walls.

This they did with less than exactness. Never had the city been bombed twice in the same night. Some of the soldiers appeared in the exercise yard clad in only underwear and thong sandals. Even in the dim light of the auxiliary power plant they looked uneasy. The big substation near the prison had never been a target before. That thought hung heavily on their minds.

Sergeant Troh put their worries to Lieutenant Vi. "Could it mean that the Americans have changed their plans and intended to invade?" he asked anxiously.

Vi tried to reassure his sergeant. "I doubt that very much."

"What else could account for this heavy bombing of the rail yards and the power station? Will they come by way of Haiphong?"

Others reported to duty stations without their weapons. Angry sergeants and corporals shouted at them and sent them off again, which touched off more confusion among the complement. Flying too high to be heard as more than a whisper, the silver birds of the US Air Force and Navy delivered crippling blows to the marshaling yards and oil storage tanks of Hanoi. Curtains of bombs rained down on antiaircraft installations, and the sky turned into a magic light show of tracers and exploding shells.

Surface-to-air missiles roared upward, to be confused by chaff sown by the invaders, and deflected to explode in the countryside. The ground rocked and heaved. No one thought to search the interior of the prison. Locked away, weakened by a starvation diet, the prisoners presented no threat. As abruptly as it had started, the rain of explosives from the sky ceased.

In the distance, the commandant of the Hanoi Hilton, Colonel Dao Nguyen Dao, heard the wail of fire brigade sirens. The entire eastern horizon was a wavering orange. Then he looked away from his window at the sound of a knock.

"Yes?"

"Comrade Colonel, the Russians are here again."

A pained expression formed on the face of Colonel Dao. "What do they want?"

"They are at the main gate with a tractor. They want in to their hidden room."

Sighing, Colonel Dao nodded his assent. "Let them in." Another thought struck him. "How, by the Great Buddha, did they get through the bombing?"

His aide shrugged. "I do not know, Comrade Colonel."

"Nor I. I suppose I should be present to greet them." He roused himself from behind his desk and reached for his garrison cap.

Podpolkovnik Rudinov wore a scowl when Colonel Dao joined him at the outer gate. "*Slizistyi Amerikanski solip'shim*," he cursed. "Have they ever bombed twice in a night before?"

"No, comrade, they have not. Nor have they ever bombed a power plant so near the prison."

Frowning, Rudinov posed another question. "Then why have they done so now? Could it be that they know . . . ?"

Colonel Dao jumped ahead of his visitor. "About what you have here? Impossible! Even I did not know until you enlightened me, Comrade."

Rudinov produced a grim smile. "Never mind. We will be leaving here before long. In fact, considering this escalation in bombing, I think tonight would be ideal."

"What?" Colonel Dao blurted. "Isn't it required that our government be advised before any such move?"

Rudinov took on a patronizing expression and spoke in a condescending manner. "It is not required that we advise our client states of any decision made by us, Comrade Colonel. Now, Comrade Borkoi and I must go to the—ah—object."

Wordy Wordsworth looked up from his examination of the hydrogen bomb. In a tone of wonder he announced his discovery to the others. "Someone has been getting this bomb ready to detonate. The electronic sequencer is already installed. This is going to be a lot more delicate a task than I expected."

"How's that?" Archie asked.

"We can't simply cut some wires and ding the hemispheres. We have to remove the sequencer, or destroy it."

"Which is easiest to do?" Tonto Waters inquired.

"Destroy it."

Tonto urged them. "Then, you guys get to it."

Without hesitation, Wordy began to pack Semtex plastique under the sequencer. He nodded to Archie. "Start cutting the wires. Remember the continuity."

"Right. Uh—tell me, Wordy, what happens if that sequencer gets activated."

Not looking up, Wordsworth answered calmly. "You might last long enough to see a bright flash."

Archie let out a grunt. "Huh—that's what I thought."

With a soft snick the sidecutters in his hand closed on the white wire. Quickly Archie reached down six inches and cut the same wire again. Then he moved on to the next. While he worked, Wordy placed a gob of plastic explosive on one of the hemispheres. He wrapped a third piece around one of the four guide rails.

With that accomplished, Wordy stuck a small electric squib into each of his charges. These he wired together in series and attached the end leads to a small detonator box. He looked up at Archie.

"Ready. Stand clear."

Archie and Wordy climbed down from the trailer, then turned away. With a deft crank of the T-shaped handle sticking up from the box, the explosives went off in rapid succession. When the small amount of smoke cleared, they rushed to the bomb. Wordy peered down intently.

"Beauty. Not even Einstein could set this one off."

Immediately, he replaced the Lexan cover, easing it into its two-lipped gasket. Then he lifted the access port cover into place and began to screw it down. He had started on the last one when Doc Welby popped through the door.

"I hear footsteps headed this way from the main corridor."

Tonto reacted at once. "Cover the bomb with that tarp and let's *di-di* outta here."

"How?" Doc asked.

"Through that big door, like I figured out to do."

Quickly Archie and Woody raised the tarp and put

it over the bomb, then stepped down off the low-boy trailer. Tonto was already at the door, with Doc at his side. When the others joined them, Tonto slapped a button with a thick thumb and the overhead motor began to wind.

After the bottom edge had raised three feet, Tonto motioned the others outside, then hit the lower control and slid under the descending metal edge. At once they flattened themselves against the wall and inched their way around the bulwark out of sight. With a solid thud, the door settled into place.

Podpolkovnik Rudinov, accompanied by chief Soviet technician, Viktor Borkoi, arrived in the bomb's secret chamber well after the damage had been done. Because of the SEALs' careful work and meticulous attention to detail, the Soviets remained unaware of it. A quick look around revealed the chamber to be vacant. He spoke to Borkoi through a disapproving scowl.

"Apparently the bombing raid has scared off your fellow technicians. Foolish of them. We must move the bomb at once, of course. Can you finish the work on the way?"

Nettled at this lack of confidence in his abilities, Borkoi answered sharply. "Naturally. Even if I have to ride astraddle of the bomb."

Images of that caused Rudinov to loosen up a little. "You may rest easy until we reach the villa." Then he turned to a Russian sergeant who had accompanied them. "Go out through the big door and tell the driver to bring in the tractor to pull this trailer."

Within two minutes the big Zil diesel tractor rolled

in through the open door. The driver expertly maneu-
vered it into position and dismounted from the cab.
He began to turn the crank that would lower the trailer
gooseneck onto the fifth wheel. When the fitting on
the end thudded into place, he gave the locking arm
a stout yank, then he and the sergeant connected the
air brake lines and electrical cables. That accomplished, the driver returned to the cab.

At a signal from Rudinov, he revved the engine and
put the big rig into gear. Slowly it began to roll toward the tall door at the far end of the bunker.

Far removed from the horrors of the Hanoi Hilton,
Petey Danvers lay on his bed, smoking his fourth joint
of the morning. Through the haze that clouded his
mind, he watched animated figures cavort on the television screen. Boris and Natasha were plotting against
Bullwinkle again. The furry brown moose seemed sty-
mied by the machinations of the Russian accented su-
perspies. *If only he could concentrate on what it was
they were saying*, Petey muzzily considered. Faintly
he heard a rat-ta-tat knock on the door. His current
live-in, Judy, would see to it.

"Mister Peter Danvers, please," a deep, masculine
voice came after Judy opened the door.

Unnerved by the leather ID folder she stared at,
Judy tried to stall. "He's—ah—resting. Can you
come back later? Maybe tomorrow?"

The unseen speaker caught a strong whiff of ma-
rijuana smoke. "Sorry, Miss. We need to see him
right now."

Cutting like a spearpoint, the tone of the man's
voice registered on Petey's dim conscience. Brushing

hair out of his eyes, he stared at the big Peace poster on the wall. Who could be in that big a hurry? Oh, Jeez, the pigs!

Petey Danvers swung his feet over the side of the bed and came unsteadily to his feet. Dimly he heard a slight scuffle as Judy tried to close the door. Petey started to the open doorway to his bedroom when it suddenly filled with two men in suits. They had shoulders wide enough to be defensive linemen on the Chargers. Petey turned on his heel and started for the window. His scoot was out back. Fire up the Suzuki and he'd be out of here.

In deep bass the words of one of the suits filled the room. "Peter Danvers? FBI. You are under arrest for conspiracy against the government."

Screaming at the top of his lungs, Petey Danvers ran to the window and dove through the screen.

Ten minutes later, the SEALs and Woody returned to find the overhead door standing open and the room beyond empty! For a moment, they stood in stunned silence. Then Doc Welby broke the quiet with a stammered question.

"M-My God, wh-what happened to it?"

"They took it," Wordy supplied.

"But why?" Doc wanted to know. "Why take it now?"

"Secrecy," Tonto offered. "If the plan we heard of from Jason Slater is at all accurate, the big shots will want to keep it totally secret from their people. All hell would break loose if the North Vietnamese found out that their own government had been cold enough to set off a hydrogen bomb in their country.

Wordy, is there a way they can still make it work?''

Wordy considered that for only a fraction of a second. "There is, given time."

"Maybe this is to our advantage. What we need to do now is find that bomb and either make it totally useless or . . ." A sudden inspiration struck Tonto. "Or, steal it back again."

Archie Golden looked at Tonto Waters in consternation. "You're outta your friggin' mind. How are we going to get it back, let alone handle a hydrogen bomb?"

Tonto gave him a blissful smile. "You've got two claymores, right? And we have two IBSs and a submarine. There can't be too many people with that lowboy. With that radio you've got we can take it off wherever we find a good place. Piece of cake, right, Doc?"

Doc Welby nodded numbly. Now they were going to chase after a hydrogen bomb.

CHAPTER 21 _____

BACK OUTSIDE the prison, the SEALs split up into teams of two and faded into the night. Except for the fires from the bombing, darkness lay over the whole city. Tonto Waters and Wordy Wordsworth crossed into an alley, comfortably free of the threat of a probing beam from a prison spotlight due to the continuing power outage.

Taking the opposite direction, Archie Golden and Doc Welby darted between a series of deep shadows. When they reached an intersection, Archie held up and took a quick look around the corner of a storefront. With a curt gesture he brought Doc up to his side.

"It looks clear. Only two blocks to reach the van."

Johnny Yu would be waiting for them at his last delivery point. From there, they would attempt to catch up to the convoy that bore the nuclear weapon. Privately, Archie still thought Tonto's idea sheer madness. How could they ever pull it off? Sucking in a deep breath, he stepped around the side of the building and started off down the street toward the restaurant where the Chinese-American CIA agent waited.

Tonto Waters realized that he had overstepped his bounds. When he and Wordy stopped at the far end of the alley, he moved up close and spoke softly into the ear of Wordsworth.

"Look, sir, I realize that technically you are the ranking man on this mission. But, we've done a lot of this kind of thing, and a lot more lately, than you. If you want to countermand my decision to go after the bomb, that's all right. I'll obey your orders. On the other hand, if we do go after it, things might go better if I call the shots."

Wordsworth did not even hesitate. "You've got it, Chief. I'm just along to play with the nuke."

"Right, sir, sure. That's why you brought along that knockout juice and all the other spook shit. And why Johnny Yu was waiting for us."

"You figure things out pretty good, don't you, Chief?"

Tonto grinned. "You got that right, sir. Momma Waters never had any dumb children."

Wordy surprised Tonto as he cracked the first joke any of the SEALs had heard from him. "Yeah, only ugly ones."

"Ah—we'd best be movin'."

Johnny Yu waited inside the large restaurant where he had delivered his baked goods earlier that night. He had no concern of being discovered. The cooks and scullery boys did not report for work until 0400. An amused smile creased Johnny's wide, round face

at the thought of what they would find. The bombs
that had taken out the power plant had landed so close
that bamboo artwork had been knocked from the
walls, a dividing screen toppled and broken, and pots
hung from the low, overhead rafters had been dislodged from their hooks. Plaster dust had sifted down
from the walls, and one wall had a jagged crack that
ran from ceiling to floor. Yes, he would be long gone
before they discovered the damage. His instructions
had been to wait until 0215 hours and no longer, then
depart. If the SEALs were not there by that time, they
would not be coming.

While Johnny waited, he reflected on what cover
story he could use on the sergeant at the checkpoint.
He recalled their conversation of earlier. Yes, that
would do fine. Something the randy noncom would
appreciate and, more importantly, believe. A rustle at
the rear door drew his attention back to the present.

A moment later, the stocky, curly-haired SEAL entered. His name was Tonto, like in *The Lone Ranger*.
In his childhood, Johnny had been an avid fan of the
adventures of the masked man on the white horse. Not
the faithful Indian companion this one. He was a
killer. What the special forces guys at Bragg had
called a cold motherfucker. Yet, Johnny sensed a
warmth and friendliness beneath the hard exterior.

It suddenly hit Johnny. What the guy did bothered
him. Not enough to make him quit, but sufficient to
prick his conscience from time to time. That made
Johnny Yu experience more comfort around him. He
stepped forward.

"Howdy, Tonto. You boys have a good time?"

"Oh, yes, just dandy. Wordy's out in the van. The other two should be here any time."

"Then it's back to the bakery and you guys go home?"

"Not . . . exactly. First, we have to catch up with a convoy of the bad guys."

Johnny Yu could not believe it. "You're kidding."

"Nope. They took our toy away before we could verify the damage."

Shaking his head, Johnny Yu walked up to Tonto Waters. "Get a grip, man. There's a lot more Injuns out there than cowboys. How many do you figure are in this convoy?"

"No idea. There can't be too many, though."

Sighing his resignation, Johnny Yu concluded, "And if I'm going out with you, I have to come along, right?"

"Yep. First we have to dig up the gear we buried and then hit the road south."

"Why south?"

Tonto smiled mirthlessly. "Need to know. But, what the hell, you're stickin' your neck way out on this. We've been told they plan to set off the bomb somewhere near the DMZ, inside North Vietnam."

"What . . . bomb?"

"That's the nasty part. It's a hydrogen bomb, US-made. That way we get the blame."

Johnny Yu spoke solemnly. "Jesus, Mary, and Joseph."

Something occurred to Tonto Waters. "What about your wife? She can't go with us."

"Arrangements have been made. She has a place to hide until she can make her way to the South."

"All right, then. We're going to have a busy night."

At that moment, Archie Golden entered the kitchen from the back door. "We're all set."

Francie Song had not slept for even a moment all night. An abiding fear clung to her that her Kent Welby was in terrible danger. She could see it hovering all around him, but could not make out the form or nature of the hazard. She had not felt this way on any of the other days the platoon had been gone from Tre Noc. Somehow, shortly after darkness fell the previous evening, this frightening premonition stole over her and she began to weep. She cried herself dry some time after midnight. Then she lay abed, eyes red-rimmed and burning, sobs choked in a tight throat.

It was all so *real*. She could feel the guns pointed at Kent Welby; her flesh ached with the impact of imagined bullets. Gray mist surrounded him and she could tell where he was. At one point, near 0300 hours, her mind registered the faint sound of softly rustling surf. Shortly after that, she began to weep again. A small, soft, warm hand touched her shoulder.

"Momma, why are you crying?" Thran asked, black eyes big with concern and confusion.

Francie swallowed down the latest knot. "I—I can't tell you. Not exactly. Only that I fear for our Kent Welby. He is in frightful danger."

Thran beamed an encouraging smile in his childish innocence. "He will not be hurt. He is the bravest man in the world."

Francie sat up and took her son in her arms. She held him close, rocking back and forth until his head drooped on her shoulder. Then she placed him beside her and stared at the dark ceiling for several minutes before she, too, laid down and drifted off to sleep.

At the checkpoint, the same sergeant came out to inspect Johnny Yu's van. Impassively, he looked the baker in the eye, intent on his face and any reactions he might see there.

"You are late, Comrade Baker," he accused.

Johnny Yu gave him his cheeriest smile. "Ah, yes, Comrade Sergeant. I was delayed at my last customer. I discovered there a young, newly opened lotus blossom that quickened my wand." He rubbed his crotch to reinforce the impression of a man who had recently made the Clouds and Rain.

Sternness filled the sergeant's voice. "Your wife had better not learn of it."

"Oh, she will surely not. I took the precaution of taking a long bath before leaving."

"A wise man. You say that she was young? How young?"

Johnny produced a wicked leer. "Her gully has only recently learned of the woman's curse."

Surprise and delight registered on the face of the sergeant. "*That* young? You lucky fellow. Tell me, were you the first to enter the silken gates?"

"Alas, no. But, I was second, guaranteed. She told me that she was introduced to her future work by a gentle young boy, under direction of the clever old woman who had purchased her from her parents in the country."

Sighing, the sergeant shook his head in regret. "It is too bad that the old ways are dying out under the enlightened rule of our Communist leaders. They are entirely too prudish, don't you think?''

Always cautious for conversational traps such as this, Johnny Yu lowered his voice and spoke in a conspiratorial manner. "Careful, Comrade Sergeant. Neither you nor I wish to be caught in an indiscretion by anyone who might overhear. Isn't that right? Oh, by the way. I had this left over. It would be a shame for it to go to waste. A dozen rice cakes, dipped in honey. Enjoy them as a gift from your friend. Now, may I say good night?"

"Yes. Good night, Comrade Baker.'' Clutching the white box, he waved the van through expansively.

Thirty minutes went by in the retrieval of the radio set, the Sliders, and the rebreathing gear. When all had been loaded in the van, Johnny Yu started off along the southern road. Once on the way, Tonto Waters spoke what was on his mind.

"It would help if we got verification that this is the route they took, and soon."

Johnny Yu agreed. "Right. And it would be an advantage if we had military transportation and uniforms. The closer to the border we get, the more soldiers are around."

Confirmation came first, from one of two soldiers manning the next checkpoint south of Hanoi. When the van slowed to a stop, Archie Golden got out of the rear door and shot one of the guards with his suppressed Browning, while Tonto Waters held the other at gunpoint. The interrogation was swift and efficient.

Speaking in flawless Vietnamese, Wordy Wordsworth asked, "Has a tractor and lowboy trailer passed through here recently? It might have been with one or two more military vehicles.''

Johnny Yu listened attentively, attuned to any subtle nuances in pronunciation that might indicate the man lied. The young soldier blinked and eyed the fat, nasty looking suppressor on the end of Tonto's pistol. Licking his lips, he bobbed his head up and down.

"Yes. Three trucks and a scout car. One was as you described.''

"Who went in them?''

"Two of our army's generals and a Russian, a *Spetznaz* officer. Also some *quai lo fann* who looked like scientists.'' When he said the last, he looked directly at Johnny Yu. Johnny nodded, acknowledging that he had been correctly identified as Chinese.

"These foreign barbarians? How many were they?'' Johnny asked.

"Two, I think. Not more than three.''

Wordsworth asked the next question. "How long ago?''

"Not more than twenty minutes. They were driving quite slowly. Hardly ten miles an hour.''

Since the checkpoint was at an intersection, Wordy asked next, "What direction did they take?''

"South.''

"Can you tell me anything else?''

"No.''

"Thank you, you have been most helpful.'' Then, by necessity, Wordsworth raised his suppressed Browning and terminated the soldier. "We'll drag them off in the bushes and disassemble the guard box and barrier. That should confuse anyone who might come after us.''

Tonto tapped the face of his watch. "That'll take time."

"At the speed they are going, it won't matter."

Tonto nodded. "You've got a point, Wordy."

Ten miles down the road, an aged Zil 6×6 had parked at the side of the road. The NVA driver and his assistant had stepped out to answer the call of nature, while four others dozed in the back. They looked up casually when a black van pulled up behind the truck as they zipped their flies.

Soft pops came from the muzzles of two Brownings and the NVA soldiers died in the ditch where they stood. "Check the back of the truck, then let's get them out of those uniforms," Tonto urged.

Archie Golden and Kent Welby stepped on grab irons and raised above the tailgate of the truck bed. Inside they found the sleeping soldiers and swiftly shot each in the head.

"There was four of 'em back here. We've all got uniforms now," Archie announced.

Quickly, Johnny Yu dressed in the driver's uniform and Wordy Wordsworth fitted the tunic and helmet of the other on his overlarge frame. Tonto and the SEALs dressed in the rear of the vehicle and then the Chief prompted the next actions.

"Put the bodies in the van and then let's boogie."

With that accomplished, he and the other two SEALs climbed into the rear of the truck. Less than a minute later, they went on their way.

Unaware of any pursuit, or of the tampering with the bomb, Rudinov and Borkoi went on their way to the as-yet-undisclosed ground zero. Borkoi chain-smoked through half a pack of strong Russian cigarettes. Seated beside him, Pyotr Rudinov made a face.

"Smoking those will kill you at an early age, don't you know?"

"What about you? You smoke cigars."

"Yes, occasionally. *Joya de Monterey*, fine Cuban cigars. And I don't inhale. *Spetznaz* taught me that."

Suddenly the lowboy trailer fishtailed wildly. More to himself than to the officers riding with him, the driver shouted, "*Pahsmatreet'yeh!*" Then repeated, "Look out! A damned tire has burst."

Rapidly he began to downshift, fighting all the while, one handed, to control the wavering vehicle and its deadly cargo. Rudinov and Borkoi exchanged troubled glances. Gradually, the tractor slowed. With a final hiss of air brakes, the careening vehicle stopped.

Grumbling, the driver climbed from the cab of the tractor and went to inspect the damage. At his back, the two Russian officers released heavy sighs of relief.

"*Vorgemoi emoi!* I almost filled my drawers," Viktor Borkoi panted out.

Pyotr Rudinov smiled familiarly. "A close thing. Surely if it had fallen it would not have gone off accidentally?"

Borkoi shrugged. "Who knows? The devices are not tossed around casually to find out. Especially I would treat one that had fallen into the ocean with considerable respect. Remember, everything is ready for it to fire, except for the time initiator to start the sequencer."

Their driver returned with the bad news. "Most of

one tire has been shredded off the wheel.''

"Can we proceed without it?" Rudinov demanded.

"Yes, Comrade Lieutenant Colonel. There are dual wheels all around. All I must do is free the rest of the casing.''

Rudinov glowered. "Then get to it.''

Borkoi spoke again. "There is something else that concerns me more. That is if the remote timing devices will even work. Already I have examined one and found it defective. That leaves only two with which to get the job done. Fifty-fifty is not good odds.''

Rudinov thrust out his lower lip and responded darkly. "Then see to it that they get the job done. We have less than forty kilometers to reach the villa of General Hoi.''

The gap was closing, Tonto realized ten minutes later. Through the open rear of the requisitioned truck, he saw a long strip of shredded tire in the middle of the road. He pointed it out to Archie and Doc.

"I'll lay odds that came off the lowboy.''

Archie contemplated it a moment. "Yeah, Tonto, that fits. The real thing weighs close to five thousand pounds.''

"Add the weight of the trailer—and from what I saw of the tires they looked damn near bald—you get a blowout on a road like this.''

Doc grinned at the Chief. "You oughta be a detective, Tonto.'' He paused to take a swallow from the canteen of one of the dead soldiers. Suddenly Doc spluttered and jerked the container from his lips. Rice wine. No wonder they had to stop and take a leak. He wiped his mouth with the back of his other hand and spoke to Tonto again.

"We must be getting damned close to the DMZ. Could it be they are taking it into the South to set off?"

Tonto smiled at the thought. "Now that we're committed to stealing back the bomb, if they do get it across, our job will be a lot easier."

"We will stop five hundred meters from the villa, on this side of that little hillock ahead," Rudinov informed the driver of the lowboy tractor.

When the driver had done as directed, Rudinov and Borkoi dismounted from the vehicle. At once the technician mounted the lowboy trailer and pulled back the tarpaulin. While he unscrewed the fastenings of the control hatch, General Hoi Pac stepped out of the scout car and bustled over to Rudinov.

"Why are we stopping here?"

Rudinov gave him a crooked smile. "It is quite simple. We wish to prevent the curious from discovering the bomb before it is too late."

Suddenly, and painfully too late, General Hoi realized that his precious villa was to be Ground Zero. Immediately he burst forth in hot protest. "You cannot do this! With an eight kilometer fireball, too much of the People's Republic will be damaged. And I must protest in the strongest manner that it is totally unnecessary to destroy my headquarters in the bargain. You must move farther south, let some of it spill over beyond the DMZ. That will anger the Southern government against the Americans as well."

Rudinov gave him a long silence before replying.

"That is a reasonable suggestion, General. However, it is our decision that the hoax will not be believed if your country does not receive some significant damage." Frost coated his words.

"Has the villa been evacuated in our absence?" Hoi demanded.

"Certainly not." The sneer in Rudinov's smile was not lost on the Vietnamese general either.

Right then General Hoi Pac lost it entirely. His face flushed deep reddish-purple. He blew up his chest like a puffer fish, and began to scream at the KGB man. "I will not allow it! I will not be party to the murder of my brother soldiers of the People's Republic and of its citizens. I shall have my troops place you under arrest."

At that threat, *Podpolkovnik* Rudinov smiled icily and calmly drew his 9mm Makarov pistol, which he pointed at a spot squarely between General Hoi's eyes. "As the Americans, who so dearly love to rhyme their colloquialisms, say, *If you try, you will most surely die.*"

In the next instant, the presence of even more difficulties announced itself in the angry shout of Viktor Borkoi. "*Vorg tfy propast!*" Then he repeated it, "Goddamn it! The bomb has been sabotaged."

Rudinov nearly strangled on the word as he demanded, "*What?*"

"Someone has destroyed the electronic sequencer, cut one of the guide rails, and dented a hemisphere. It will take at least two weeks to get parts and effect repairs. In the end, we might not be able to detonate it at all."

CHAPTER 22 _____

WORDY WORDSWORTH tapped Johnny Yu on the shoulder and then indicated the unfolded square of paper in his lap. "According to this map, we are getting dangerously close to the headquarters of a General Hoi."

Unflappable, Johnny Yu calmly replied, "Yes, I know."

Tonto Waters had stuck his head through the unzipped flap in the cover of the truck bed and shoved it into the open window space at the rear of the cab. "D'you think that the bomb is being taken there?" He considered and then rejected that idea. "Naw. No general's gonna have a thing like that sittin' around his headquarters."

Wordsworth looked over at Tonto. "And what if they did take it there?"

Tonto reasoned that out promptly. "With only five of us, it would be suicide to go in after it." And immediately he began to work out a way they could manage it.

* * *

Podpolkovnik Rudinov became instantly furious. "How can that be?" His voice raised an octave as he continued with what seemed to Borkoi to be rhetorical questions. "When could it have been done? Who could have gotten into *that* place and done the damage?"

A sudden, cold intuition told him. "Those damned Americans. They did it. Those SEAL *yoludoki* did it. *Yeb vas*, Lieutenant Marino of the SEALs." His fury at high tide, he shrieked the words in English. "Fuck you, Marino!"

With equal swiftness, the rage within Rudinov subsided into cold, deliberate purpose. "You said it can be repaired?"

"Yes."

"Then do it, Viktor Vassilivich. Do it at once."

Borkoi shook his head. "I am sorry. I cannot. Some, yes, but to achieve the perfection we need . . ." His shrug told the rest.

"But there is a way to reach critical mass?"

"Of course, Pyotr. But it could be dangerous. The bomb may not go off. The charges I would have to use might merely rupture the container and spill radioactive plutonium all over the place."

"Or it might go off prematurely?" asked Rudinov ominously.

Borkoi sighed. "There is that." What he refrained from informing the KGB officer was that he could not effect proper repairs here. He needed technical equipment and precision machining not available in North Vietnam.

He need not have worried about his omission. While Rudinov continued to harangue him about making immediate field repairs, the SEALs arrived from around a bend in the long drive to the villa.

Shivering in the cold, barren room, he watched as a sheet of chill rain slashed against the plastic material that covered the broken windows of his miserable hovel. The cubicle smelled of mold, mildew, human urine, and feces. A fugitive! Petey Danvers a god-damned fugitive. How could it happen to him? He was a leader, a Party member. He controlled four cells in San Diego. God, how wretched it felt.

After escaping from the FBI at Judy's pad, he had split fast as hell out of Pacific Beach. He'd taken the road over Mount Solidad and picked up Pacific Highway to Clairmont Mesa Boulevard. From there he had gone into Linda Vista. Petey had located this abandoned building, one of hundreds built on the mesa as Navy Dependent Housing during World War II, and settled in.

He rolled his motorcycle up the steps and into the ground floor apartment, where it would remain out of sight. *Hell*, Petey thought glumly, he had not even had time to grab his stash, or a blanket, or the five thousand dollars paid him by Comrade Fulton. He had maybe twenty dollars and change in his pocket. What would he do for food? He dared not go out to buy some. The friggin' FBI would search for him everywhere. How had they gotten onto him anyway?

Petey did not give thought to the long closeups shot of him and shown on television all up and down the coast after the demonstration at the Embarkadero at Long Beach.

He hadn't felt this low since he was a little kid.

The last time Petey Danvers had cried was when he was eleven and a speeding car had run over and killed his dog. Right now he wanted to bawl and wail like he did then.

If only he had a joint, or some acid. Yeah, something to take away the tension and fear, the terrible sense of abandonment and defeat. Yeah, a nice little acid trip would be great now. Yeah, cool. Drifting in a warm spot among the purple and chartreuse clouds. *"Wouldn't you like to fly . . . in my beautiful . . ."* Sniffling, missing the drugs that could soothe him, Petey dabbed at his brimming eyes with the hem of his tie-dyed tank top undershirt.

Outside, a plain sedan rolled to a stop across the street. Two men in suits were seated in the front. After a short pause they got out of the vehicle. The one wearing a hat nodded toward the duplex opposite.

"That's the one."

"You're sure, Al?"

"Yep, Dave. An old woman down the street, a Mrs. Eudora Washington, said she saw it all. First white man in the neighborhood outside of plumbers or other service types since the navy left. Just rolled a bike in there and disappeared inside."

"We might as well get it over with."

Al looked at his companion. "You know, you're hanging me way out on this one, comrade."

"Can't be helped," the other man responded as they climbed the three steps to the minute porch. "He knows too much. And, he's a junkie. If the FBI got ahold of him, they'd make him spill it all. Then a whole lot of us would be history."

Reaching out, he opened the sprung door and they went inside. Quietly they climbed the stairs, to where the bedrooms were. They kept to the inner edge to avoid betraying squeaks. In the short hall, they turned first to the right, found the room empty. They went back to the left to the second and found Petey Danvers sitting on the filth-littered floor, legs drawn up and arms wrapped around his shins. His chin rested morosely on his knees.

Al stepped to one side and his companion spoke, which shattered Petey's reverie. "Say good-bye, Petey."

With that, Yevgeney Gorochke, the man Detective Al Carstairs and Petey Danvers knew as Dave Fulton, raised the suppressed .22 caliber Colt Woodsman and shot Petey Danvers through both eyes.

AK-47s spitting steel-jacketed slugs, the SEALs roared down on the parked vehicles. One swath, fired by Archie Golden, swept four Soviet soldiers off their feet. At once, he turned the selector lever to single fire and took aim at more obscure targets, hunkered down behind the sidewalls of the two Zil 6×6 trucks.

Right behind Archie's full rock-and-roll volley, a British Mk 5 fragmentation grenade flew from the hand of Doc Welby. Four seconds later it went off with a sharp roar that masked the screams of the Russian troops shredded by the shrapnel. Doc had time to shout a warning to Chief Waters.

"Tonto, on your left!"

Tonto Waters turned in time to see Viktor Borkoi snatch the Makarov pistol from his holster and charge it. Before the Soviet technician could take aim at

Tonto's exposed body, the chief stitched Borkoi from crotch to eyeballs with the chattering AK-47 in his hands.

Stunned by the sudden fury of the onslaught, Generals Thrun and Van only now reacted. They leaped from the scout car and began an ungainly run toward the top of the drive. Johnny Yu recognized Thrun as Chief of the Directorate of Information and chopped him across the kidneys with four fast rounds from his Kalashnikov. Only then did Johnny remember to take the six-by out of gear and step on the brake. Pyotr Rudinov fired only one round from his 9mm pistol, which struck Johnny Yu in the right shoulder, before he found himself confronted by the muzzles of two AK-47s.

What is happening here? Pyotr Rudinov thought in an instant of confusion and panic.

The NVA Zil truck had appeared around the curve in the lane to the villa without warning. At first he thought nothing of it. A routine patrol, no doubt. Then the firing started. At last it registered on him. The men inside the truck were far too big to be Vietnamese. And their faces were smeared with green camouflage grease paint, with lines of brown and spots of black.

Vorge moi, it is the SEALs! Resolutely, he drew his Makarov and chambered a round. Above him on the lowboy, Viktor Borkoi screamed, a short, horrible sound, and fell in a loose-limbed sprawl. A line of exit wounds, ugly red blossoms, ran along Borkoi's spine. Rudinov broke off his momentary paralysis and took a shot at the driver of the Zil.

The truck grated to a stop as the bullet struck. Dust

enveloped Rudinov. When it cleared, he stared into the menacing muzzles of two Kalashnikov assault rifles. Presented with no other choice, he lowered his pistol and meekly raised his hands.

General Hoi Pac watched the death of General Thrun in a numbed state of disbelief. Not ten minutes ago he had been threatened by the KGB Lieutenant Colonel. Now they were all under attack. *But by whom?*

It did not occur to Hoi that his old nemesis, the Navy SEALs, had come to pay a call. Not until the small force of only five men took out the entire force of twenty Soviet soldiers, the drivers of the trucks, and Technician Borkoi, did he realize that indeed these were Americans. He watched, stricken to the core, as Rudinov surrendered without a struggle. Not conversant with the language, he did not understand what Rudinov said when he spoke in English.

"I am a citizen of the Soviet Union, and a noncombatant in this conflict. I demand that you release me at once to contact my Embassy in Hanoi." He waved a hand at the lowboy trailer. "That is property of the Soviet government and in my custody. It must go with me."

For a moment, everything stood still. Then a tall, lean American in green face spoke. "I suppose that under international law, you're right. You may go, *Tovarish Podpolkovnik* Rudinov." He hooked a thumb at the low-slung trailer. "But that goes with us. I believe it belongs to our country."

He knows my name! Rudinov thought in total shock. Who is this man? It was not his counterpart, Jason

Slater. He would recognize that face anywhere. Although certainly he is CIA. Mere naval enlisted personnel would never be provided with the identity and rank of a member of the *Komitet*. Rudinov's fair complexion washed even whiter with this realization. The American agent was speaking again, this time in Russian.

"We will be leaving now. I suggest that you do not render assistance to any North Vietnamese troops who might follow us." He turned to what had to be the SEALs who had plagued the Soviet plans in the Delta for nearly a year. "Get on the lowboy. Tonto wants to take it with us, so we will."

With that, the small party of Americans headed for the tractor-trailer rig. All but one, who walked over to the scout car, reached in, and yanked out General Hoi Pac.

"Well, look what we have here. This one I think we take with us."

During the lull after the blitz of the SEALs, Johnny Yu had his shoulder wound treated and bandaged. "Want a shot of morphine?" Doc Welby asked him.

Johnny Yu gritted his teeth and shook his head in the negative. "I'll do. Who's gonna drive?"

Tonto Waters spoke up, having considered the same question. "I worked on delivery trucks my last year of high school, and for two years after. I figure I've got the most experience."

Tonto Waters climbed to the driver's seat and Johnny Yu squeezed into the center, followed by Wordy Wordsworth in the shotgun seat. Archie Golden and Doc Welby, with General Hoi Pac trussed and stashed under the tarp covering the bomb, took positions at the rear of the trailer. With a blast of diesel exhaust, the tractor-trailer crawled to a turnout, reversed direction, and rolled down the long drive.

Behind them, *Podpolkovnik* Rudinov did not even consider reaching for one of the dropped AK-47's of the dead soldiers. He would content himself to wait for the reaction force that would surely soon come from the villa.

Lieutenant Commander Barry Lailey came down from Binh Thuy to Tre Noc shortly before nightfall. With him, he brought papers to initiate an investigation into the alleged desertion of Lieutenant Carl Marino, QMC Thomas Waters, MM/3C Richard Golden, and the rest of the Alpha Squad, Alpha Detachment, Team 2 SEALs. He found the offices closed as usual at 1630. His task would have to wait until the next day. With anything but a cordial welcome, he had little choice than to spend his time in the bar at the Phon Bai restaurant.

There he observed a strikingly attractive young Vietnamese woman. The more he looked at her the more familiar she seemed. Then he recalled. One of the SEALs, in Alpha Squad at that, had an affair going with her. He had been instrumental in getting her hired by the Tre Noc Riverine Force headquarters. Lailey made a mental note to the effect that after his inquiry had been officially acknowledged, he would have to interrogate her. Surely she knew something about this disappearance. She could be a Viet Cong agent and responsible for it.

No, he liked it better that they had not been captured by the Cong, rather that they had deserted on their own initiative. Lailey downed the last swallow of the so-called scotch he had been served and winced. What did they flavor it with? It tasted like iodine.

"I'll have another," he told the barman. "And whatever the lady is having."

His scotch was duly delivered and the bartender poured mineral water from a bottle of Golden Tiger into a fresh glass for Francie Song. He spoke to her and she looked up. Her smile was distant at first, then warmed when she recognized him. Or perhaps failed to, Lailey amended. He gestured to the empty stool beside him. She rose and came over. Her smile broke a little as she neared.

"I am grateful for the refreshment. But, I am sorry, I do not sit with strangers."

"But, don't you work here?" Lailey asked, confused, thinking her to be a part-time B-girl or a prostitute.

"No. I do not. I work for you Americans at the Riverine base."

Barry Lailey turned on what for him was a radiant smile. "That's interesting. I'm Lieutenant Commander Barry Lailey, from Binh Thuy."

A slight frown between her eyes revealed that Francie had heard the name, albeit not spoken with respect or reverence. "I am called Francie Song."

Bluntly, Lailey probed. "Your father was European?"

Francie hesitated. "Yes. He was killed in the fighting against the Viet Minh. I took my mother's name when the French were deposed. I was only a girl at the time.'' She looked away, studied the scant collection of bottles on the back bar.

Suddenly acutely uncomfortable with this, Lailey sought to change the subject. ''Are you acquainted with many of the sailors on the base?''

Francie's smile was more a grimace of stress than an expression of warmth. ''Only a few. Those I work with, of course.''

Abruptly, Lailey dropped a 20 piaster note on the bar and stood to leave. ''I'm the—ah—intelligence officer. Perhaps we'll meet again. Now, please excuse me, I must go in for dinner.''

Halfway through the garlic-steamed prawns and sautéed vegetables, a single siren began to wail in the direction of the Tre Noc base. Shortly after, mortar rounds began to drop into the compound. *Odd*, Lailey thought, *the Cong are starting early tonight*. Well aware that the Cong did not usually fire on the village, Barry Lailey stayed where he was until the last shell had echoed into silence for a good five minutes.

Then he roused himself from the table, paid his tab, and hurried out toward the distant main gate. He had no sooner arrived than he was forced to dive for a bunker as another projectile made feathery warbles through the air and dropped down by the docks. A half dozen more swiftly followed. Lailey ground himself into the floor of the sandbag-and-palm log shelter.

''What the hell's going on?'' he demanded of Captain Fred Haskins, the newly appointed CO of the Riverine Force, who hunkered beside him.

''Not the usual fare, I've been told. It might be we'll get a probe at the wire tonight.''

*   *   *

Twenty minutes later, whistles began to shrill and bugles to blare out in the darkness on three sides, beyond the wire. The mortar barrage slacked some, the strident *craaaak-bam!* of their detonation replaced in part by softer plops as illumination rounds went off high above the compound.

Sappers, who had already crept into place and slid bangalore torpedoes under the concertinas of razor wire, ignored them as they quickly fired their infernal devices. Gouts of dirt and wire geysered skyward as explosive charges went off along the outer defenses of the complex. Myriad yellow flickers from Type 56 assault rifle fire lit the near edge of the jungle. Satchel charges sailed over the triangle of concertina wire to land on the roofs of low bunkers near the perimeter.

Those went off with thunderous roars that punished ears and misted the air with a dense cloud of dust and pebbles. The roof of one collapsed entirely, exposing the occupants to the weapons in the hands of Viet Cong and NVA regulars who swarmed through the breaks in the wire. During the day, the survivors would later find out, the accommodating *papasans* who kept the kill zone free of all obstructions had industriously emptied all the cans of rocks and cut the telltale wires, removed trip wires from the claymores, and turned them inward. The same had been done for the land mines. They had done it so skillfully, while performing their usual tasks, that no one had suspected. Now the enemy reaped the harvest of their efforts.

Sporadic fire began to come from the guard towers. An M-60 chattered first, followed by the throaty roar of a .50 Browning. Tracers of red-orange and green sped in opposite directions. More satchel charges went off. The screams of the wounded and injured were nearly drowned out by the increasing volume of the firefight. Crouched in the gateside bunker, Barry Lailey reached out tentatively for an M-16 that rested against an overturned table. He secured it in time to look up and watch a satchel charge spin into the underground room.

Lailey went flat, arms over his head, mouth open wide. The enormous blast of the package of explosives singed his hair and deafened him for the time being. Dazed, his chest aching, eyes watering, Lailey groped again for the M-16. He reached it in time to empty half a magazine into three VC who stepped boldly into the bunker. *Not good*, he thought calmly. Then he realized that the table had saved him. Its canted surface had deflected most of the force of the blast upward. Above it, three palm log beams hung broken and dislodged from their moorings.

"Shit!" Lailey spat. "Captain Haskins, are you all right?"

After a long, tense moment, a groan answered him, then, "I think my leg's broken."

"Can you move?"

"Yeah, Commander. I can. Hurts like hell, but I can."

"You've got to get to your command post."

"Don't I know it."

"I'll help you. If they throw another charge in here, we're history."

Outside, in the trench that connected them with another bunker more inboard, Lailey and Haskins found the bodies of three of the Marine guard force, as well as half a dozen NVA regulars in their sickly, gray-pea-green uniforms. This one was not going away easily. Shouts and screams came from everywhere. And the discordant shriek of the whistles came from every quarter of the compound. Limping, an arm around Lailey's shoulder, Captain Haskins moved toward the next bunker.

Lailey, the M-16 at the ready in one hand, did what he could to speed them up. The second wave of the assault began as Haskins reached the undamaged bunker. Lailey left him there and turned to head for the SEAL compound when six VC rushed directly at him. They yelled frantically and fired from the hip as they advanced.

CHAPTER 23 ⎯⎯⎯⎯⎯⎯⎯⎯

FRANCIE SONG had half a flight of stairs to reach her apartment when the first mortar rounds burst in the Tre Noc compound. Automatically, fear for the safety of her beloved Kent Welby struck at her heart. Then she remembered that he was not there, and apparently not in Bangkok either. She pushed that aside and hurried to the apartment. Thran would be frantic over the bombardment with her not there.

She no sooner opened her front door than she saw her son. He stood, trembling visibly, at the edge of the palm matting that covered the floor, barefoot, in his dark blue school uniform shorts and short-sleeved white shirt.

"Momma, why are they doing it so early?"

"I do not know, Thran. Do you want to go to the shelter?"

Thran blinked, thought a moment. "No. I am afraid one will fall on us in the street."

A rippling crack from the bangalores, followed by the crackle of small arms fire, blanched Francie a pasty, gray-white. She reached out and tousled her son's thick, black hair. "Yes. I think it is wise for us to stay inside. Put out all of the lights."

Obediently, Thran went from one kerosene lamp to another, blew on the wicks, and turned them down. Francie even extinguished the votive candles. Quickly she returned and locked the door. Then she put an arm around the shoulders of the boy and led him to her bedroom.

"I am afraid something very bad is happening," she told him in an unsteady whisper.

Thran remained silent. He had seen enough war in his few years to know better than to speculate.

At the first point where Tonto Waters stopped the slow-moving tractor to let Archie Golden plant some of his nasty surprises, the Chief broached a troublesome subject with Wordy Wordsworth.

"You know, Wordy, nice as it would be, I don't think we can take General Hoi with us."

"Tonto, remember he commands all of Vinh Province. He would be a gold mine of information. Give Jason and Bobby three days with him and he'll be rappin' it off like a tobacco auctioneer."

Tonto produced a thoughtful frown. "You know them from somewhere before, don't you?"

Wordy produced a crooked, rueful smile. "Yeah. We went through the Farm together."

Tonto brightened. "Then Pope an' me had the right of it. You're not just a nuclear whiz-kid and ex-Blankethead. You're a spook, aren't you?"

Wordy's smile became strained. "Let's leave it that I have ties to the Company. Seriously, it would be far better to take Hoi with us."

Doc Welby got in his bit. "Wordy's right, Tonto. If they wring out Hoi, we can really play grab-ass with a whole lot of NVA heavies."

Tonto snorted. "All right, you've convinced me. We'll keep him."

Archie finished stringing trip wires across the road, at a level to catch the radiator grill of any pursuing vehicle. One went to an M-18 claymore, the other to a rope of C-4, rigged to cut down a waist-sized palm so that it would fall across the roadway. He hurried to the rear of the trailer and jumped aboard.

"Let 'er rip! But Tonto . . . don't back up."

Slowly the tractor-trailer gained speed. Tonto ran through the gears, watching the tachometer and speed gauge. The needle reached 2,700 rpm and the speedometer indicated 13 kph. Recklessly, Tonto gave it more throttle. Redline on the Zil was 4,000 rpm. The second dial registered 90-plus kph. Good. Good. But still not fast enough.

Ten minutes later, the crack of the C-4 and the spang of the claymore came from behind them. *That should buy us some time*, Tonto thought. Wordy intently studied the map. Brow puckered, he ran a finger along the route they followed. At last, he tapped Tonto on the forearm.

"About three klicks ahead, there's a side road that leads down to the coast. There's no indication of any buildings or houses. That doesn't mean there aren't any. But this was made from last month's overflight."

Tonto decided instantly. "So we take it."

Led by Colonel Dak, the quick reaction force came racing down the road from the villa. *Podpolkovnik*

Rudinov flagged down the lead scout car and climbed in beside the agitated NVA officer.

"General Hoi? Where is he?" Dak demanded.

Rudinov eyed him evenly. "They took him with them."

"Who?"

"Why, the American SEALs, of course. They took the General and..." Security considerations amended his reply. "The object we were bringing here."

So agitated he abandoned his usual caution, Dak blurted, "You mean the hydrogen bomb? Oh, General Hoi told me about it. After all, I am the intelligence officer." Only then did Dak realize what Rudinov had said. "SEALs? You mean the American navy?"

"Just so. A number of them attacked us and took away the bomb you were not supposed to know of, and General Hoi in the bargain." Rudinov was loath to reveal that only five men had demolished twenty Soviet soldiers and only one had taken a wound. "We need to pursue at once."

"Of course. Driver, continue at all reasonable speed."

Rudinov snapped immediately after. "At full speed, driver."

Fifteen minutes later the blunt grille of the scout car activated the trip wire on the claymore, then the C-4. Due to the slight delay, the small light-armored vehicle sped past the deadly traps unscathed. Behind it, the four truckloads of NVA troops did not fare so well.

Nine-millimeter steel balls slammed into the lead truck. A dozen punctured the radiator, two flattened the right-hand tire. A shower of thirty stripped away the windshield and imbedded in the faces and upper torsos of the occupants of the cab. A dead man at the wheel, the Zil wavered drunkenly and made for the side of the road. The blown front tire made the rear flail around and provided space for the second vehicle to whiz past while the driver tried frantically to brake the truck.

He managed in time to take the falling palm trunk across the bed of the Zil, crushing the life from half a dozen NVA regulars. The rest were frozen in terror. That gave time enough for the grenades tied to the upper trunk to explode. Stunned by the ferocity of the SEALs, *Podpolkovnik* Rudinov could only stare in aching disbelief. Slowly the sound of the carnage faded away.

Rudinov swallowed hard. His cold eyes turned on Colonel Dak. "Quickly, find out how many troops are left who are able to go on."

"How can we go on, Comrade Colonel? One truck is destroyed, the other has its radiator smashed."

"We run that truck until it burns up. It is a Zil, Comrade Colonel Dak. It will run forever." Despite the bloody situation that surrounded them, Rudinov could not resist that bit of irony. "We will find these SEALs and destroy them," he added darkly.

Lieutenant Commander Barry Lailey awakened to a thunderous headache. Darkness swam around him, marked by pinpricks of light. He was moving but he was lying down. How could that be? Then, a more compelling question. Where was he? In a blinding flash it all came back to him.

Tre Noc had been attacked. He vividly recalled six

NVA soldiers rushing toward him. They had been firing. Had he been hit? Was he in a medevac helicopter? No, there was no vibration or roar of engines. Where, then? Lieutenant Commander Lailey regained his hearing.

Voices spoke low and in Vietnamese. Barry Lailey became conscious of a strain in his arms and ankles. With considerable effort he forced his eyes to focus on the precious little light that filtered down to him. He saw a sagging bamboo pole directly above. At least one man had to be at each end of it. Suddenly he realized that he hung from that rod like a trussed pig. The truth of his condition numbed him. He was a prisoner!

"Where are we taking this one, Lau?"

"To Five Bunker, Chou. He is an important American. Comrade Frahn will want to question him."

Lailey could not understand the words spoken above him. Nevertheless his next thought reached the correct conclusion. Better if he had been killed. For all his vanity, Barry Lailey knew far too surely that no one could hold out forever in an interrogation. Torture would come first. Then, if he survived that, most likely sensory deprivation and drugs. Sooner or later he would break.

And he knew too damned much. His knowledge could severely cripple the Navy's mission in the Delta, and endanger the lives of many others. Could he take it upon himself to deny them the information? His ego rebelled at the idea of suicide. More than that, Barry Lailey looked upon suicide as the coward's way out. Abruptly the column—there had to be more than two men, he reasoned—halted.

A pale, red glow registered on his upraised knees. Movement came again. His head canted downward suddenly and Lailey realized that they were going underground. The red luminescence remained after he heard the muffled thump of the camouflaged cover being put in place. The ground leveled under them and Barry Lailey swayed from side to side. His captors continued until another downsloping ramp took them deeper into the earth. The tunnel walls seemed to squeeze Barry Lailey. He began to sweat.

Funny, he thought with giddy detachment, *I never knew before that I had claustrophobia*. His skin began to itch. Sudden loss of equilibrium made his stomach churn. Abruptly the bulwarks widened into a large room. His bearers slid the pole from their shoulders and let him drop painfully to the floor of the bunker. With a sputter and hiss, a gasoline lantern sprang to pale, yellow light, then surged to actinic brightness.

A figure approached and bent over him. "Welcome to Number Five Bunker, Lieutenant Commander—ah—Lailey," a smirking Asian said in English as he examined the name tape on Lailey's tiger stripes.

"Crank it down," Archie Golden shouted from the trailer.

Tonto Waters rounded the corner onto the narrow dirt road and then braked. Archie jumped off and went right to work. He set a claymore, then another on the opposite side of the route. He aimed them to angle along the trail, saturating it to the intersection. Next he rigged the trip wires.

With that accomplished, he placed four grenades at the head level of people seated in a vehicle and wired them to snag a front bumper. After a satisfied look at his handiwork, Archie jumped back on the lowboy and shouted to Tonto.

"Haul ass."

Tonto ground through the gears. The Zil tractor gained speed at a time-eating pace. Slowly the vehicle and its trailer disappeared over the crest of a long downslope. Tonto Waters could smell the salt tang of sea air. They had to be less than a mile from the Gulf. That reminded Tonto of something more important even than the bomb. He turned his head to shout through the opening.

"Hey, Doc, crank up that locator beacon. Give it ten seconds, then off for a minute, then on again. Repeat it three times. They should get a fix by then."

Ahead, a steep grade presented itself. The ground to either side of the road showed sandy patches with tufts of saw grass waving in the stiff onshore breeze. The salt odor grew stronger. The diesel engine labored as it strained into the climb. Tonto pressed the accelerator to the floor. Suddenly the distance-flattened sound of detonating C-4 reached their ears. The claymores had been tripped.

In a ripple, the grenades popped one after another.

"Damn, they're still coming," Tonto swore aloud.

Podpolkovnik Rudinov saw the bright flash behind them a fraction of a second before the sound of the exploding claymores reached his ears. He swiveled in his seat in time to watch fragments of canvas and slivers of wood fly from the sides of the already damaged Zil truck.

It lurched forward, a dead hand on the steering

wheel. In a staccato undulation, four hand grenades detonated a second apart and ended the work of the mines. Screams, shrieks, and moans came from the shattered vehicle. In a heartbeat, the chances of stopping the SEALs vanished before the Soviet officer's eyes. Five of them in the scout car. That was all the manpower they had.

"Keep going," he urged the NVA driver.

Young, inexperienced, and decidedly frightened, the young driver turned to stare at Rudinov. "But, Comrade Colonel . . ."

"DO IT!"

Colonel Dak nodded his approval. He understood men like Rudinov. He saw himself as one. They preferred action over indecision. Technically he outranked the Russian, yet prudence dictated he let the Soviet officer give the orders. When this affair reached its conclusion there would be an inquiry, naturally. The less his name appeared in official reports, the better.

And, if they failed to stop the Americans, General Hoi would be lost. The man who seized the initiative and organized a pursuit would not be overlooked in finding a replacement. For that, he would gladly take second seat when it came to the bungling of it all.

"Slow down," Rudinov commanded suddenly. "They may have left more booby traps behind." He smelled the sea and knew the Americans had nowhere to go from here.

"Now hear this. Now hear this. Lieutenant Marino to the con. Stand forward to the con, Lieutenant Marino."

When Pope Marino reached the operating control center of the *Sunperch*, he found Captain McDade bent over the high-back, padded chair of the radio operator. "Marino reporting, sir," Pope said by way of attracting the commanding officer's attention.

McDade stroked at his bare chin as he turned. "Good. We have contact with your people, Marino."

Pope correctly read the frown on the skipper's brow. "Only what, sir?"

"They're not where they are supposed to be and it's daylight up there."

That brought a scowl to Pope's forehead. "Any idea why?"

McDade smiled. "I suspect that they are in some deep shit up there."

"Are we going to follow regulations and wait until dark to surface?"

Eyeing Marino carefully, McDade pursed his lips and made his decision. "Considering they are damned near a hundred fifty miles south of the Red, no. We head there now. When we reach the spot, we can decide on when to surface."

Wordy Wordsworth pointed ahead. "We couldn't ask for anything better. Pull on down there on the sand, Tonto, and swing sideways to the water."

Tonto cut him a sideways glance. "Won't we get stuck?"

"Keep the speed up and we won't. That winch won't off-load the bomb any other way."

Gritting his teeth, Tonto accelerated and the rig bounced and jolted over the dividing point between solid ground and sand. The tractor lugged down, but kept rolling. The vehicle churned forward until it straightened out, the left-hand wheels at the water's edge. At once, the SEALs dismounted. Tonto studied the low, slow swell of the Gulf of Tonkin and waved Doc to him.

"Better send the signal again. I don't see anything of an antenna."

CHAPTER 24 _____

DOC WELBY set up the transmitter and keyed the locator beacon again. Meticulously he went through the routine of sending three times. He waited a full four minutes before shutting down. Then he looked up at Tonto, his face drawn with worry, dark blue eyes clouded with uncertainty.

"No answer."

"So I gather," Tonto replied dryly. "Well, we can't just stand here. Keep workin' on it, Doc. The rest of us will go up to the crest and wait for anyone who got away from that last go-around." He nodded to Archie. "Have you got any of that stuff left, Arch?"

Grinning, Archie hefted the bag. "A few. Couple of blocks of C-Four, some grenades."

"Good. Go ahead with Wordy and Johnny and put them in place. Doc and me will stuff tarps around the bomb to change its shape. Wouldn't do to let those underwater sailors know what it is and let the word get out."

* * *

Lieutenant Colonel Rudinov peered beyond the mud-smeared windshield of the scout car. The narrow lane they followed bent around a sharp curve. Beyond it should be the long grade down to a cramped shelf of beach. What did these *Amerikanyets pastooch* expect to do? Rudinov chuckled silently. Yes, they were cowboys right enough. Cowboys in the navy.

Then it struck him like a fist in the center of his forehead. Navy. SEALs. *They are going out by submarine!* Countermanding his previous order, Rudinov shouted at the driver again. "Get going as fast as you can."

Roostertails of gravel spurted from the rear wheels. Rudinov clutched the AK-47 to his chest and stood to gaze beyond the limit placed on him by the seat. When he did, a line of lower tree limbs masked the ridge ahead. After they cleared the obstruction, nothing could be seen at the crest.

Archie Golden prowled inside his versatile pack and produced a small pair of binoculars. They resembled opera glasses in size, yet held powerful lenses that provided nearly the same magnification as a pair of 7x50's. With them, he studied their backtrail from the military crest of the ridge. After ten seconds, he grunted.

"Some of them are still comin' on. You'd think, after all the stuff I put out there, that those jokers would get the word."

Tonto Waters, who had joined those on the slope only a minute before, sucked at a tooth and wished they had something besides C-Rations to eat. Then he gave his opinion. "I'd say we have that Russkie on our hands.'' He turned to Wordy. ''No disrespect, sir, but you are full of that 'honor among spooks' crap. That sumbitch knows that he'd be off to the salt mines if he loses that bomb. Those people are fanatics. Hell, they treat their own people worse than they do anyone else.''

''You really think Rudinov is with whoever is coming, Tonto?'' Wordsworth asked.

''Bet my next pay on it.''

Archie got in his view. ''Good thing I put those blocks of plastic on remote detonators. Did you see those gray and black tiger stripes he was wearing? That's *Spetznaz*, their special forces. Those are some bad dudes.''

''Yeah, but Wordy here says he's KGB. Don't necessarily mean he is qualified, ya get me?''

''All the same, I'll be glad for any distance between him and me when I set those off.'' Archie returned to his study of the approaching scout car.

It looked battered and dinged in a superficial way. The lightly armored vehicle would look a hell of a lot worse before long. Archie fingered the radio control that would set off the explosives. Somehow that comforted him. He turned again to Tonto.

''We'd best draw back when they start up the grade. I don't want that thing landing on us when it goes.''

Tonto and Wordy silently agreed with that. They motioned to the other SEALs and together the small force slid back down the face of the headland. From out on the sand, near the lowboy, the growl of the engine could be clearly heard. Archie waited, silently counting off the seconds, then raised the safety cover

and pressed the red button. Only a fraction of a second
delay followed, while the nose of the scout car rose
above the rim. Then the ground rocked from the force
of enormous twin explosions.

Podpolkovnik Rudinov felt the scout car lift a heartbeat before the sound of the explosions struck his
ears. The armored belly of the vehicle, intended to be
proof against land mines, buckled but did not give.
The low-slung carriage vaulted into the air and the
heavier engine compartment dipped downward. A
scream of raw terror came from the driver. Three of
the five occupants in the rear spilled out over the
sides.

To their misfortune, they landed on trip wires that
dislodged the pins on two grenades. Again the thick,
steel plates of the scout car saved the occupants. Despite the numbing effect of the primary explosions,
Rudinov faintly heard the ping-ping of fragments
striking the belly of the vehicle. A sudden thought
chilled him: *the gas tank!*

No, he reasoned, *that would be safely inside the
sheet of protective material*. A quick look out the
windshield showed the ground hurtling upward toward them. Rudinov had time to brace himself and
throw his arms up to cover his face before they struck.

A loud crunch and groan rose from the impact point
as the bodies of the passengers hurtled forward to
slam into any obstruction in front of them. Rudinov
felt a sharp, hot pain in his left arm. Then a cloud of
sand and steam enveloped him and his head slammed
into the dash. Blackness shrouded him at once.

*   *   *

Archie Golden pumped his clenched right fist into the air and did a little dance. "Yes! Yesss! Write *da sve-dahnya* to that Russkie puke."

From beyond him, down by the tractor-trailer, Doc Welby shouted excitedly. "I got them. I got a signal."

At once, the SEALs and Wordy converged on the site. Archie hauled out his field glasses and scanned the sea from atop the lowboy. "I don't see an antenna."

Doc switched to a voice frequency, muttering, "I wish Repeat was here. He's the RTO." Then he spoke into the mike. "Momma, this is Junior. Do you copy? Over."

Static answered him. He repeated the call sign. More static. Doc tried a third time. "Momma, this is Junior. Do you copy? Over."

Static again, a stronger burst that broke off abruptly into a faint voice. "Junior, this is Momma. We read you three-by-three. Send locator again. I say again, send locator. Over."

Doc twisted the dial and keyed the locator beacon. Then quickly back to voice in time to hear, ". . . ior, we have you at ten knots off our present position. We are closing. Stand by. Momma out."

That left the SEALs alone, with the injured and unconscious enemy some three hundred meters from the truck. Tonto spoke for all of them. "Damn. That means we're stuck here for half an hour."

A continuous ringing in his ears sounded like the bells of St. Basil's, back before the State had banned such public displays of religiosity. For a moment, Pyotr Rudinov did not know where he was. Then it flooded back in painful detail. He grasped at each individual impression.

The narrow road to the beach. The scout car. There had been an explosion, a mine of some sort. The damaged vehicle careening through the air. The sudden, violent contact with the earth. More aware now, Rudinov discovered that his left forearm throbbed unmercifully. So did his forehead. With effort he opened his eyes, to find the lashes crusted with blood.

That accounted for the numbing waves of agony that emanated from his skull. He had struck his head on the dashboard. Carefully brushing away the dried blood, Pyotr examined his left arm. To his intense disappointment, it had been broken. He recalled, during the next pair of throbs, the sharp pain that had come when the scout car rammed into the ground. Around him now he heard the groans and sobs of the other occupants.

One had fallen partway out of the vehicle, his upper body crushed under the left side when it came to rest. Colonel Dak sat hunched forward in the rear compartment, elbows on knees, while blood dripped from an obviously broken nose. None of them had escaped injury, Rudinov quickly ascertained. He moved and fresh pain shot up his arm. Rudinov decided to speak to Dak.

''Colonel,'' he said in Vietnamese, ''do you have a handkerchief? If so, you can stuff a couple of ends in your nose and stop the bleeding. Then you can assist me. It seems I have broken an arm.''

Dak glowered at him a moment, then rummaged in a hip pocket. He came out with a neatly folded pristine square of white. This he opened, tore a strip, then divided that portion in half. Gingerly he went about inserting the cloth into his nostrils. Pain forced tears into his eyes. With that accomplished, he spoke rustily to Rudinov.

"Considering your injury, and the condition of the rest of the men, I have one question. What, if anything, are we going to do now?"

Lieutenant Colonel Rudinov raised his head to stare beyond the wreckage of the scout car. "We've come this far. And we are only a few hundred meters from the enemy. I say we make certain they do not escape."

Dak nodded and turned to the NVA soldiers who slowly regained consciousness. "If you can walk, get out of the car. We are going after the Americans."

Four young faces turned to him, their expressions incredulous. Groaning, one pulled himself free. Then a second. Eventually four bloodied, torn, uncomfortable soldiers stood before their colonel. Dak glanced inward at the driver as Rudinov climbed from the ruined vehicle. The Russian saw the direction of his gaze and shook his head.

"He is dead. Broken neck."

Dak sighed. "Take what weapons you can find. We will spread out and attack the Americans."

"Come right to one-niner-zero." Stan McDade ordered the helmsman.

"Right to one-niner-zero, aye."

"All hands, prepare to surface."

Static crackled from a speaker on the bridge to which the radioman had piped the voice channel from Junior. "Momma, this is Junior. We have three friends we're bringing home to supper. One of them is really big.''

Capt. McDade looked to Lieutenant Marino. ''What does that mean?''

''I think I know. And unfortunately you have no need to know, Captain.''

''Hunh! I suspected this was some sort of spook deal. I won't press you, Lieutenant.''

''Fine. I'm going down with our landing party. Permission to leave the bridge?''

''Go ahead.'' Then McDade turned to his duties. ''Stand by to blow forward ballast. Planesman, come to twenty degrees on the bow. Surface to decks awash.''

The rating on the plane wheel responded with alacrity. ''Twenty degrees, aye. Surface to decks awash.''

Captain McDade waited a slow five count, then, ''Take 'er up.'' Compressed air made a roar as it forced water out of the ballast tanks.

Four SEALs of Alpha Squad waited at the forward main hatch along with Lieutenant Marino. A seaman pushed through them with polite apology and spun the wheel that sealed the hatch. Water spilled down in a chilly cascade. He went up the ladder another rung and threw back the hatch.

Moving quickly, he climbed onto the deck. Foam-flecked, clear water with a greenish tint washed around his rubber-soled shoes. He bent down inside the sub and gave a heave on the heavy packs that came next. Pushed by the SEALs, they popped out. Above the sailor, Captain McDade appeared at the gunwale of the conning tower. He put large, powerful binoculars to his eyes and studied the beach.

His first sweep confirmed the presence of an unexpected object, a lowboy tractor-trailer rig with some
bulky object aboard. His second located the team that
had gone ashore three nights before. Then McDade
stiffened suddenly on his third pass. He stared intently
at six figures moving toward the Americans. Then,
quickly, he bent to the intercom tube.

"Pass the word for Lieutenant Marino. His men on
the beach are taking fire from the enemy."

When Pope Marino heard that, he punched the
switch on the nearest intercom. "What kind of fire?"

"Small arms," came the answer.

Marino grabbed a lifejacket and strapped into it,
then took an M-14 from the deck beside him. As an
afterthought, he scooped up a canvas bag of MK 5
British handgrenades. Up the ladder he went. When
his head appeared, he hailed the others. "I'm coming
with you."

Ping! Ping-ping! Nearly spent slugs rang off the thick
metal siderails of the lowboy. Tonto looked up to see
six men in uniform rushing at them.

"Incoming!" he shouted. Then, "How the hell
many lives do those guys have?"

At better than three hundred meters, the range was
too much for the Type 56 rifles of the NVA soldiers
and the AK-47 Rudinov had brought along. They fired
as they came anyway. Rudinov sought the CIA agent
who had spoken with him. That one had to die.

Wordy Wordsworth and the SEALs waited until the
enemy came into range. Then they opened fire. One
of the NVA troopers went down. A second cried out
and staggered. A third dropped to his knees, though

he kept on firing. Tonto Waters took aim on a Vietnamese officer and squeezed the trigger in a three-round burst.

A grin flickered for a second on Tonto's face as he saw green cloth puff up from the right side of his target. The NVA colonel jerked, then came on, assault rifle held low. Carefully he ticked off three-round bursts. Tonto shot again . . . and missed. Cursing his accuracy, he wished for his Ithaca. The frame of the trailer rang like a carillon. Archie hurled a grenade.

It exploded without visible effect. Faintly over the roar of gunfire, Tonto thought he heard the soft purr of the electric motor of a STAB. A second later, the volume of gunfire from their side doubled. Tonto risked a quick look behind him.

What he saw was the sweetest sight in the world. Two STABs sped toward the beach, with SEALs aboard, firing over the heads of those ashore at the charging enemy. Tonto let out a whoop and Archie threw another grenade. To Archie's right, Johnny Yu let out a grunt and clapped a hand to his left thigh.

"Damn close, pilgrim. Two inches to the right and I'd never sire another kid."

Beyond Johnny Yu, Wordy Wordsworth dropped the last of the NVA soldiers. That left Rudinov and the NVA colonel. They wisely withdrew. Each walked backward and fired as they worked their way out of range. Tonto left Johnny and Archie to plink at them. He hurried toward the arriving STABs. Quickly he pointed to the trailer.

"Make fast to the side of that trailer. We've got a load to transfer."

"Aye, Chief," called Zoro Agilar at the helm.

Chad Ditto jumped out of the small boat and joined Archie at the rear guard. A second later, Pope Marino and Randy Andy arrived and knelt to fire at the retreating enemy. For a moment, Pope locked eyes with the tall, blond warrior in the *Spetznaz* uniform. A chill ran along his spine. Then he began to tick off rounds, one at a time.

Podpolkovnik Pyotr Rudinov went rabid with fury as he watched the bomb being winched off the trailer and onto a double-pontoon inflatable boat. He and Colonel Dak crouched behind the ruin of the scout car, well out of range and helpless to prevent what was happening. Unable to contain himself longer, Lieutenant Colonel Rudinov spat his words angrily.

"Is there a radio close at hand?"

"I am afraid not, Comrade Colonel," Colonel Dak answered breathily. "The closest is back at the villa."

Rudinov watched in impotent fury while the rubber boats approached the submarine. Water skimmed over the skidproof foredeck of the submersible vessel so that the first, more lightly loaded boat skimmed up the rounded side and grounded on it. It might as well be his career they were taking with them.

"It will be impossible to accuse the Americans of invading your country and stealing back their own hydrogen bomb—one no one is supposed to know about anyway. And now, thanks to that submarine, soon no proof that it ever was here will exist." Rudinov paused to slam his uninjured fist against a blown tire.

"To add insult to injury, during the firefight, when we made our withdrawal, I caught a glimpse of a man

I have grown to despise. I know,'' he hastened to add, ''a soldier is supposed to remain objective and impersonal. But, this SEAL officer, this Lieutenant Marino, has plagued me constantly for the last year.''

In spite of his pain, Colonel Dak produced a knowing smile. ''He is the one responsible for the failure of General Hoi's escalation plan last year?''

''Oh yes, he is. That's quite astute. And I swear to you, by the God we good Communists are not supposed to believe in, that the next time I see Lieutenant Marino it will be as a corpse.''

CHAPTER 25 ———————

"SONAR TO bridge. Contact at three-zero-zero. Single screw, making high turns, closing rapidly."

"Bridge, aye," the third officer, Lieutenant (j.g.) Cramer, responded. Then he spoke into the intercom. "Captain to the bridge. We have sonar contact at three-zero-zero."

Captain McDade sat down the coffee mug with which he warmed his hands more than drank from. "So soon? We're not ten knots from where we took on the team."

Carl Marino cocked an eyebrow. "We had a hell of a lot of radio traffic. More than called for in the plan."

McDade nodded. "Any plan of battle falls apart at the first contact with the enemy. I know that only too well. Ayup, duty calls."

McDade reached the bridge as the sonarman sang out again. "Second contact at zero-eight-four. High speed screw making max turns. Headed our way and closing."

At once McDade stepped to the twin stainless steel

tubes of the search and attack periscopes. "Up periscope."

The well-oiled mechanism hummed and slid smoothly upward. The captain of the *Sunperch* stepped to the instrument, dropped the focus and ranging handles into place, and peered through the eyepieces the moment they cleared the well. Rising with the periscope, he swung through an arc that covered both bearings. Quickly he located one enemy then the other, and stepped back from the device.

"Patrol boats. Down 'scope." McDade raised his voice as he reached an instant decision. "Prepare to dive. Angle on the bow at twenty degrees down, flood all ballast. Rig for silent running. Dive! Dive! Dive!"

Five heart-stopping minutes went by.

Ping!-Bong! Ping-Bong! The enemy sonar had made contact.

Sluggish for only milliseconds, the *Sunperch* canted at a sharp angle and continued to nose downward. In a silence broken only by muttered orders, a race for life got underway. Back in their quarters the SEALs exchanged worried glances. They had been through this before and did not enjoy the results.

Archie Golden had visions of depth charges tumbling through the water. Then he recalled that one of the submariners had told him the Vietnamese patrol boats carried only two ash cans each. They also carried a pair of tube-mounted, deep-running torpedoes, with more stowed below. *How about that for a chilling thought?* he asked himself.

Naval Lieutenant Goh Vohn sat at the tiny chart table in his low-ceilinged cabin aboard the Antisubmarine

Patrol Vessel *Spring Wind*. His sonar operator, crowded in next to him, tapped at the cluttered screen of the obsolete Soviet-made detection device and resolved the confusion into a single point of greenish light.

"It is there, Captain," he proudly told Lieutenant Goh. "An American submarine."

"Excellent, Comrade Sonarman. This time it will not escape us."

Sonarman Bei looked at his superior with surprise on his young face. "Do you think it is the same one we encountered four days ago?"

Goh tried to keep from sounding condescending. "They do not have so many submarines that the Tonkin Gulf resembles carp in a garden pool. Yes, it is most certainly the same. What puzzles me is what it is doing here. Why in so close to the coast?" Goh sighed. "We will probably never know. Our job is to kill it."

"It will not escape us below the thermal layer this time?"

"No, Sonarman Bei. We are on it entirely too soon. Feed course, bearing, and range to Senior Torpedoman Trahn when you have established them."

Proud of his ability and his shipmates, Bei answered eagerly. "The very instant, sir."

Lieutenant Goh left his desk and went on deck. "Prepare depth charges. Drop both on the first pass. Our sister boat, *Spring Rain*, will make the second pass. Once the American is crippled by the depth charges, we will finish it with a torpedo."

*   *   *

Abruptly, Sonarman Eckert looked up from his console. Fear did not figure into the gaunt expression on his face as he spoke the fateful words. "First craft has just passed over us, sir." He paused a second. "Depth charges in the water, sir."

Captain McDade checked the depth gauge. They had not yet reached the thermal layer, let alone gone below it. "Steady as she goes. Increase angle on the bow to thirty degrees."

"Second boat approaching now," Eckert sang out.

WHAM! To the SEALs it sounded like the depth charge had gone off inside the submarine. Reactively, the *Sunperch* swayed from side to side. *WHAAM!*

Pressure plates bulged inward on the outer hull. A water line burst in the forward torpedo room. Hydraulic fluid squirted from half a dozen breached joints in control lines. Cookware clattered noisily in the galley.

"Jesus, get us out of this," Chad Ditto muttered softly.

Hail Mary, full of grace, prayed Doc Welby silently.

On the bridge, Sonarman Eckert quickly yanked the headphones from his ears and looked at the captain. "Two more charges in the water, sir."

Falling at a measured rate, first one then the second depth charge detonated. The lights went out throughout the *Sunperch*. One of the charges had reached a spot close by the conning tower. The force of its blast, which compressed water into a multiton sledgehammer, breached a hull plate and sent a thick, greenish geyser into the upper compartment. In the wavering red emergency lights, water gushed down over the men on the bridge until Lieutenant (j.g.) Cramer dashed up the ladder and grabbed the hatch. He yanked it to and quickly spun the wheel of the watertight mechanism.

Above, the patrol boats circled like wolves. A larger vessel approached. Lieutenant Goh lined up the torpedo shot.

"Steady . . . steady. Now, fire!"

At his command, compressed gas launched the old Soviet projectile into the water at a steep angle off the port bow.

Down below, Sonarman Eckert reported the deadly event. "Torpedo in the water, sir. Descending on course to our position. Running hot, straight and true . . . . No. Wait a minute. It's—it's turning. It's done a one-eighty. And . . . it's rising. Now it's veering again. It's headed for a third, larger vessel."

Every face wore stunned expressions as the torpedo headed away from the *Sunperch*.

From the deck of the *Spring Wind*, Lieutenant Goh stared in helpless fascination as cavitation bubbles formed a silver wake off his port bow. The torpedo rushed to the surface, broached, then leveled out, nose down, its rudder fins set to send it directly to the frigate. He stared in horror as it struck the vessel broadside, amidships, and erupted with a tremendous roar and a towering fountain of water.

Even louder, the sound of the secondary explosion when the boilers went raced across the water to his ears. Lieutenant Goh swallowed hard, his mouth suddenly dry, and he muttered a proscribed prayer to the Buddha to protect him from the wrath of his superiors. But why bother? It was karma. His karma, and all bad.

Before his wondering eyes, the keel snapped and the frigate swiftly went down with all hands. Idly, Lieutenant Goh wondered if the bullets of the firing squad would hurt.

Sonarman Eckert pronounced the eulogy for the Vietnamese frigate. "They just sank their own ship, sir." Then, moments later, "The vessel has broken up, sir. She's going down fast."

Captain McDade cut his gaze from one to another of his three junior officers on the bridge. Then, quietly he mouthed his most profound relief. "Gentlemen, there *is* a God." To Eckert he added, "Put that out for all hands."

Eckert keyed the annunciator system. "Now hear this. Now hear this. The gooks sank their own ship. She's broken up and going down."

Slowly at first, then rising in enthusiasm, the crew and passengers began to cheer. "Hot damn. There's a kiss for Poppa Ho," Chief of the Boat Walt Hayward, shouted up to the bridge through the hatch to the deck below.

Eckert's next words were most welcome. "The others are pulling off, sir."

"Hobbs," Captain McDade addressed his executive officer. "Lay a course for Saigon. I'll take the con."

*   *   *

Barry Lailey ached in every part of his body. He had been beaten with slit rods of bamboo, punched, slapped, starved, and deprived of all necessities for three days. At least he thought it was three. Kept underground, he had lost all track of day and night. His captors had only given him the exact minimum of water to keep him alive. So far, they had learned nothing, Lailey thought with a hot flash of pride. He, on the other hand, had learned much more than he had expected.

Six others from the Riverine Force had been captured with him, but not an officer among them. That set his brain to working. If the best offense is a good defense, he reasoned, he had better start now. When Colonel Frahn entered the tiny interrogation cell, Lailey spoke first for once.

"I want to see the Red Cross representative."

Frahn smirked. "Whatever for?"

"I want to file a protest. Under the articles of the Geneva Convention, as an officer I am entitled to be quartered with other officers, not with enlisted men. You are violating that term."

Colonel Frahn had not expected this. His country was not a signatory of the Convention. Surely this lieutenant commander knew that. He responded with feigned anger. "That is preposterous. There are no other officers held here."

Lailey nodded and forced a smirk. "Thank you. That was something I wasn't sure of before."

Swiftly, the open palm of Frahn's gloved hand slammed into Lailey's left cheek. "What is your function with the American Navy?"

"Lailey, Barry, NMI, Lieutenant Commander, five-

five-nine-six-zero-seven-three-four-three.''

Colonel Frahn motioned the two thick-muscled louts who hulked in the background. Slowly, methodically, painfully, the beating began again.

Two nights later, the *Sunperch* rendezvoused with a light cruiser off the shore of South Vietnam. Preparing to leave, the SEALs shook hands in turn with Captain McDade and Wordy Wordsworth, who would be remaining aboard. They saluted both of the officers, and it was Tonto Waters who had the last word. His compliment sounded downright sincere, until he completed it.

''Wordy, you done good . . . for a blankethead.''

When the laughter subsided, Stan McDade spoke to Pope Marino. ''Would someone be kind enough to tell me what the hell I'm supposed to do with that *thing* you brought on board?''

Pope nodded to Wordsworth. ''That's why Wordy is staying aboard. He'll tell you where to take it.'' Pope drew himself up and saluted. ''Permission to leave the boat, sir.''

''Permission granted. Good luck, SEAL.''

From there, the SEALs, and their prisoner General Hoi, went by STAB to the cruiser. In late afternoon, they flew by chopper off the stern of the cruiser to Saigon. They reunited with the rest of the platoon at Ton Son Nhut. Their smug expressions revealed to everyone that they had recently pulled off one hell of a big one, but no one asked what that might be. After a quick chopper ride to Tre Noc, they set foot on solid ground that looked somewhat more devastated than they remembered it. That's when they got the word from Jason Slater, who had come down to meet them.

"A large party of VC and NVA regulars hit the base while you were gone. They—ah—took a few prisoners along with them. Six guys from the Riverine Force. The seventh one was Barry Lailey."

"Hey, that's great," Archie Golden exclaimed.

Tonto Waters did not see it quite that way. Nor did Carl Marino. Tonto expressed it first. "Not so great, Arch. We gotta get him back."

Archie frowned. "But he's such a bastard."

Pope Marino put in his attitude. "Yeah, but he is *our* bastard. And remember he is a SEAL and a brother. We never leave one of our own behind."

"That prick did," Archie groused.

Tonto took it up next. "An' Pope went back and got 'em out. And that's why we've gotta do it for Lailey." He produced a wicked grin. "Won't he just love it when it's us who saves his ass?"

Lieutenant Marino turned to Jason Slater. "What do you have so far? Any intel on where they took him?"

"Yes, some," Slater responded. "But don't you guys need some rest?"

Pope shook his head. "We got some on the—ah—chopper. And it will take at least a day to set up the op to snatch Lailey out of their hands. We can rest while we work. Give us what you've got."

By then, the conversation had moved inside the Platoon office, with Alpha Squad crowded around the map table. Jason Slater stood at the head of the table and picked up a pointer, made of a shaft of bamboo with a .50 caliber casing on the base and the slug on the tip. "Assets have advised us of a large underground bunker located at about here.'' He pointed to a spot some five klicks from the west bank of the Bassiac. He went on to describe the location and the estimated number of VC sympathizers in the surrounding area.

''You'll note I did not indicate any pacified vills around Number Five Bunker. That means you'll have to get in and out by air.''

Tonto nodded enthusiastically. ''Yeah. Pope, it's worked good every time before. What about a parakeet op?''

Pope considered it a moment. ''Okay. We can modify it to fit the situation. It's the most flexible tactical element we have.''

''Bear in mind, Pope, that you'll be facing some forty to sixty VC. This won't be any cakewalk.''

Pope produced a humorless smile. ''Then maybe we'll drop a few cobras down their vent pipes first.'' He went on to outline their needs. ''It will take at least two squads. And four gunships. Can we get that many laid on? Also at least three Slicks. And what about some Black ponies?''

Jason Slater tapped the palm of one hand with his pointer. ''I'll make the arrangements myself. When do you want to go?''

Pope had his answer ready. ''No later than day after tomorrow.''

CHAPTER 26 ————————————

ALPHA AND Bravo Squads loaded aboard two of the slicks. The door gunner on the port side of one swung his M-60 into place, while on the other the starboard gunner set up. Crouched by the inward-facing doors, Tonto Waters and Anchor Head Sturgis gave each other a thumbs-up as the last men boarded. Standing above them, the crew chiefs spoke into their boom mikes and the jet engines spooled up.

Rotors turned faster in response and the ungainly aircraft strained to break free of the ground. They would be going in at treetop level, Pope Marino had told them at the briefing. The Slicks would hold back while the Cobra gunships trashed the surface above and all around the VC bunker. Then the Hueys would rush in and the SEALs would take to the ground by repelling lines. Their extraction would be by a new device, created for Seal Team One. They called it simply McQuire rig.

It consisted of a single standard rape line, fitted with loops ten feet apart along the line. Using specially prepared pieces of parachute harness the riggers had stitched together, the SEALs and the men they would be bringing out, could strap themselves into it like web gear, and later use it to secure them to the rope. Then they would safely ride all the way back to Tre Noc—or at least that was what the pilots had told them during the practice sessions.

To their surprise and pleasure, it worked exactly as expected. Designated members of each squad carried spare pieces of the harness rig for Barry Lailey and anyone else they brought out. The rpm reached lift capacity and the helicopters lurched into the air. It would be a tense forty minute ride.

Colonel Frahn looked out the large window of the bamboo hut that sat under the trees. It would be nightfall soon. The drone of insects had already begun to diminish—except for the mosquito population, which would triple after dark. He had every confidence that this would be the moment when he broke the stubborn navy officer. What would make it so is that he would be given his first meal.

After five days of starvation he would be primed to accept a favor and cooperate in gratitude. Frahn ended his silent gloating to concentrate on a distant buzzing sound that had impinged on his consciousness. What was it? From that far off he could not tell.

Gradually the sound grew in volume. As it did, it broke up into the whop-whop of helicopter rotor blades. His eyes widened as he counted the number of individual aircraft. That many could not be friendly.

Colonel Frahn went to the window to call out an alarm when two dark shapes popped up above the trees. Tiny flickers of yellow-white came from two remote control turrets as the 7.62mm multibarrel Minigun and the 30mm three-barrel cannon opened up. From the four stores pylons, the first of 76 2.75-inch rockets roared to life and hissed off their hardpoints to streak toward the knoll under which existed Number Five Bunker. Suddenly two more AH-1G Cobra gunships joined in.

An instant later the first rounds struck. Colonel Frahn felt the detonations of the 30mm shells through the soles of his boots. He watched while the incoming ordnance advanced across the bare ground, erupting gouts of dirt to a height of ten feet. The nearest dark green monster peeled off and lined up on the three room hut where Frahn looked on in horror as the hail of bullets closed in on him.

In the blink of an eye, the sawed mahogany planks of the veranda blew up in clouds of splinters. Thatched palm roofing disintegrated into a haze of fragments, then the matting in front of his legs shattered and blasted inward. Intense pain seized his thighs and the NVA colonel went down hard, shot through both legs. From somewhere he heard a terrible scream. After a moment he realized it was his own voice. Then fiery punches slammed into his belly and chest and a thick wave of blackness swarmed over him.

"Cherokee One, this is Cherokee Four. Over."

"Cherokee One, go."

"We just splashed a gook officer type in a hut over here. Over."

"Rocket the damn thing, Four. Cherokee One, out."

"Cherokee One, Cherokee Two. Over."

"Go, Two."

"Longjohns has found the entrance. Over."

"Cherokee Two, this is One. Tell him to knock politely. Over."

At once, the AH-1G designated Cherokee Two turned on its axis and puffs of white smoke appeared at the rear of two of the missile pods. The 2.75-inch rockets streaked toward the target when fired by the weapon operator, seated in the nose of the chopper. When they struck true, a salvo of four more instantly followed.

A veritable Old Faithful of dirt and small rocks shot into the air where the concealed entrance to the bunker had been. "Good show, Longjohns," the flight leader praised from behind his own weapons man in Cherokee One. "Spread out, guys, and start our first orbit."

"This is Four. Roger that, One."

"Three, roger."

"Two, roger."

Buzzing like angry wasps, the four gunships began to make a circuit of the clearing and first hundred meters of jungle. Their deadly venom shredded the foliage and shattered trees. In their lethal onslaught they blasted the life from twenty-five VC from the local militia.

Their second pass finished off the wounded. "Chauffeur One, this is Cherokee One. You may curb your passengers."

Climbing abruptly, the four AH-1Gs set up tight

circles while their weapons officers watched the ground expectantly. After the fury of their runs, nothing stirred. Flames crackled in the collapsed hut and a thin column of smoke rose above them. The three Huey Slicks moved into position above the savaged entrance to the bunker.

Tonto Waters slid down the rape line, his legs loosely wrapped around its supple length. The boots over his head belonged to Chad Ditto. Above him came Pope Marino, followed by Archie Golden, Doc Welby, and Zoro Agilar. Below him, Randy Andy Holt touched boots to ground.

A quick look to Tonto's starboard side revealed Anchor Head Sturgis and his squad streaming earthward. The moment Tonto reached the dirt, he unslung his 12-gauge Ithaca and started for the bunker. Randy Andy covered his sector with a Stoner. The belt of ammo lay waiting on the feed tray. Andy Holt saw faint movement to his left front and cut off a five-round burst.

A thrashing in the undergrowth answered him and an NVA regular staggered out into the open and fell on his face. Tonto reached the bunker and hurled an M26 fragger down the opening. It went off with a muted *krang!* then the lower half of Tonto's body disappeared below ground. Shotgun leading the way, Tonto went down the steps in a cautious rush, reached a lateral tunnel, and poked the scattergun around the corner.

Number four buckshot spat from the muzzle and the Ithaca bucked in Tonto's hands. Ears ringing despite the sound-deadening plugs he wore, Tonto heard

the screams of at least two wounded men. He pumped
the action and fired another round. Silence followed.
Three more SEALs had joined him by then.

"What's the holdup, Tonto?" Anchor Head asked
lightly.

"Waiting for an invitation," a grinning Tonto answered laconically.

Barry Lailey heard some heavy stuff going off above
him. It gave his spirits the first lift since he had
conned the verification of no other officers out of Colonel Frahn. When the big rockets slammed into the
bunker face, he knew for certain who had come after
him. Well, hell, he admitted to himself as he grinned
in expectation, he wouldn't even mind if it turned out
to be that prick Carl Marino. Then grenades began to
go off down in the bunker.

From his cell, Lailey could dimly follow the fighting as the NVA troops struggled to repel the invaders.
More grenades went off, punctuated by the staccato
chatter of automatic weapons fire. Suddenly there
were shouts in English outside the cell doors.

"Out! Get out—get out—get out! Move—move—
move."

Lailey was ready, hunkered down in the low cubicle. The brighter light of the communal room of the
bunker streamed in and Lailey bolted into the open.
To his surprise he found his speculation had become
fact. That impudent BMC Waters was shoving some
sort of harness at him.

"Put that on, Commander. Hurry. We ain't got a
lot of time. Strap it up tight."

With fingers numbed by torture, Barry Lailey fumbled into the webbing rig and adjusted straps. A carabiner snap-link D-ring hung from the center of the chest strap. *What the hell was that for? He'd find out*, he supposed. Then the rescue team started to herd the freed prisoners down the long tunnel to the entrance.

Outside, Lailey blinked in the red glow of a setting sun. Abruptly from above, a Cobra gunship fired a ripping burst from a 40mm cannon. It thoroughly trashed a section of jungle. From the screams that came to Lailey's ears, he estimated some VC militia had gotten what they deserved. With a loud whopping, three Huey Slicks skidded across the sky at treetop level and closed on the center of the clearing.

Pope Marino spoke into the handset of the radio on the back of Repeat Ditto. "Chauffeur One, this is Warbird. Some of our passengers are in bad shape. Bring one down to load them. Over."

"Roger that, Warbird. One descending."

Lailey saw that two of the three choppers trailed long lines with loops worked into them at regular intervals. With the assistance of the two teams, those former captives who were in good enough condition stepped into loops, hooked up for safety. Those helping them soon followed. Chief Waters secured Lailey and took the position below him. Crew chiefs in the open doorways watched for thumbs-up signals from the last SEALs to hook up. When they got them, the birds lifted swiftly and whisked away in the direction of Tre Noc.

Back at the base at Tre Noc, jubilation was unrestrained for an unprecedented twenty minutes. Cold beers came from the platoon bar, to be passed out to the rescued riverine sailors. Their CO welcomed them personally and offered effusive congratulations to the SEALs. Lieutenant Commander Lailey grudgingly sought out Pope Marino.

"I hate to admit this, but I owe you one. Thanks for coming after us. But, then, that's what you guys do. I'm giving a bottle of VSOQ cognac to each of the helicopter pilots. You and the rest of your platoon will each receive one, too. Now, would you mind telling me, what in the bloody hell were you really doing?"

With a straight face, Lieutenant Carl Marino looked Lieutenant Commander Barry Lailey in the eye. "I'm sorry, sir. But you have no need to know." *God, how he loved doing that.*

After a thorough cleanup of weapons and men alike, and the beginning of a long rest, the SEALs of Alpha Squad received their mail. Quite a lot had accumulated during their two-week-plus absence. In it, Kent Welby received two letters from his wife, Betty. The first was the one that confirmed that she still wanted a divorce. He experienced extreme relief until he opened the second, the letter she had written him shortly after the squad left for the Philippines. Doc Welby examined it with mounting dread.

Dear Kent,
I have had long talks with my mother and, of course, father. They have caused me to see where I was wrong about a lot of things. Most importantly to us, I now believe it would be the

worst possible thing for both of us if we were to divorce. In your last letter, you said you would abide by whatever I wanted. The answer is, darling, that I want you and will wait for your return. I love you more now than ever before. I will advise my attorney that once and for all, absolutely finally, I will not go forward with the divorce.

All my love,
Betty

Aghast over this turn of events, Doc stared wordlessly at the blank concrete block wall of his quarters. What could he tell Francie? What about the baby on the way? Darkest gloom descended upon the shoulders of Kent Welby.

Gloom could also describe the mood of Tom Waters. A letter from home informed him that his father was in the hospital for a risky heart operation. During his teen years, father and son had not been close, yet Tonto now believed that he understood his father—and he respected him. An ache in the area of his own heart formed, only to intensify when he opened his second letter.

It came from Eloise Deladier. Her message was short and cryptic. *"Dearest Thomas,"* was her salutation. *"I regret to tell you that I will be out of touch for at least a month. I have an assignment from* Le Monde *that will make my career as a journalist. When I return to your part of the world, I will contact you from Saigon. With love and fond memories, I am . . ."* She signed it simply, *Eloise.*

Tonto Waters knew without doubt that in fact she was off on an assignment for French intelligence. Would he ever see her again?

Back in Binh Thuy, given a cautionary clean bill of health by the doctors, Lieutenant Commander Barry Lailey was cleared for limited duty. While browsing his desk, he came upon a notation relating to something called *Operation Artful Dodger*. It had been logged in and signed as received by his assistant S-2 on the day after had been taken captive. Two things stood out glaringly to him. Reference was made to the CIA and to Alpha Squad, First Platoon, SEAL Team 2. Intrigued, Lailey buzzed for his assistant.

"Herb, what the devil is this about?" Lailey asked when the young lieutenant entered.

Herb Sellers took the offered memorandum and read it quickly. "I'm not certain, sir. It's some super-secret CIA spook thing, and we were told we have no need to know. Except that it involved movement of personnel assigned to this command."

Lailey put it together instantly, his fury growing as he added up the pieces. "By God, that's where they went. It's too bad I can't keelhaul that damned Marino over this. It says there that the operation was a success. I suppose that means some sort of commendation and maybe a medal or two?"

"Oh, no, sir. Much too sensitive an operation for that to happen."

A beautific smile washed the anger from Lieutenant Commander Lailey. At least he had the satisfaction of knowing they had been deprived of any glory. Damn, how it rankled to owe Marino for his freedom. But, there would be another day and he would find a way to even the score.

SEALS
THE WARRIOR BREED
by H. Jay Riker

The face of war is rapidly changing, calling
America's soldiers into hellish regions where
conventional warriors dare not go.
This is the world of the SEALs.

SILVER STAR
76967-0/$5.99 US/$7.99 Can

PURPLE HEART
76969-7/$5.99 US/$7.99 Can

BRONZE STAR
76970-0/$5.99 US/$6.99 Can

NAVY CROSS
78555-2/$5.99 US/$7.99 Can

MEDAL OF HONOR
78556-0/$5.99 US/$7.99 Can